Ashes of Life

ERICA LUCKE DEAN

Ashes of Life

First Print Edition: March 2015

ISBN-10: 1940215463
ISBN-13: 978-1-940215-46-4

Red Adept Publishing, LLC
104 Bugenfield Court
Garner, NC 27529
http://RedAdeptPublishing.com/

Cover and Formatting: Streetlight Graphics

To our Mady,
For being just bad enough to inspire an entire book
but not quite bad enough to get arrested for it. (Not yet, anyway.)

ASHES OF LIFE

Love has gone and left me and the days are all alike;
Eat I must, and sleep I will,—and would that night were here!
But ah!—to lie awake and hear the slow hours strike!
Would that it were day again!—with twilight near!

Love has gone and left me and I don't know what to do;
This or that or what you will is all the same to me;
But all the things that I begin I leave before I'm through,
There's little use in anything as far as I can see.

Love has gone and left me,—and the neighbors knock and borrow,
And life goes on forever like the gnawing of a mouse,
And to-morrow and to-morrow and to-morrow and to-morrow,
There's this little street and this little house.

Edna St. Vincent Millay

Give sorrow words. The grief that does not speak whispers
the o'er-fraught heart, and bids it break.

William Shakespeare

CHAPTER 1

MADDIE

TWO CASKETS FLANKED THE CHURCH altar: dark wood—mahogany, maybe—for Dad and a warm honey oak with white satin trim for Mom. So many flowers surrounded them, my nose stung from the mixture of scents, or maybe it stung from my grandmother's perfume, sprayed on thick to mask her alcohol-laced breath. Grandma Rosie and Aunt Shannon both reeked as though they'd spent the entire morning at a bar.

Alex sat, unmoving, across the aisle from me. My stepmother's perfect auburn hair draped over her shoulder like a scarf as she stared into her lap. Her hands rested over her flat stomach, but I knew what she hid under those bony fingers. And she could pretend all she wanted, but her stomach wouldn't be flat for much longer. She didn't even bother wearing black to her own husband's funeral. Instead, she wore a stupid purple cashmere sweater and gray slacks—not a stitch of black, unless you counted her soul.

Father John recited a closing prayer, and the organist played a low, mournful melody as people exited the sanctuary, turning their backs on my parents… and on me. When most everyone had left, the immediate family—and *she*—was allowed a few private moments. My aunt and grandmother got up and headed straight to my mother's casket. No one from my dad's family came. His parents had passed away years ago.

"Maddie? Would you like to come up?" the priest asked.

I sucked in a deep breath and stood, but the world spun, and I stumbled. Alex looked up at me with her emotionless green eyes but never made a move from her seat. Regaining my footing, I marched toward my father first.

"Hi, Daddy." I didn't really know what else to say. He was gone. His body was in the box, but my *dad* was gone. I kissed my fingers then pressed them to his heart. "I love you." Then I wiped my eyes and went to see my mom. My grandmother and aunt stepped aside but hovered close by. "Mom," I whispered. "I-I'm…" I burst into sobs, wishing I could crawl into the casket with her and shut tight the lid.

Alex's mother put her arm around me. "She'll miss you just as much as you miss her."

I doubted it. Did the dead even have the capacity to *feel* anything? I glanced at my stepmother. Some of the living didn't seem to feel much as it was.

She gave my shoulder a light squeeze then stepped back, allowing me some space to wipe my eyes and nose with my already well-used tissue. That was when Alex decided to stand and go to my father's side. I watched her put her hands over his, but if she said anything, it was too quiet for me to hear. Grandma Rosie *tsked* and left the sanctuary with Aunt Shannon close on her heels, probably both in search of a drink.

"We'll take care of your parents until the ground thaws in the spring," Father John said, reminding me we had to wait months before burying them.

"Thank you." I swiped my sleeve across my eyes to dry my tears. "I think I'll go find my friends now."

"Very good." He smiled then turned toward my stepmother. "Alex, would you like to join the others for some refreshments?"

My dad's new wife, his *widow*, didn't move. "I'll be there in a minute."

The old priest nodded, making the loose skin on his jaw bounce. "Take as much time as you need."

With one last look at my mom and dad, I left. On the way to the reception area, I nodded at Alex's parents, refusing to read too much into their sad smiles. Father John held the door then walked me through the lobby and all the way to the fellowship hall. I was barely ten steps inside before people surrounded me, offering their condolences. I felt like the french fry all the seagulls fought over at the beach, but the attention always seemed to come with a lot of shit.

Mrs. Jarvis—the lady who lived down the block from Mom and me—latched on to my wrist. "Oh, sweetie, your mother was such a wonderful woman, and we're all going to miss her."

One of the guys from Dad's golf club patted my head as if I were the family dog. "I bet your dad's already found a prime course, wherever he is."

"Your parents loved you so much, Maddie. It's just so, so sad," said a woman I didn't even recognize.

Each comment, laced with well-meant but unnecessary pity, made me want to run away, screaming. None of these people knew my parents as I did. None of them knew *me* the way my parents did, especially Mom. The nearly uncontrollable urge to bolt from the room as if a horde of zombies was bearing down on me swept through me, and I had to force myself to breathe through it.

"Hey." Haleigh hugged me. One of her corkscrew curls caught in my eyelashes, and I smothered a laugh. "I have to admit, I thought it would be weird having your parents' funeral together, but Father John did a nice job."

"Yeah, he did. And nobody had to sit through two services. But now I just want to get out of here. I can't stand all these people looking at me like I'm the most pathetic thing they've ever seen." I wrapped my arms around myself. I'd worn my black sweater dress, the one Mom'd bought for me to wear on New Year's. We'd done our annual shop 'til you drop at the after-Christmas sales, and she'd found it on a clearance rack. The fit, the style, everything about it was perfect.

"You don't look pathetic. You look stunning right now, and you should totally show off that dress later."

Part of me knew I should have probably stuffed the dress in the back of my closet and never thought of it again, but no matter how badly I wanted to, I just couldn't do it. I didn't have anything else to wear for the party, and Mom *did* buy it to show it off. She'd been so happy when I modeled it for her that day.

"Maddie, I'm so sorry for your loss." My school principal put her hand on my shoulder. "I wanted to let you know that, in light of your current circumstances, we're not going to take any action regarding last week's incident. However, that doesn't mean I want to see a repeat of it." She stared down at me, raising one penciled-on brow in a perfect arch.

"Thank you, Mrs. Walker." I forced a smile. *So kind of you to remind me of my transgressions at my parents' funeral. Bitch.*

"And who are you staying with?" She looked around the room as if scoping out my possible caregivers.

"With Haleigh's family."

"Oh…" She glanced between the two of us. "Well, I'll make a note of that in your record, but if you need anything at all, please be sure to let me know."

"Okay." I shrugged.

She patted my shoulder again then went over to Haleigh's parents. The three of them kept glancing in my direction, and I knew without a doubt they were talking about my *situation.*

Poor Maddie, the troubled sixteen-year-old orphan, whose parents died in a car accident together. She's going to need lots of support and… a keeper. She's going to need to talk to someone and tell them all about her feelings.

"I could really use a hit right now," I whispered in Hayleigh's ear.

Hayleigh went wide-eyed. "Maddie! We're at your parents' funeral."

I rolled my eyes. "My point exactly."

"I get it. But you might want to be careful. You could've been expelled if it weren't for—" Her mouth fell so far open I could see her uvula—a word I'd learned in biology the week before.

"My parents dying?" I stared her down, watching her face turn every shade of red in the color wheel. I had no idea why I was punishing Haleigh for the shit day I'd had. She hadn't done anything wrong.

She stared down at the floor. "Mm-hm."

"Sorry. I just… I don't even know." Then I bumped her with my shoulder. "Did your mom say we could use her car tonight?"

Haleigh smiled. "As long as the snow holds off. But I wish you had your license. I hate driving at night."

"Yeah, maybe I can get it in April." That seemed like such a long way away, and I wasn't even sure who'd take me. Mom and Dad had made me agree to wait until I turned seventeen because they didn't think I was ready to have my license. *I'm pretty sure they didn't expect to die before then.* I know I never expected to lose them so soon.

"What are you two girls conspiring about over here?" Grandma Rosie slurred her words, and I wondered where she'd found more alcohol in the short time since the service ended. The church most likely didn't keep a stocked bar, unless you counted the communion wine. But I wouldn't have put it past my grandmother to raid that when no one was looking.

"Probably some party with booze and boys. Maybe we should crash it." Aunt Shannon winked at me, though she had trouble re-opening her eye, as if she were moving in alcohol-induced slow motion.

I tried to guard myself against the offensive smell oozing off the two of them, but it was impossible when my grandmother wrapped her twig-like arms around me, and her bleached-blond hair fell in my face.

"You know you can come with me if you want, to live I mean. We'd have such a great time." I had to help her stand upright as she let me out of her grasp.

"Oh, that would be fun!" my aunt squealed a little too loudly. "It'd be just us girls, and we could give each other facials and watch Hugh Jackman movies. God, that man makes me wet."

Ew, gross! "Um, thanks. I'll keep that in mind." I grabbed Haleigh's hand. "I should probably go say hi to some people, so..." I took a step back, pulling my best friend with me.

"Okay, sweetie. You just let me know," Grandma Rosie said, though it came out more like, *Okay, sheety. Yoused lemme know.*

I hadn't even made it halfway across the room when my former ballet instructor cornered me. "Maddie!" Miss Nicole pulled me into a hug, enveloping me in her familiar gardenia perfume. "I'm so sorry, sweetie. Your parents were such wonderful people. I've missed seeing them—and *you*—since you stopped dancing." She finally let me go and took a step back. "My God, has it been three months?"

"Time flies." *When your life is falling apart around you.* "I've missed you too."

"Why don't you stop by the studio? You never did see the new floors. No more warped wood."

I'd sooner spend a week in detention. "Sure. I'll do that. I, uh, should go say something to my, uh, stepmom before she leaves."

"Okay, good." She pressed a kiss to each cheek before setting me free again. "I'll see you soon."

I turned around to make my escape and ran smack into Brody Allen, all six feet, blond hair, and brown eyes of him. His soft dark sweater clung to his lean muscular chest, and he smelled like sweet pine with a hint of chlorine, probably from spending most of his time swimming with the school's team.

"Sorry, I—"

"You have nothing to be sorry about." Brody winked at me with that skeezy half-grin of his perched on his kissable lips. "I'm the one who's sorry about your parents. My dad's really shaken up by it too. He keeps saying he's going to sell his golf clubs and take up fishing instead." Michael Allen and my dad had golfed together every week, from the moment the snow melted until the course was too cold to walk, so I'd known Brody half my life. The guy went through girls like Grandma Rosie went through six-packs, and he was exactly what I wanted at that moment. *Sign me up for self-destruction 101—only bad boys need apply.*

Brody ran a finger across the back of my hand, and my mouth turned dry. Sweat trickled down the back of my neck as if someone had turned up the furnace to its boiling point. "Thanks. Um, I think my dad would want him to keep playing, though." If the look in Brody's eyes was any indication, I was about to become his flavor of the week.

"Let me know if you need anything. I'll even cover your next stash," he whispered in my ear then kissed my temple and stepped back. "So, are you two coming to Drew's party tonight?"

Haleigh giggled and turned a lovely shade of pink. I managed to nod just before another well-wisher appeared.

"I'll see you later, then." He winked and walked away. I knew he probably practiced that wink for hours in front of the mirror, but I couldn't help the butterflies in my stomach when he directed it at me.

CHAPTER 2

ALEX

"Oh, Alex, it's just so sad. So unbelievably tragic," my mother whispered, dabbing at her eyes with a crumpled tissue as she shifted her gaze between the two glossy caskets. "That poor girl lost both of her parents. Where will she go? Who will take care of her?"

Never mind the fact that *her* only daughter had just lost her husband in the same tragic accident. Leave it to my mother to worry about David's daughter—the girl who couldn't look anything more like his ex-wife if she'd been born as the woman's identical twin, right down to her perfect, long brown hair, amber eyes and oh-so-cute button nose. What would happen to *my* unborn child?

"I'm sure she'll be fine, Mom. Kids are resilient, right? Practically all of Lake Edna showed up to support *her*." I forced a smile, but based on my mother's expression, I'd failed miserably.

She clasped both my hands in hers in a vise grip. "Oh, my dear girl. You've lost just as much. I didn't mean to suggest you haven't. But David left you a piece of himself, and I just know you'll be a wonderful mother. I can't wait to spoil my grandbaby. But I worry about poor Maddie. I can't imagine losing both parents that way. Do you know what arrangements have been made for her?"

"I'm just the stepmother. Why would anyone bother to tell me?" Once I'd wrestled my hands free, I dug through my purse in search of my cell phone, keeping busy to avoid meeting her scrutiny. I knew I was being childish, but at that moment, standing alongside my husband's casket, I couldn't find it in me to care.

The low battery warning flashed up at me. Of course, I'd forgotten to charge it, again. *Life goes on, right?*

Mom gave a resolute nod. "I'd like to talk to her, if only to make sure she has someplace to go."

"I'm sure she'd like that." *She'd like anything if it meant avoiding having to talk to me.*

"Come on, Helen. Let's give the girl a few minutes to grieve… alone." My father stepped forward and motioned for my mother to follow him. He always had perfect timing and seemed to know the right things to say.

"Promise you'll come eat something?" Mom's mossy-green eyes pleaded with me. "You haven't eaten since—"

"I promise." As if food was something I was even remotely interested in at that moment.

My father pulled me into a hug and whispered in my ear. "I'm so proud of you, Sweet Pea. Life wasn't fair, taking him too soon. And for you to have to plan not just David's funeral, but hers…" Dad glanced at Sarah's casket, and I was thankful the funeral director had closed it before leaving the room.

"Thank you, Daddy. I didn't do anything special. It's what David would have wanted." My eyes burned with unshed tears, and I blinked them back before stepping out of his embrace. "Can you give me a few minutes to say goodbye?"

"Take as much time as you need. We'll wait for you in the fellowship hall." My father pressed his lips to my cheek then patted my shoulder before turning to lead my mother out.

A shaft of sunlight broke through the stained glass windows, bathing David's casket in a kaleidoscope of colors. My fingertips ran over the warm mahogany finish as I inched my way toward the opening where he lay, motionless, as if he was simply sleeping, not—*dead.*

Why, David? Why did you push so hard for me to go on that trip? I could have stayed home—should have stayed home. I had a bad feeling. If I'd only followed my instincts… listened to my gut… maybe you'd still be here.

The control I'd fought so hard to maintain slipped, and my body shook with quiet sobs. I grabbed the hem of my sweater, twisting the cashmere between my fingers, struggling to rein in my emotions. I refused to break down here, where *they,* the strangers who'd never bothered to get to know me, could watch it unfold in front of them. I reached out with trembling fingers to cup David's chilled face, stroking my thumb against the faint stubble peppering his jaw.

"Why was she in the car with you?" My heart stuttered, threatening to break all over again. "You *lied* to me, David. You brought me to this godforsaken place, halfway across the country, and you left me here alone. You said we'd *grow old together*. How can I ever forgive you?" More tears threatened to fall, but I squeezed my eyes shut, trapping them.

Three months. We'd been married for a moment, and he was gone.

With one last jagged breath, I pulled myself together and brushed David's hair to the side. They'd parted it all wrong. I straightened his silver tie, tucking the end into the V of his black suit coat. "Who dressed you?" If I hadn't known better, I'd suspect he'd done it himself. He'd always had a knack for crooked ties and misaligned buttons. I gave his lapel one last pat then pulled my hands back to wring them together.

"Mrs. Barrett?"

A deep voice drifted into the quiet sanctuary, and I turned to face the source.

"I'm sorry. I didn't mean to interrupt you. I just wanted to pay my respects."

I didn't recognize the tall, slender man in front of me with golden-brown hair and a gentle smile. "It's okay, I was..." After a quick glance at David's casket, I turned back to the man's blue eyes.

"No." His forehead wrinkled. "You don't have to say anything. I'm intruding on your grief." He shoved his hands into the front pockets of his charcoal dress pants, shifting his gaze—and my own—to his polished black shoes.

I took his moment of inattention to swipe at the traces of moisture beneath my eyes. "Were you and David friends?"

"Uh, no... we only met in passing. Sarah had nice things to say about him, though. I wish I'd had a chance to know him better."

The mention of her name set my jaw on edge. "So you and Sarah were...?" I waited for him to fill in the blanks.

His face flushed crimson, and he pulled a hand from his pocket to rake it through his thick hair. "We… uh… knew each other from the hospital. We went out a few times. She was a nice lady, but her heart was somewhere else. She'll be missed." He was obviously uncomfortable, but I had no desire to ease his discomfort.

I struggled to come up with something appropriate to say about the woman I barely knew. "I'm sure she will be. It's clear from today she touched many lives."

"They'll both be missed. And God… *Maddie*." He sank his hand deep into his pocket to jingle his change, leaving his hair in complete disarray. "I can't imagine what she must be going through. First the divorce, now this. Poor kid. What's going to happen to her now?"

For what could have been the hundredth time that afternoon, I forced a smile. "I'm sorry. I don't know. I'm sure her family will want to step up. Her grandmother and aunt are here today. She'll be fine—in time." I had to remind myself that he didn't know about the other child who'd lost a father in that same tragedy. Almost no one knew.

His head bobbed a few times, but he said nothing.

"I should really…" I nodded toward the double doors leading to the vestibule, desperate to escape the attempts at polite conversation that made me realize I hadn't really given one moment's thought to my stepdaughter's fate.

He stepped aside. "Oh, sure. Of course. I should get going anyway. My shift starts soon, and well, again, I'm very sorry for your loss."

With one last nod, I turned to walk out of the sanctuary. I still had to find my parents and suffer through forced socializing with the Michigan natives who had been *so* welcoming to me during my time in their town.

The back of my neck prickled, and I glanced over my shoulder to see the man still standing in the aisle. He flashed a warm smile, and I realized he'd never introduced himself.

My gray pumps clacked against the tile floor as I reluctantly marched toward the fellowship hall, leaving my husband, his ex-wife, and the stranger behind.

Clearly, the fine parishioners of Saint Michael's had funded several additions to the old building, so there were multiple corridors I had to choose from. I followed the sound of somber voices until I reached my destination.

"There you are!" My mother grabbed a hold of my sleeve, tugging me toward my father and a few people I recognized but couldn't place. "I thought you'd gotten lost. Come... have something to eat." She thrust a dried-out cucumber sandwich into my hand. "We were just chatting with Mrs. Walker."

I blinked a few times, compelling my brain to fire on a few more cylinders while I ran through the possibilities of who the woman was. The name seemed familiar, but I couldn't recall the angular face made harsher by the severe bun tugging her skin taut across her sharp bones.

Mrs. Walker extended a hand to me. "My condolences. I'm the principal at Lake View. I knew both Mr. and Mrs. Barrett. They were such loving, attentive parents. I'm confident they wanted the best for Maddie, so let me assure you, I will do everything in my power to make this transition easier for her. I hear she's going to be staying with a friend for a few days. The school will need you to sign some papers, but we don't need to discuss that today."

My attention shifted from Mrs. Walker to my parents then to Maddie standing beside the buffet table across the room. Her amber eyes locked with mine for a moment. She resembled her mother so completely I had a hard time looking at her without drowning in a sea of inadequacy, so I turned back to her principal. "Why would I need to sign papers? She has her grandmother and her aunt. Wouldn't one of *them* be better suited for this conversation?"

"Oh." Mrs. Walker blinked at me, and I struggled to avoid staring at her drawn-on eyebrows. "I just assumed since Mr. and Mrs. Barrett listed you as the only other contact, you would be taking care of Maddie."

An involuntary burst of laughter bubbled out of me. "That would be the worst possible scenario I could think of. I can't imagine Sarah would've wanted *me* making life decisions for *her* daughter." The one time I'd met her, she couldn't keep the disdain from her expression if she'd tried, and she obviously hadn't tried.

"Of course. I understand. Would it be all right if I contacted you next week just to make sure all the necessary papers are signed?" She carried on as if she hadn't heard a single word I'd just said.

"Sure." Turning up the corners of my lips was such a chore when all I really wanted to do was to curl into a ball and disappear. "That would be fine. But if you'll excuse me..."

I couldn't get away from her fast enough, but I'd barely gone a few steps when a familiar, friendly voice stopped me in my path. "How ya holding up?"

I twisted my head around to greet my favorite barista—and only friend—in that godforsaken town. "Natalie," I said her name on a sigh, relieved to have at least one person in the wretched place I could actually confide in. "I'd be a hell of a lot better if I had a decent cup of coffee."

"Well, you won't get one here. They didn't exactly ask *me* to cater this shindig." Natalie bumped my shoulder with hers.

For the first time that day, a genuine smile broke through, and I let myself relax. "I'll be sure to speak to the establishment about that the next time I hit the confessional." As if I'd *ever* hit the confessional.

"Yeah... if you ask me, He owes you one." She drew me into a one-armed hug.

"I'm not sure *He* keeps track like that, but thank you just the same." I hugged her back before taking in her out-of-character appearance. Instead of her signature coffee house apron worn over snug jeans, a form-fitting sweater, and bright-red Converse sneakers, the bubbly blonde wore a sedate white blouse, pressed black pants, and a pair of conservative pumps. "You clean up nice." She'd even combed and subdued her typically tousled hair into a stylish chignon. "Thank you for coming. I think you might be the only person here who isn't looking at me like I devour small children."

Natalie shrugged. "Hey, what else was I going to do all day when my best customer was otherwise engaged?"

I glanced around the room at the sour faces paying too close attention to our conversation. "Believe me, I would have rather spent the day drowning my sorrows in espresso."

"Well, first thing Monday morning, we've got a date. You, me, and the biggest damn cup of decaf I can pour." She patted my stomach, reminding me of my self-imposed ban on caffeine for at least the next six months.

"As soon as I drop my parents off at the airport, you're on. I only hope I survive until then."

"Okay… come on." Natalie tucked her arm around mine, tugging me toward the buffet table. "Let's get you a cup of this crappy coffee before you chew your own arm off to escape."

CHAPTER 3

MADDIE

Deep snow banks reflected the headlights back at us, and I leaned my head back and closed my eyes as Haleigh navigated the winding road north to Drew's house. His family owned an old Victorian just outside the city limits, far enough away from neighbors that no one would complain about a bunch of kids at a noisy party.

I needed the noise. I hated how everyone talked about me in whispers lately. *Hello, I'm here!* Alex's parents were the only ones who'd come right out and asked me where I wanted to go. Even though what I really wanted wasn't possible, at least they'd asked. Alex, on the other hand, barely said a word to me and shot me dirty looks from across the room. She must have been adopted or something to have such nice parents. I pitied that poor baby.

"You sure you're up to this? We don't have to go if you've changed your mind." Haleigh bounced her leg so hard against the seat I thought she might sprain her butt cheek.

I tilted my head in her direction then held my hands out, pretending to weigh my choices on two sides of a scale. "Let's see... go to a party with cute boys, no adult supervision, and plenty of drinks to help little orphan Maddie forget her troubles. Or spend the night crying and wallowing in self-pity. Tough call, but I think I'll go with boys, drinks, and no adults."

"I'm not going to drink." She stared straight ahead with her hands gripping the steering wheel at ten and two.

I rolled my eyes. "What. Ever."

"You can't pass out. I'll never be able to get you up to my room when we get home."

Home. I had always thought of Haleigh's house as a second home, but as of a few days ago, I didn't even have a first one. Sure, my mom's house was still there, along with the Kool-Aid stain in the sofa that Mom knew about even though I'd flipped the cushion to hide it, my secret stash of Cheetos and Red Bull, and the scent that was all Mom—like dark chocolate and cut flowers—floating in the air like dust motes. But *she* wasn't there. And as for my dad's house, that hadn't felt like home since he'd moved *her* in.

"Okay. I promise I won't pass out." If I hadn't been buckled into my seat, I would have crossed my fingers behind my back.

"Good."

A few minutes later, we pulled up to the three-story Victorian. Haleigh parked her mom's Impala between a black pickup and a red Mustang. We left our coats behind, and the freezing air pricked my skin as I climbed out of Haleigh's car. Haleigh hugged close to my side until we reached the main entryway. A few kids leaned against the railing on the large front porch, as if it wasn't the middle of January in northwest Michigan, sipping from red Solo cups and steaming up the air around them. The big front windows vibrated from the music pounding inside.

Aside from the dark wood floors, moldings, and staircase, the inside didn't look anything like the outside. Sleek white leather sofas faced each other on either side of a white marble fireplace, giving the room a futuristic feeling rather than matching the gingerbread house we'd stepped into.

Two girls dance-stumbled on the matching sofas while Pitbull's latest song played. A couple girls I recognized from school brushed past us carrying more red cups, and the craving I'd had all day reared its head. "I'm going to get a drink." I stepped away to search for the liquor, but Haleigh grabbed my arm.

"Don't forget. You promised me," she shouted over the thumping bass.

The problem was I wanted to forget more than I wanted to honor my promise. "I know. I know. Now go find some hot guy. You know you want to." I waggled my eyebrows at her.

Her mouth dropped open. "Maddie!"

"Kidding. But seriously, go dance. Have fun, and I'll catch up with you later." I smiled as I shook her off, hoping she'd take the hint without making a scene.

She let go of my arm, and I followed the stream headed to the back of the house like a school of salmon looking to spawn. A large dining room opened into an even larger kitchen where at least fifty people maneuvered in front of the big silver keg. I sighed, knowing it would be a long wait before I got my turn.

"I wondered when you'd get here." Brody pressed his warm hand into the small of my back and flashed a toothy smile. "Hey, Luke," he shouted over the crowd. "My girl, Maddie, needs a drink."

His girl? Luke, another member of the swim team, filled a cup. The crowd of kids parted, obeying an unspoken rule about who got their drinks first, and Brody took the cup from Luke and gave it to me.

As soon as the beer was in my hands, I sucked it down as if I'd just crossed the Mojave in the summertime, finishing half the cup before taking a breath. I hated the bitter taste, but it felt so good going down. "Thanks."

"No problem, but you might want to slow down there, lightweight." He put his large hand on my waist, making me feel small in comparison.

My cheeks flamed, and I took another sip of my drink. "Just thirsty. I'll be good in a minute."

"Thirsty. *Right*. You want another one before we go dance?"

I coughed a little but managed not to choke or spit all over him before swallowing. "You want to dance with me?"

"Maddie, in that dress, every guy here wants to dance with you." Then he pulled me a little closer, his hand still on my waist. "I'm just not going to let them." My knees went weak, and I fumbled with the cup before he took it. "I'll go fill this for you. Don't go anywhere until I get back." I nodded, and he parted the sea of people.

"He's using you." I jumped at the deep voice coming from behind me.

In a dark corner of the dining room, a boy sat with his legs propped up on a polished chrome chair and a pad of some kind in his lap, his face hidden by shadows.

I wasn't in the mood for any more *helpful* advice. *Besides, I'm using him right back.* "Why do you care?"

Corner guy shrugged.

I darted my eyes back to where Brody was filling my cup. Luke handed him something, and Brody slipped it into his pocket before topping off my beer.

"Ten to one that's molly, and if I were you, I wouldn't drink anything more he gives you," corner guy said, and I knew that voice, but as hard as I tried, I couldn't quite place it.

"Well, you're not me, and I've had a really shitty day, and I don't need some asshole telling me what to do. I'm going to drink and smoke and fuck whoever I want, and I'm not going to let anyone, especially some creep in the corner, give me crap about it."

"Suit yourself." He dropped his feet to the floor then stood and folded a pad of paper—mystery item solved—in half and shoved it into his back pocket.

I caught Brody's eye, and he held up a finger.

I jumped again as corner guy leaned into the light to whisper in my ear. "They're picking rooms upstairs to make sure they don't bust in on each other."

I noticed the cheekbones first. The guy could have been sculpted from stone for all I knew. But the smirk definitely screamed "human," and I most definitely recognized *that.* "Grey Daniels?"

"Madison Barrett." He drew out every syllable.

"No offense, but what are *you* doing here?" Of course, I knew Grey. We had class together—he was my damn lab partner. But seeing him outside of class… outside of *school* seemed… *weird.*

"Haven't you heard? Every party needs a creepy guy in the corner to give the pretty girl crap." I couldn't tell whether he was mocking me or calling me pretty. "Sorry about your parents, by the way. But there are a lot better ways to deal with that kind of pain."

Yeah, but I don't have a razor blade handy, and I'm not a fan of my own blood. I prefer the less messy cutting, the kind that happens on the inside where no one can see it. But of course, Grey couldn't read my mind. "Thanks for the tip, but I know what I'm doing."

"Sure you do." He shot a glance toward Brody then sauntered out of the room as Brody handed me my drink.

Did the school loner really just warn me about the school golden boy?

"What'd Daniels and his broody eyebrows want?" Brody stared at Grey's retreating figure through the crowd of partygoers. "I seriously don't get what girls see in him. Does anyone actually believe that tragic hero vibe he gives off is real? I blame those stupid vampire books."

"Oh, please. He's more the sensitive artist type. Don't tell me you're jealous." A jolt of giddiness flowed through me. "You have nothing to worry about."

"Good." Brody brushed my hair from my shoulder, spreading the tingles like hot butter. "Let's keep it that way."

I turned to see if Grey lingered on the fringe of the room, but I couldn't see him. "Does he come to all your parties?"

"Nah. I mean, we give an open invite to the entire swim team, but he rarely comes. Dude's a freak. Kelsey dragged him here tonight."

"Oh." I glanced down at the cup in my hands. How ironic… the *freak* was sitting alone in the corner while the *nice* guy was trying to get me drunk. "What'd you put in my drink?"

Brody winked. "What makes you think I put something in there?"

I crossed my arms and waited.

"I didn't put them *in* your drink. I'm not that kind of guy, but…" He pulled a small white capsule out of his pocket. "It's molly, and I'm willing to share."

I hesitated for a moment, then a flash of my parents in their caskets crossed my mind. I took the pill from his hands and held it up in a mock salute, popping it in my mouth before bringing the plastic cup to my lips for a big swallow. "Here's to forgetting."

I rolled onto my back and draped my arm over my eyes. The smell of sausage drifting up from downstairs did nothing to help the queasiness. Not that I had anything left to throw up.

Haleigh's mom banged on the door. "Time to get up, girls! Breakfast is ready."

"Why is your mom yelling?" I hugged the pillow to my face, taking cover beneath the downy stuffing.

"She's not," Haleigh snapped.

What crawled up her butt?

I uncovered my head and gaped at her. She sat cross-legged on top of her faded old Hannah Montana sheets as if she wanted to strike me down with laser beams. "Why are you pissy?"

"You don't remember any of it, do you?" She shot up and swung her legs off the bed. The movement made me dizzy even though I was lying down. I had to close my eyes.

She'd had twin beds as far back as I could remember, and I'd always considered the one on the left to be mine, my home away from home—or lately, the only place that felt like home. "I remember Brody getting me a drink and dancing with him. And I remember Grey Daniels being a creepy jerk."

"So you don't remember that creepy jerk saving your butt or you doing your darnedest to get Brody Allen to take your virginity... or breaking your promise to me." She mashed her hands to her hips, staring at me as though I'd given her father a lap dance.

"I almost *what*?" I sat up, and the whole room spun. "I seriously feel like the entire football team walked over my stomach."

Haleigh made a huffing noise then stomped to her dresser to grab a hair tie from a Mason jar and pulled her curly hair into a messy ponytail. "Serves you right," she whispered.

"Please, Hale," I whined. "Tell me what happened."

"Fine." She plopped onto her bed. "I was in the living room, and you stumbled in with Brody. You were completely out of it. I tried talking to you, but you blew me off. You were too busy dancing—if you can even call it that—with him. You had a drink in one hand and the other one under his shirt. A while later, I went to find you, and you guys were headed upstairs. I tried to stop you, but you told me to find my own guy. Grey was coming down the steps with Kelsey Monahan, and you called him a freak and then..." She caught her bottom lip in her teeth.

"And then *what*?" Like one of those Facebook GIFs playing over and over in my head, I saw myself puking on Grey's black Vans. Though why could I remember *that* of all things was anyone's guess. "No! Not his shoes!"

"Ah, she remembers. Brody and Kelsey both got grossed out and left you there on the steps. Grey helped me get you to the car, but not before you puked a bunch of times. Then he followed me home and helped me sneak you up here. I cleaned you up as best I could, but I think your dress is ruined. And you are totally washing those sheets." She nodded toward the Nutcracker bedding her mom had gotten me for Christmas a few years earlier.

I realized I was still wearing the black sweater dress, and the smell of my own vomit hit me like a punch in the face. I covered my mouth and nose then tried to pull the dress off one-handed. Haleigh sighed then grabbed a pair of sweats and a T-shirt for me as I shoved the dress into her garbage can.

"My mom's going to—" I stopped, half-naked, and stared at the dress in the trash. *My mom's going to... nothing. She's not going to ground me for getting drunk. She's not going to lecture me about my poor choices or how she was my age once. She's not going to call my dad to say, "Deal with your daughter." And she sure as hell isn't going to get mad about a stupid dress. Not ever again.*

Haleigh took a step toward me, but I waved her away. "Maddie, I—"

"It's fine. *I'm* fine." I felt the blood draining from my face. I had no idea where it had gone, though, because I was suddenly cold all over. "We'd better get downstairs, or your mom will come back and wonder what's going on."

"Yeah, okay."

I snatched my clothes and marched into the bathroom to wash my face and rinse out my mouth. My toothbrush sat beside Haleigh's in the holder, and my favorite toothpaste lay alongside it, courtesy of Mrs. T., who knew I hated the blue gel kind. A few minutes later, I sat with Haleigh, her mom and dad, and her little sister at their kitchen table, pushing sausage around my plate and nibbling on a piece of dry toast.

"You two are awfully quiet this morning." Mr. Thompson didn't look up from his morning paper. He held it up so the real estate section faced the table, but we all knew he had the Sunday comics open on the other side. "How was your movie?"

Haleigh cut her eyes toward me. "It wasn't my kind of show."

"Maddie, you've hardly eaten a bite." Mrs. Thompson fretted over me like the second mom she'd been since my preschool days.

I blinked back tears and forced a smile to keep from hurling. "I'm not really that hungry."

"Okay, sweetie. I understand." She practically had "worried" tattooed across her forehead.

The grief card worked in my favor, but using my parents that way made me even more sick to my stomach. "I think I'm going to take a shower." I pushed my plate away and stood.

"Haleigh, where's the boy?" Hannah—her incredibly perceptive four-year-old sister—asked.

Haleigh and I shared a glance. Her parents stopped eating and stared at us.

Mr. Thompson's fork clattered to his plate. "What boy?"

The color drained from Haleigh's already pale face. "Dad, I don't know what she's talking about."

"But I saw him go in your room." Hannah shoveled another syrupy bite of pancake past her lips as if she hadn't just dropped a major bombshell on the breakfast table.

Mrs. Thompson jumped up, clearing dishes from the table with what could only be a burst of nervous energy.

My skin prickled as I dissected the expressions on their faces. I loved Haleigh's parents—they'd taken me in when my world was crumbling—and I hated lying to them, but I didn't want to see Haleigh get in trouble for helping me. "She probably saw me come in with Haleigh last night. I had my hair up."

"Like I'd be dumb enough to try to sneak a boy in *here*." Haleigh took a huge gulp of her juice, probably wishing it was spiked. "Not a chance."

Mr. and Mrs. T glanced at each other but dropped the subject… for the moment. "Maddie." Mrs. Thompson stopped me before I could get out of the kitchen. "Bring your dress down. You'll probably want it cleaned after wearing it all day, and Haleigh can take you to your house today to get a few more clothes. There's a winter storm warning, so I want you two to go first thing."

Shit. "Okay." I went upstairs and grabbed the dress out of the trash then found a plastic bag under the bathroom sink. There was no way I wanted Mrs. Thompson to get a hint of the vomit stench, so I tied the bag closed around the dress and figured I could drop it at the cleaners myself.

Just before noon, Haleigh and I headed out. We didn't talk much, and when we got there, she stayed in the car while I ran into my house to get more clothes. Several of the things I wanted to wear were dirty and mixed in with my mom's in the hamper. I froze, staring at the blue blouse Mom had worn the day before the accident. I shivered, telling myself it was from the cold, and jammed what I needed into a duffel bag and ran back out the door.

As an afterthought, I grabbed the mail. I had no idea what to do about it or who was going to handle that stuff, but I didn't want it sitting in the box. We stopped at the only dry cleaners open on a Sunday on the way back to Haleigh's house then spent the rest of the day catching up on the last season of *The Vampire Diaries* on Netflix. I couldn't help fantasizing about sharp fangs sinking into my throat and hot blood oozing out of me, drop by drop, until there was nothing left but never-ending darkness. Thankfully, the subject of a boy in the house never came up again, and I went to bed shortly after dinner.

I heard Haleigh come into the room and crawl into the other bed about twenty minutes later. "Maddie?"

I rolled over and hugged my pillow, blinking against the blackness. "Yeah?"

"You should thank Grey tomorrow. If he hadn't helped me, I never would have been able to get you home."

"Sure." My eyes drifted shut.

"And I don't think I ever told you this, but..." She shifted on her bed, making the mattress creak.

Despite the darkness, I sat up to face the sound of her voice. "What?"

"I'm glad you weren't in the car with them."

That made one of us.

"I guess you just scared me last night. I know it sucks that they're gone, but I don't want to lose you."

"Thanks, Hale. I love you, too."

CHAPTER 4

ALEX

"DAVID?" I NESTLED MY FACE into my husband's pillow, drawing in his scent—the faint blend of eucalyptus, leather, and clean sweat—as the alarm chased away the last vestiges of the dream. For that brief moment, he was still there beside me. The feel of his arm tucked around me faded as the incessant beeping echoed off the walls.

After fumbling along the top of the nightstand with my eyes closed, I managed to slap a hand down on the button. I ached from being in the same position too long—curled into a tight ball in the center of the bed—and stretched my limbs, relishing the cracking in my bones. I kicked off the flannel sheets cocooning me and sat up.

The house was too quiet. No water running in the other room like most mornings when David would beat me to the bathroom, saving me just enough hot water to grab a quick shower before work. No eighties tunes sung off-key with gusto as he went through his morning ritual. *No David.*

He was gone. My heart skipped a beat before setting off at a thundering pace. My skin prickled as if I stood too close to an open flame. Not just *not here* but never coming back. *Gone.* I couldn't catch my breath and felt as if a heavy rope had been tied to my waist, dragging me under. How would I ever really breathe again without him?

"Alex? Are you up, honey?" My mom's voice came from the other side of the door. "We need to leave soon."

I forced my lungs to pull in air, choking back a sob before I could trust myself to speak. I cleared my throat. "Give me a few minutes to get dressed, and I'll be down."

I dragged myself out of bed and into the real world. My arms weren't long enough to hold myself together. I had no idea how I was still alive when inside, I was crumbling. Every intake of breath felt like a betrayal. And yet, I *had* to carry on. If not for me, for the baby. He would have expected that much. *The baby.* Not something we'd planned—we hadn't even discussed marriage yet when I'd found out—but the minute I told him, he'd proposed. Not a second of hesitation.

Somehow, my feet carried me to the closet. David's battered green-and-white Spartan sweatshirt hung to my knees, and I had no intention of taking it off. Nor did I plan to bathe. And I didn't bother with clean underwear because, in the grand scheme of things, no one really cared. I pulled out the first pair of jeans I could find—not what I would usually wear out in public, something I'm sure everyone in town would note.

As I passed David's dresser, his familiar smile caught my eye. He had his arm around Maddie in the photo—beaming at her in her frilly ballet costume. The picture couldn't have been more than a few years old; Maddie looked around thirteen or fourteen. He'd been so proud when he spoke of her scholarship to the dance academy. And heartbroken when she'd given it up just after we'd gotten married.

I forced my gaze from the happy father and daughter to the mirror. My reflection sneered back at me as I pulled my unwashed hair into a half-assed ponytail then twisted it around itself until I could tuck it into a messy bun. Even in my zombie-like state of mind, I was aware of my out-of-character behavior and complete disarray. I simply couldn't bring myself to care. Instead, my heart ached for the pictures that would never be. Pictures of my husband with *our* child.

I floated from the bathroom, down the stairs, and to the front window in a daze. A light dusting of snow covered the ground. Not enough to close the roads or the airport but enough to give me pause. *Had the roads been worse on Wednesday? Was David distracted while he drove? What were his last thoughts before…?*

"Did you hear me, sweetheart?" Mom's voice filtered into my consciousness, and I turned from the window to face her. She parked her rolling suitcase and an overnight shoulder bag on the floor by the front door.

"No, I'm sorry. I was just thinking." Thinking about how, no matter how cold it might have been outside, it had nothing on the chill in my bones. I could have climbed into the fireplace and still not felt the heat.

"Don't think today. Just get a little something in your stomach." She patted the slight swell between my hips. The barely noticeable bump seemed to appear overnight. "If not for yourself, for my grandbaby. I'm getting too old to worry so much."

"You're not so old."

She tilted her head and eyed me. "You can't fool me, you know. You haven't been eating, and all this stress isn't good for either of you. And don't try to pretend you're fine. I heard you retching this morning."

"Just a little leftover morning sickness." I picked up the white angora sweater draped over my mother's suitcase. The light floral fragrance of her favorite perfume floated in the air as I folded and refolded it, only to toss it back onto her luggage. "It's been a difficult few days, but I'm not the first person to lose—"

"Hey." My mother gripped my hand, lacing her fingers with mine the way she did when I was small. "I'm not worried about other people. I'm worried about you."

"Mom, I'll be fine."

"Are you still planning on seeing the lawyer today?" She gave my hand an extra squeeze.

I pried her fingers from around mine and took a step back. "Yes, I have an appointment this afternoon. I thought it best to get it out of the way."

"Well, I do wish you'd take a few more days to mourn before tackling the business end of things. I don't like that you're going alone. You know, I *could* stay for another—"

"No, really." My lips formed a grim smile. "I need to do this on my own, and you and Dad need to get back to California where the temperatures are somewhere above freezing. If you stick around here too long, you could get snowed in for the entire winter."

She waved a hand toward the window. "Oh, I don't mind the cold that much."

I laughed. "Now I *know* you're lying. You don't even like ice cream."

"That's because my teeth are sensitive. It has nothing to do with the weather."

"Please don't worry about me, Mom." I stepped forward to wrap my arms around her. "I'm a big girl. I'll get through this just like everyone else does. Now, I imagine we need to find Dad and get you to the airport before you get bumped from your flight." I squeezed her tighter, wishing for an instant they'd miss their flight so I could keep them just a little longer.

"Oh, your father called a cab. It should be here soon."

I let out a breath, not sure if I should be relieved or annoyed. "I told you I'd take you. You didn't need to call a cab."

"Nonsense. You've been through enough this weekend." She pressed her lips to my forehead and lingered. "Besides, you don't need to chauffeur us around in this horrible weather."

I knew she was thinking I couldn't handle driving on the same icy roads that had killed David, and maybe she was right. Maybe I couldn't. The thought of getting into a car on snow-covered roads made me shudder, but the reality of being alone in that house was worse than anything else I could imagine.

I bobbed my head a few times. "Okay. You're right."

"Do you have everything you need?" My dad stepped out of the kitchen with their coats slung over his arm and glanced at Mom and me. I knew he'd waited to come out until we'd had our moment. I guess being married to my mother for over thirty years had given him more than his share of insight into the feminine mind. I'd always teased David that it might take thirty years, but I'd get him trained.

The sadness in Mom's eyes cut me as she picked up her wrinkled sweater and pulled it over her head. "I'm all packed up and ready to go."

A loud honk sounded from the driveway. "Perfect timing." Dad helped Mom into her coat before tucking me under his chin the way he did when I was a kid. "You take care of yourself, Sweet Pea. And call us if you need anything."

"I'll miss you, Daddy."

"We're only a phone call away." Dad kissed my forehead before letting go of me to pick up the bags.

"Oh, Alex." My mother sobbed into my shoulder as she grabbed me for another hug. "Please eat. Don't let yourself waste away. David wouldn't have wanted that."

"I promise. No wasting away."

The horn honked again.

Dad checked his watch. "We'd better go. I have no doubt we're already on the meter."

From my front door, I waved as my parents climbed into the yellow cab and disappeared down the street. The emptiness inside me grew the farther away they got. For the first time since Wednesday, I was completely alone, and as much as I told myself that was what I wanted, I knew better.

I grabbed a coat and my keys, and before I'd decided where I was going, I'd backed out of the garage in my charcoal-gray Cayenne—the only Porsche equipped to handle the brutal Michigan winters. Even as a steady blanket of snow fell, the roads were still mostly dry as I weaved around the small town with no real destination in mind.

No sooner had the bright neon sign caught my eye, than I'd made the turn into the parking lot of my favorite coffee shop, Bean There, Donut That. As I entered the quaint building—a diner in its previous life, complete with shiny metal counters and red vinyl stools—I shook the snow off my coat and stomped my boots.

Natalie stuffed a giant blueberry muffin into a brown paper bag and handed it to an older gentleman. "Here ya go, Stanley. I threw in a few extra blueberries this morning, just for you."

Stanley beamed at her and pulled his coat tight before heading back into the cold. The morning rush had ended, and aside from the few stragglers grabbing steaming cups to go, I was the only customer in the place.

"Well, there she is. Hello, stranger." Natalie greeted me from behind the counter with a toothy grin. "How ya holding up?"

"Other than getting tired of people asking me how I'm holding up, I'm holding up just fine." The fake smile had become a permanent fixture on my face.

"Sure you are." Natalie's features morphed into a rigid scowl. "That's why you look like you slept in your clothes and haven't bathed in days."

"What did you expect? Dolce trousers and Ferragamo shoes? It's barely in the double digits out there, and it's been snowing since October."

Natalie wiped a trail of crumbs from the counter. "And that's stopped you from wearing the high-end shit before? Not a chance, princess. But hey, far be it from me to keep you from self-destructing. You're allowed, under the circumstances."

"Thanks. I was hoping dressing incognito would keep the natives from hunting me down to lynch me in the town square." I hopped onto one of the red vinyl stools to face my only friend in town.

Natalie laughed as she poured me a cup of coffee. "No one wants to lynch you."

"It certainly doesn't feel that way. First, I take the most eligible bachelor in town... the guy half the single women are pining for—including his ex-wife, as it turns out—then I dress inappropriately at his funeral."

"Who says it was inappropriate? You wore what David would have wanted you to wear. Wasn't he the one who said, 'Don't wear black to my funeral'?"

"Right, no one but you knows that, do they?" I swirled a splash of cream into my cup and wondered if my husband had somehow known his time was drawing near when we'd discussed funerals just weeks before his death. "And why was he with Sarah, anyway? People are probably already gossiping."

"They could have been together for any number of reasons. They had a child together. And as for what everyone else thinks... fuck them. I couldn't give a shit about what those old crones have to say, and you shouldn't either. David loved you, and he'd be absolutely livid to see you walking around like this." She tugged on the sleeve of the Spartan sweatshirt. "This isn't you, Alex."

I yanked my arm back. "Well, *this* still smells like David, and I'm not quite ready to take it off. Thank you very much."

"Sweetie, I'm not trying to push you. I know you need to take time to mourn. But don't let it drown you. Okay?"

My head bobbed a few times as I stared into my murky cup. "I won't."

"You know—" A smirk danced across Natalie's crimson lips. "—Now that I think about it, you *are* perfectly dressed for mopping my floors. I had to fire that kid I had working for me. The little shit showed up drunk last week."

My mouth fell open. "That high school kid? He couldn't be more than sixteen."

"Seventeen. But trust me. They start younger and younger all the time." She bumped my elbow. "So, whatta ya say? Grab a broom and a mop, and keep me company today?"

"Can't." I took a gulp of coffee. "I have an appointment with David's lawyer before lunch."

Her eyes widened as she raked them over me. "You're going home to change first, right?"

"I don't see why I should."

Natalie shook her head as she muttered what sounded like, "*Drowning*."

The offices of Howard, Barnes, and Schultz were located in an old brick building just off Main Street. From what I understood, old man Howard had been David's family attorney for years. He'd even represented David in his divorce. I'd met him at the funeral, but this would be my first time seeing him in an official capacity.

The man clasped my hands in his and squeezed. Instead of a suit, he'd dressed in a pair of khaki trousers and a forest-green sweater as if he'd come in on his day off to meet with me. Lines marked his round face, making him look sad. "First of all, I want to offer my condolences again. David was more than just a client. I've known him since he was a boy. His father was one of my dearest friends."

"Thank you." I wriggled my fingers free of his grip and settled into the leather chair across from him.

"Now, I'm sure you're aware David has left you the house on Grant Street, but since Mrs. Barrett..." He coughed loudly then reached for his cup and took a sip. "I mean, the former Mrs. Barrett has also passed, you would inherit the house on Maple Drive as well."

"Wait." I felt a sharp twinge, and my stomach roiled. "Why would

I inherit Sarah's house? Shouldn't that go to someone in her immediate family?"

"Well, David owned the Maple Drive house. Had he preceded Mrs. Barr—Sarah—she would have inherited that residence, but since he did not, it would go to you along with the rest of his estate—the bank accounts, stocks and bonds, and the automobiles. Of course, he's provided for Madison. He even added a provision for future children." Mr. Howard's eyes zeroed in on my midsection, lingering for a moment longer than was polite, before shifting back to my face. "But until Madison reaches her twenty-first birthday, you would be in charge of her trust fund."

The twisting sensation intensified. "Why would *I* be in charge of that?"

"As her legal guardian—"

"What!" My heart skipped a beat. "What do you mean? I never agreed to that." My stomach gurgled and churned, making me regret that last cup of coffee. My mind raced as I tried to remember a single conversation about me acting as a guardian for his daughter, legal or otherwise. I drew a great big blank.

Mr. Howard frowned. "I would have thought David had discussed this with you?"

"No." I blew out a breath, gripping the edge of my seat to keep my hands from shaking. "David most definitely did *not* discuss this with me."

"There are other options, of course, but it's my hope that you wouldn't consider those." A bead of sweat formed above his brow, and he shuffled the papers in front of him, avoiding eye contact. "As the only *suitable* family member, were you to refuse to take responsibility of the minor child, she would revert to the custody of social services."

Social Services? Did he just say Maddie would become a ward of the state? "Are you saying if I refuse, she goes to foster care?" My voice came out in a squeak.

His eyes locked on mine, and I read the sadness—or was it disappointment?—in them. "In a nutshell, yes."

"What about her grandparents? Her aunt?"

His lips curved into a weak smile. "I realize you hadn't been married for long, but did David ever mention he had no living relatives?"

I leaned back in my chair, my insides still twisting uncomfortably. *Panic attack, or morning sickness rearing its ugly head again? Maybe I should find a restroom.* "Yes… yes of course, I knew that. But what about Sarah's mother or sister?"

He shook his head. "Both David and Sarah were very specific in their wills that Maddie *not* have extended access to either of those individuals. There is a long documented history of substance abuse and legal trouble that I would rather not get into at this time."

My skin prickled, and my hands went to my stomach. I wasn't even sure I'd be ready when our baby came, and David had left his daughter to me? I didn't know the first thing about taking care of a teenager, specifically, a teenager who'd made no secret of her distaste for me since the very first day her father had introduced us.

Heat spread across my chest and up my neck until I felt it in my hairline. Black spots swirled in my vision as the sparse contents of my stomach threatened to come back. I stood on unsteady legs. "I don't feel well. Is there a restroom?"

Mr. Howard bolted out of his chair to my side, taking my arm in his as he guided me across the room. "Right through here." He ushered me through a door then closed it behind me.

Dry heaves wracked my body as I fell to my knees in front of the polished white porcelain. Other than the coffee from this morning, there was nothing left to bring up. I sat on the cold tile floor for a few minutes until I was sure my body had finished its assault on me then lathered my hands with lavender soap and took a few sips of water directly from the sink, hoping to wash away the sour taste in my mouth. My stomach clenched on itself, and I suddenly wished I'd taken my mother's advice to eat something. The baby wasn't due for six months, and already I'd done a terrible job as a parent. Too many days had passed since I'd finished a meal, and it was obviously taking its toll.

Once I'd dried my hands and smoothed my hair back into the messy topknot, I stepped out to apologize to Mr. Howard. "I'm so sorry. I just wasn't prepared—"

"Nonsense." He waved off my apology, his gaze resting on the baggy sweatshirt covering my abdomen again, and I wondered if David had told him before... "You've just lost your husband. It's understandable under the circumstances."

If anyone else said "under the circumstances" to me, I'd explode. "Really, I think I just need a day or two to process this. Can I call you next week to discuss my options?"

"That would be fine. Do you know where Madison is now? Should I find someone to take care of her until you've made up your mind?"

"She's with a friend. She should be fine for a few days. I'll check in with them tomorrow." The pain in my abdomen grew stronger, the nausea morphing into something sharper, and I gripped the hem of my shirt, twisting it in my hands. My skin crawled with the overwhelming need to get out of there before a full-blown panic attack set in.

I held out a hand to Mr. Howard, and he took it in both of his. "Call me next week, Alex. Don't worry. Things will work themselves out. In my experience, they usually do."

"Thank you." I tried to smile but was certain it came off as more of a grimace as stabbing pain attacked my insides. Before he could say anything, I turned and hurried out of the office and to my car.

I'd barely turned the key in the ignition when another wave of pain washed over me. Something was very wrong. I pulled my phone from my front pocket and hit the autodial.

"Bean There, Donut That, how can we help you today?"

"Natalie? I need your help."

CHAPTER 5

MADDIE

IT SNOWED OVERNIGHT BUT NOT enough to cancel school. *Why couldn't it be a blizzard like the weatherman promised?* Monday was my first school day after… well, just after, and I would've rather been anywhere else—well, *almost* anywhere. The tension built in my neck as my classmates either gave me sympathetic smiles or whispered behind my back.

"You survived." Brody leaned against the locker next to mine, perma-smirk etched across his handsome face, and I imagined slapping it off and leaving shock in its place.

With one last glance at the picture of Mom and Dad from my last ballet recital taped to the back, I slammed my locker door and spun the dial to engage the old-fashioned lock. "No thanks to you. As soon as I wasn't fun anymore, you ditched me."

"Yeah, sorry about that. I don't do so well with the whole puking thing. Terrible gag-reflex." He actually *looked* apologetic for two seconds before flashing one of his toothy grins. My knees betrayed me by going wobbly when he leaned down and whispered, "Next time less beer, more molly."

Sounds good to me. I stepped back as the five-minute warning bell rang. "I have to get to class."

"Before you go, I brought you an 'I'm sorry' gift." He handed me a brown paper bag.

I stared at the crinkled bag then at him. "I have my own lunch." He rolled his eyes, so I opened the sack and saw the plastic baggie full of neatly rolled joints, as if he'd taken pride in his work, looking for a gold star. "Shit!" I closed the bag. "If I get caught, I'll get expelled for sure this time."

"So don't get caught." He winked before walking away.

"Wait," I called to him as the halls cleared. "Do you know where I can find Grey?"

"Daniels?" I almost wished he'd get mad. *Or jealous.* But he laughed. "You already ruined his shoes. What do you want with him now?"

I stood straight and poked my chin out. "I just need to tell him something."

"Huh... try the east lot near the art wing." Brody ducked around a corner.

I shoved the bag into my backpack and went to first hour. By third hour, I was sick of hearing how sorry everyone was for me, and I counted the minutes until I could smoke myself into a beautiful daze. I decided to skip fourth hour and headed toward the art wing to find Grey, killing two birds with one stone, since the east lot was the smoker's hangout. But I wasn't keen on standing out in the snow.

"Madison?"

I pivoted to see the sharp lines and cold stare of the principal headed my way. "Uh, yes, Mrs. Walker?"

"How is your day going?" She reached a hand out as if she was about to pat my head like a lost dog but dropped it to her side before touching me.

It was about to be just fine. "All right, I guess. Everyone's been nice." *But I wish they'd leave me alone and that I wasn't the pathetic girl whose parents just died.*

"Good, I'm glad." She flashed a fake, 'I'm just being polite' kind of smile, her red lips reminding me of the Joker—the Heath Ledger one. *Why so serious, Maddie?* "I was wondering if you knew how to get a hold of your stepmother. I've tried the home phone and her cell, but she hasn't returned my calls. Does she have a work number?"

"You could try my Dad—" The breath in my lungs whooshed out. *Did I really just say that? It's only been five days. What the fuck am I even doing here?* "I'm sorry, Mrs. Walker. I don't know how else to contact her. She works from the house, but if you left her a message, I'm sure she'll call you back." I swallowed back my blueberry Pop-Tart. "Is there a problem?" *Had someone seen Brody give me the weed?*

"No. No problem. I need her to sign a few forms now that—"

I folded my arms and stamped down the urge to flee. "She's not technically my stepmom anymore, you know? She has nothing to do with my life." *Except for the devil's spawn she was carrying, linking us forever.* I shuddered.

"Yes, well, I'll just wait awhile, and if I don't hear from her then..." She looked like she was trying to work out a puzzle in her head.

"I'm pretty sure I won't be talking to her anytime soon, but if I do, I'll make sure she calls you."

"All right. Thank you, Madison. Everything okay with the Thompsons?"

"Yep." I forced a smile.

She nodded a couple times. "The tardy bell is about to ring. If you have trouble with your fourth hour teacher, tell her you were talking to me." She spun on her heels and marched down the hall, leaving me an alibi for what I was about to do.

The art wing was located in the basement of the school, and as I went down the steps, the stench of paint and glue assaulted my senses. I heard a bunch of guys talking and laughing. At the other end of the hall, I saw Grey. He sat on the floor scribbling something in a notebook, his messy brown hair falling in his eyes. As usual, he seemed completely oblivious of the little blonde staring at him from a few feet away, as if he was Harry Styles or something.

"Uh, hello," one of the other guys said, and Grey raised his head to look at me. I'd never noticed how blue his eyes were, like the lake on a sunny summer day—almost a perfect match to his blue button-down.

Grey's mouth dropped open as he stared up at me. "Madison? What are you doing down here?"

I gripped the strap of my backpack, feeling the sticky remnants of the "Dance is Life, Life is Hard" sticker I'd tried to pick off like old nail polish. "I was, uh, going out for a smoke."

"Hmm..." He lowered his eyes to his pad of paper. "I only drink when I smoke, and I only smoke when I drink. Or is it, I only do molly when I drink? I can't remember, can you?" He looked up again.

"Asshole." I turned around and headed back the way I came. *Blondie can have the jerk.*

I heard him jump up from the floor and jog toward me, undoubtedly breaking one heart in the process. "Damn it, Maddie. Wait."

No way. I wasn't going to stand around and let him make fun of me in front of his friends, no matter what he'd done to help on Saturday or how badly I wanted the joint in my backpack.

"Stop." He touched my arm just before I reached the steps.

I spun around and glared at him. "That was a pretty shitty thing to say when I came down to thank you and apologize for—you know."

He glanced down at the worn pair of Doc Martens on his feet where the brand-new Vans should have been. "Ruining my shoes?"

I couldn't see his friends from where we stood, but I was sure they could hear us, so I dropped my voice. "I'll replace them."

"You did me a favor actually. I hated that pair. My grams bought them for me, and they never fit right."

Why that made me smile, I don't know. "If you're done being a jerk, I'll say thank you now."

He smiled and changed his whole face. Instead of distant and judgmental, a smiling Grey made me want to lean into him and stay a while. *How'd I never notice how hot he is?* "I'm done, but I did warn you about Brody."

"Well, thank you for helping me when I didn't listen."

"You're welcome." He rubbed the back of his neck.

I reached into my backpack and fished for one of the joints Brody gave me. "Wanna have a hit with me?"

His eyes widened until I could almost see the white all the way around the blue. "Are you kidding me? Did Brody give you that, too?"

"He—" I was going to lie, but I had a feeling he'd see right through it. "Yeah, so?"

He shook his head. "I told you. There are better ways to deal with the pain."

"Right, because you've lost so many parents." I shoved the joint into my bag and put a few steps between us. I wanted to run back the way I came, but I wouldn't give him the satisfaction of running off.

He shoved his hands into his pockets and stared at the scarred linoleum beneath his feet. "My mom died four years ago, and I never knew the sperm donor. He didn't stick around very long after she told him she was pregnant."

"Oh." My eyes stung. She would have died when we were in junior high, and we hadn't gone to the same school then.

He lifted his head to lock his eyes with mine. "Anyway, try to stay out of trouble, okay?"

I wasn't really thinking about staying out of trouble. I *was* thinking about the sliver of bare skin I saw when he raised his arm and how he smelled like citrus and a new box of pencils.

"Maddie?"

"What?" I shook my head. "Oh, yeah. Stay out of trouble. Speaking of which, I should get to fourth hour."

I turned to leave, but he reached for my hand and smoothed his thumb over my fingers. "You've probably heard this a lot lately, but if you need *anything*, well, you obviously know where to find me."

"Thanks, but I'm fine."

He dropped his arm, and all the warmth left my hand. "Yeah, okay."

It wasn't until the ride home that I realized I'd been thinking about *him* and not about how much I missed my parents. Somehow, that short conversation had gotten me through those last few hours, and I wondered how many more conversations I'd have to have with Grey Daniels in order to make it through the rest of my life.

CHAPTER 6

ALEX

"CAN WE GET SOME HELP here?" Natalie wailed at the nurses behind the triage desk. "My friend is bleeding, and it's running down her legs. She's pregnant."

"How far along?" The red-haired nurse asked Natalie as if I wasn't able to speak.

"Less than four months." I panted through a wave of pain.

Natalie rubbed my arm. "Do you think she's having a miscarriage? Her husband died less than a week ago, she hasn't been eating, and she started complaining of nausea and discomfort. By the time I got to her, her pants were soaked in blood, and she was in horrible pain."

"No!" Not that. Not after losing David. "Please help me."

"Get me a gurney over here!" someone yelled, and the Emergency Room was a flurry of activity.

A man burst through a set of double doors at the end of the hall, and my world stopped. My legs buckled under me. *David.*

Natalie wrapped her arms tighter around me as I slipped toward the floor. "Oh my God, I need help."

Then *his* arms were around me. "Don't worry, I've got you," he whispered in my ear as he scooped me off the floor and placed me on a gurney.

A deep shudder cut through me as if a red-hot sword was embedded in my gut and someone twisted it from side to side. "Hurts so bad." I smiled up at him through a blur of tears. "But it's okay. You're here now. Stay this time. Don't leave."

"I'm not going anywhere. Can you tell me on a scale of one to ten how bad it hurts?" His warm hands slid over my abdomen, and I reached for them, squeezing them in mine.

"Ten. *Twenty.* Can't you just make it stop?" Another twist of the sword sucked the breath out of me, and everything that had happened that afternoon came flooding back. "David, why didn't you tell me about Maddie?" I locked my eyes with his. "You know she hates me."

A deep furrow formed between his eyebrows. "Alex, I'm Dr. Hudson. Don't you remember? We met Saturday. At the fu—at the church."

I blinked up at him. I did remember meeting Dr. Hudson at the funeral. Only he hadn't introduced himself. They had the same wavy brown hair, but he wasn't David at all. Pain spiked through me, starting in my heart. "I thought you were..."

Natalie's voice moved closer. "Dr. Hudson's going to take care of you, sweetie. Ben, why is she so out of it? It's like she's on something."

"It's the pain and blood loss. Look up here, Alex." The deep resonating voice called to me, and I turned my head in his direction. His face was a mask of grim determination. "It doesn't look good for the baby. Our job now is to get you stabilized." He turned his eyes from mine and yelled to someone behind him. "We need to get an IV started, get a type and cross, find the OB on call, and get them down here, we're gonna need an OR."

"I can't lose this baby." I shook my head, tears welling up in my eyes until his face became blurry, and visions of David clouded my thoughts. He wanted more children. A house full of them. He loved his daughter so much.

Maddie.

The first words I'd heard her utter came back like a staticky radio with a fresh signal. *"Why'd you bring her?"*

I'd had such hope as we drove to the Silver Bullet Diner. Even as she'd sat in the backseat of David's car with her slight arms folded across her chest, staring at the trees as we passed by, I'd imagined us being friends if nothing else.

It wasn't that long ago I'd been a teenager myself. I could speak their language. Loved the same music. Spent time interacting with teens as I worked on the video games I developed. But as David's daughter sat rigidly across from us in the tiny booth, my hope dwindled.

Maddie glared at me, and I felt every drop of hate she directed my way. "Why'd you bring *her*?"

David wrapped an arm around my shoulders and pulled me against him. "Alex and I are married."

"You're *married*?" She laughed. Just a quick blast of air through her nose as if David's announcement was a sick joke. "No offense, but what'd you do, knock her up?"

I froze to the vinyl bench seat, my heart hammering in my chest as she gaped at us in turn.

Maddie's horrified expression made her look older than her sixteen years. "You *did* knock her up! What about Mom?"

"Sweetheart, your mom and I have been divorced for almost two years. It's time we both moved on. I know you and Alex will become great friends." David squeezed my hand under the table.

Maddie's face hardened as she locked her eyes with mine. "She'll never be *anything* to me."

"Alex, can you hear me?" The doctor squeezed my hand, and my attention snapped to him. If I squinted, he looked so much like David, and I felt safe.

I pulled my eyes from his as a sob escaped me. "I'm sorry, David. I'm a total failure as a mother. I'll never be what she needs."

"Come on, we need to roll before we lose them both."

I tried to focus on what he was saying, but it was too much. First David and now… I couldn't even think and let the darkness wash over me.

"Hey, you're awake. How are you feeling?" Natalie stood over me smiling, but I could see the worry lines in her forehead.

I tried to reposition myself, but I hurt all over. And the worst pain was the kind that drugs couldn't fix. "How do you think I feel?"

Natalie's eyes glistened with unshed tears. "Like you went five rounds with Tyson?"

"I suppose that's accurate." Playing along was easier than talking about reality.

"But would it be Tyson now, or Tyson when he was still a boxer?" She fiddled with my blankets, smoothing the white cotton over my toes.

I stared at a faint scar on the back of her hand and wondered how many times she'd burned herself serving coffee. "Does it really matter?"

"It might." She stepped away from the bed and pulled up a chair, never once dropping the façade. "He's pretty out of shape these days."

"I'll bet he could still do some damage." *Damage? Could* anything *do more damage than the one-two punch life had just dealt me?*

"Right. That's why he's doing *The Hangover Six* or whatever." Natalie blew out a breath and fixed her eyes on mine. "Wanna tell me how you *really* feel?"

I avoided Natalie's question and focused on anything but her attempt to strip my soul bare. The faded blue wallpaper did nothing to dispel the depressing mood of the sparse hospital room. Neither did the drab curtains or the Motel 6 artwork screwed into the wall. "Like someone just ripped what was left of my heart from my chest."

"Oh, sweetie." Natalie grabbed my hand in hers and gave it a gentle squeeze, careful to avoid the tubes and wires.

I pulled my hand back, and my gaze followed the path of the clear tubing all the way to the bag of fluid hanging on the rack beside the bed. A slow and steady drip fell into the tube, leaving a chill in its wake. I hated hospitals—hated the smell, the dim lights, the generic walls—and the reminder of the lives lost within them. Not even a week ago, David had lain cold and still on a gurney in this very building.

I pulled my attention from the blank wall and shook off the memory. "No one will tell me what happened, but I can feel the loss. I know the… I know I lost it." My lips refused to form the word *baby*.

"I should have Ben come back in to talk to you." Natalie jumped out of the chair as if it had bitten her.

"Ben?"

"Yeah, Dr. Hudson. He's one of my coffee customers. He was on duty last night. He took care of you." Pity oozed from her expression. "You thought he was David."

I threw my arm over my face. I wasn't sure whether I should be humiliated or heartbroken. I'd wanted him to be David. So much.

"Don't worry about it. I'll go get him." Natalie patted my shoulder then left the room.

I timed the seconds by the monitor, beeping softly along with the cadence of my heart.

"How's our patient today?" The doctor approached the bed—the man who, other than coloring and build, didn't resemble my husband much at all.

Natalie trailed behind him, avoiding eye contact.

"I'm fine." *I may never be fine again.* I'd lost my baby. *David's baby.* "How long have I been here?"

"You came in yesterday." The doctor pulled his stethoscope from around his neck and pressed the cold disk to my chest. "Deep breath."

I sucked in as much air as I could then let it out.

"Again."

I did as he asked and waited while he listened.

He tucked the instrument around his neck and ran his warm fingers over my tender abdomen. "Are you experiencing any pain?"

Pain? When was the last time I *wasn't* experiencing pain. My heart couldn't tell the difference between internal and external misery anymore. "A little."

"On a scale of one to ten…"

"If you mean physical pain, I guess a six." As far as emotional pain, I couldn't count that high.

Natalie pointed at me as if she'd caught me stealing muffins from behind her counter. "She said she felt like she'd gone five rounds with Tyson."

"Five rounds? Really?" The doctor's eyebrows shot up. "You'd go that long? I'd probably take a dive after one." He flashed the same sympathetic smile I'd seen on too many faces in the past several days.

"Well, I wasn't being literal." I wanted everyone to stop trying so damn hard. Stop making jokes to lighten the situation. Just stop.

He tilted his head to the side the way David did—as if he were trying to read my mind or crack some impossible code—and I had to pull my eyes from his face. I couldn't allow myself to imagine he was someone he wasn't. I tried to sit up but changed my mind when a searing pain erupted in my midsection.

"Are you sure it's just a six? Your face is telling me it's closer to an eight."

I'd take an eight if it would distract me from the twelve working its way through my heart. "Just tell me already. Get it over with, like pulling off a Band-Aid. Stop trying to protect me from the truth."

He shifted his weight and stared at the floor for a moment before locking his eyes with mine. "You're right. You deserve the truth. I'm very sorry, Alex, but you had a miscarriage. You're lucky Natalie got you here so quickly. Had you waited any longer, we might have lost you too."

I barked out a hollow laugh. *Would that really have been so awful?* "Well, I guess I owe my life to Natalie… and you. Thank you." It seemed to be the appropriate thing to say.

"I want to keep monitoring you for another hour or two, but as long as your vitals stay where they are, you should be able to go home today. Is there anyone we can call?"

"No." I stared at the plastic hospital-issue bracelet circling my wrist. "There's no one. Not anymore."

"What about your parents?" Natalie asked.

"They just went home." Was it only yesterday? "And they worry about me too much as it is."

The doctor's brow furrowed as he jotted notes on my chart. "I'd really feel better if someone were at home with you. You'll have a difficult time getting around for a few days. And you lost a lot of blood. We need to make sure you don't hemorrhage again."

"I can stay with her." Natalie took my hand and squeezed.

"No. You have the coffee shop. I'll be fine by myself, really," I said.

"Don't be a martyr. I'll just get Rachel to work a few extra shifts. It'll be fine."

I shook my head hard enough to see stars. I just wanted—no, *needed* to be alone. The tiny fissures beneath the surface of my soul were spreading like cracks in the ice, and it would only be a matter of time before I fell through. "I can't let you do that."

"Quit being difficult, Alex." Natalie held her hand up to halt my next thought. "You're not doing this on your own, whether you like it or not. Just accept it."

Dr. Hudson cleared his throat, and we both turned to look at him like scolded children. "What about following up with your OB?"

"I-I don't have a doctor here… not yet. I never got around to it."

"How about I stop by to check on you?" He offered with a faint smile.

"No." Natalie and I said at the same time.

"That's really sweet of you, but it's not necessary." Natalie addressed the doctor then turned to me. "I'll come stay at your house. End of discussion." The look on Natalie's face told me arguing would be futile.

"Fine." I folded my arms across my barely-there hospital gown. "Have it your way."

Natalie helped me settle into bed, fluffing my pillows for the third time.

"Stop hovering." I swatted her hands away from my blanket. Having her in my house, treating me like an invalid, was driving me crazy. "I still haven't forgiven you for ambushing me. For going along with your buddy Dr. Hudson in his plot to keep me from having a meltdown in peace. It's not even remotely fair for you to be such good friends with my doctor."

"We're not really friends. I've known him for a while. He's one of my regular customers—a coffee snob like you. He can't stand the crap they serve at the hospital, so he comes in to the shop to fuel up before a long shift. But that had nothing to do with him saying you shouldn't be alone. He's a doctor. It's his job to look out for his patients." She watched me out of the corner of her eye. "Besides, I think he likes you. He's usually reserved and much quieter."

"I'm married." I swallowed against the knot in my throat. I reached toward David's side of the bed and wrapped my fingers around his pillow, tugging it to my chest. "I mean, I still *feel* married."

"That's not what I…" Natalie stopped fussing with my bedding and stared at me. "Oh, sweetie." Her pity washed over me in waves.

I punched the pillow then smoothed it out again, putting it behind my back. "No, don't say it."

"I promise it'll get easier."

I glared at her. Would I ever stop feeling as if my entire world had been yanked out from under me? "When? When I'm ancient and no one wants me anymore? Did I ever tell you how we met?"

She sat on the edge of the bed and shook her head.

"I was at a gaming con, trying to take down some sixteen-year-old kid playing Mystic Realms. I refused to get beat on a game I designed. The kid had mad skills, but I'd finally won, doing this ridiculous victory dance. David was there scoping out the competition, so he said. In retrospect, I should have known better. He barely even knew how to *play* a video game. I mean, seriously, the guy designed networking software. But he walked right up to me, with no preamble, and asked me to dinner. He said any woman able to hold her own against a teenage boy in Mystic Realms was worth getting to know. I didn't tell him until months later it was actually *my* game."

He threw his head back and laughed. "You cheated!"

"I did not."

"That kid didn't have a chance. You wrote the program." His eyes sparkled as he stared me down. "I'm impressed."

"He'll think twice before underestimating a 'girl' next time."

"Clever and beautiful. I can only hope my daughter grows up to be as confident as you."

I wiped the tears from my cheeks as I realized David would never see his daughter again. Never know he'd lost his second child. That *I'd* lost his baby. "David was it for me. I'll never find that again."

"You're only twenty-seven. Eleven and a half months younger than I am, I might add, and if you even *think* about telling me there's no chance of me finding Mr. Right, I'll...I'll stop making you coffee!"

"Oh, no. Not the coffee." Sarcasm hurt my insides, but it felt good to smile after so long. "I just don't know how to *be* anymore."

"What do you mean?"

"Without him. I mean, I know we were married for barely three months, but even before then, we might have been apart for weeks at a time, but we talked every day. I've had to stop myself from dialing his number so many times in the past week. I have no idea how to be *me* without David." The cracks spread a little further, and I fought to keep myself together. "And now I have this new empty place inside of me. How am I supposed to—ugh!"

"I know it sounds cliché, but time really does heal all wounds. And David will always be part of you, just in a different way. And if the way Ben was purposely avoiding checking you out today is any indication, you'll have no shortage of men banging down your door when you're ready to receive them." She waggled her eyebrows.

I gaped at her and pulled the pillow from behind me to hug it to myself. "I'm not even remotely interested in *receiving* anyone." Did she conveniently forget I'd just lost my baby? David's baby. And I still had to come to some sort of decision about his daughter. I couldn't begin to imagine what I would do about Maddie, and I wasn't ready to think about it yet.

"You will be. It'll just take time." Natalie swiped the TV remote from the bedside table. "How about a *Cake Boss* marathon? We can live vicariously and calorie free."

Late Thursday morning, Natalie bounded through the bedroom door with a huge grin plastered on her face. "You'll never guess who's here?"

I stared at her but said nothing. The twinge in my stomach told me I wouldn't like it.

"Ben! He's here to check on his favorite patient." She bounced on her toes, reminding me of a high school cheerleader.

"And how many phone calls did you have to make to get him here?" I narrowed my eyes and swallowed the string of curses straining to come out. "I don't want to see him."

Natalie's mouth dropped open. I almost believed the indignant expression. *Almost.* "Are you suggesting I had something to do with his visit today?"

"Yes, I *absolutely* think you had something to do with his visit, and it's not cute." Tears of frustration filled my eyes but didn't fall. How could she think for one minute…? "This isn't some romance novel, where the handsome young doctor saves the day and rescues the poor widow. This is my life. I'm recovering from a miscarriage. And my husband *just* died! Even if I did want to get out there again *some*day, it wouldn't be *to*day. Less than a month after his funeral!"

Natalie stood frozen in place, her hands still gripping my blanket and her eyes glistening. "I'm sorry, Alex. I didn't think of it that way." Something that happened a lot lately.

I brushed her hands away and stared at her. "Maybe you should have."

A single tear rolled down her cheek, and she wiped it away. "You're right. Of course, you are. I know it's too soon. But it's okay to let people in. He's a doctor. And he knows you don't have family here. He came all this way. So maybe just let him check on you. I'm sure he's not thinking of anything other than your health. He's a really sweet guy."

Part of me was afraid if he walked through that door, I'd see David again. And I couldn't bear to see him when I knew he was never coming back. "If you like him so much, why don't *you* date him?"

"I'm not saying you should date him. Just let him be your friend." Natalie smoothed the comforter. "Besides, he's a few tattoos and a motorcycle shy of my type."

"Fine." I sat against the pillows and crossed my arms. "Where is he? You didn't leave him outside to freeze to death, did you?"

"Of course not." She waved a hand. "He's standing in the kitchen, drinking the best damn cup of coffee your pitiful coffee maker has ever made."

My mouth dropped open. I would have killed for a cup of Natalie's coffee. "You made coffee, and you didn't bring me any? I thought I was hallucinating the smell of Arabica beans the way people in the desert hallucinate an oasis."

Natalie shrugged. "I was going to use it as leverage if you didn't agree to my conditions."

I bit back a smile. "Why are we friends?"

"Because I'm awesome." She beamed at me. "And I make the best coffee in Lake Edna."

"As far as I'm concerned, you make the *only* coffee in Lake Edna."

"That I do. Now go brush your teeth so your breath doesn't smell like yesterday's garbage while I go get him."

Dragging myself out of the bed to brush my teeth felt more like running a marathon, and I wished I'd taken the pain medication Natalie had offered me earlier.

"Knock, knock." The doctor's deep voice startled me as I crawled back into bed.

"Come in." I held my breath.

The door creaked open, and he poked his head in to smile at me. His blue eyes looked nothing like David's warm brown eyes, and I let go of a breath. "You look better today." He stepped into my room dressed in a pair of faded blue jeans and a beige sweater, his signature stethoscope wrapped around his neck like a scarf. I wondered if he wore that around the house, too.

"Well, I feel like shit." My muscles tensed as he stepped closer, waiting for my mind to play tricks on me again.

He chuckled. "You'll feel better in time."

"Why does everyone say that?"

"Because it's usually true." Dr. Hudson sat on the edge of my bed, keeping a comfortable distance between us.

I tugged the blanket up to my throat. "So, Doctor… will I live?"

He rubbed his chin in what came across as mock seriousness. "You want my expert opinion?"

"Absolutely."

"Then I'll need to check your vitals… listen to your heart… all that doctor stuff." He wiped the trace of a grin from his lips.

I inhaled slowly, pulling the blankets away from my body as he stood and leaned in closer to me. "Okay, then." I braced myself while his warm hands slid across my stomach. Trying to avoid eye contact with him, I caught movement in the hallway and shook my head. *Natalie.*

"We have an audience," I whispered.

He furrowed his brow. "She's worried about you."

I nodded, keeping my eyes trained on his long fingers as they pressed gently on my abdomen.

"Any pain?"

"Some. It's not too bad. A four, tops." *Unless you count the hole where my heart used to be, I'm fine.*

"Good." He pulled the blanket over my midsection. "You seem to be healing nicely."

On the surface maybe. "So I'll be up and around in no time?"

"I'm sure Natalie will have you sitting on a stool at the coffee shop before the week is out."

"Knowing her, she'll just bring the whole shop to me."

He laughed—a rich warm sound. "You're probably right. She has a way of getting people to do what she wants."

I struggled for something to say. I didn't know how to make small talk anymore, and even *I* knew the weather in January was the only constant in the small town. "Poor Rachel. She's probably going nuts trying to run the shop by herself."

Dr. Hudson twirled the end of his stethoscope between his fingers. "Natalie told me she hired someone new. He came in while Rachel was working the other day. Nice kid, she said."

"That's good. One hurdle down." I raised my voice loud enough for Natalie to hear me. "Now, can you please tell her I'm fine to take care of myself?"

He flashed a friendly smile, and Natalie's words came back to haunt me. *He's a really sweet guy.* "Just give it another day, okay? There's nothing wrong with letting someone take care of you once in a while."

Then his lips turned down, and the serious doctor mask was back. "And you don't have to pretend it doesn't hurt. Natalie said you're not taking your meds. There's no shame in admitting you're in pain."

I crossed my arms. "Fine. I'll take the damn meds. And I'll give it until tomorrow. But then I'm kicking her ass out."

"If she doesn't leave tomorrow, I'll help you." He rested his hand over mine and squeezed.

The sweet gesture caught me off guard, and a new wave of sadness crashed over me. I wanted to close my eyes and pretend he was David for a minute, just long enough to take the pain away. But I knew it would only be worse later if I did. "Why are you being so nice to me? I'm pretty sure it's against the doctor code to make house calls in this century."

He stood and draped the stethoscope around his neck again. "I won't tell anyone if you don't."

"No, really."

"You caught me." Dr. Hudson turned away, but before he did, I caught the pink flush in his cheeks. "I'm making an exception because Natalie said I'd be cut off from coffee for a month if I didn't."

I made a point of tucking the blankets around me. "That sounds like her."

"She's a tyrant, that one." He chuckled. "Well, I'd better get going, or I'll be late for my shift."

"Thank you, Dr. Hudson."

"Ben."

"What?"

"My name. It's Ben. It's a small town. We don't bother much with formality here. Take care of yourself, Alex." He pulled out a small white card and held it up. "This is my cell number. Call me if you need anything." He placed it on the dresser then turned and left the room.

Twenty-four hours later, Natalie decided I was finally well enough to leave alone. I was more than ready for her to go home, but my peace and quiet didn't last long. A shrill ringing cut through the silence, startling me out of a restless sleep. I didn't recognize the caller ID.

"Hello?"

The man cleared his throat before speaking. "Mrs. Barrett?"

"Yes, this is Alex Barrett."

"Mrs. Barrett, this is Joseph Howard. I hope you're doing well. I was concerned after you left on Monday, and I didn't hear back from you."

"It's been a busy week." The last thing I wanted to do was rehash things with my husband's attorney. And I knew he hadn't really called to ask about my health. He was waiting for an answer from me. An answer I didn't have.

"I won't take much of your time, but we do need to discuss arrangements for Madison. The last time we spoke, you seemed unsure as to whether you would be willing to take legal responsibility for her. I was hoping you'd had a change of heart."

"Actually, I hadn't given it much thought this week." I knew it made me sound uncaring, but I couldn't admit I'd lost David's baby and then tell him I didn't want David's daughter. What kind of monster did that make me? She'd just lost both of her parents, and I couldn't bear the thought of spending a single minute in her presence. "Is this something I have to decide today?"

"No, I suppose not." His hesitancy told me he agreed. I was a monster. "But we can't delay this too long. If you're going to refuse guardianship, we'll have to make arrangements for foster care until something more permanent can be decided."

My pulse quickened as the reality of the situation sank in. "That's really the only other option? It's either me or foster care? Surely she has godparents or other distant relatives somewhere."

"I suppose there might be, but unless you're willing to take the time to make those inquiries, I don't know how we would ferret them out."

David would never forgive me if I let his child go into foster care when I could've taken her in. "What if I agreed to keep her? Not permanently... just until we find someone."

"I think that would be a reasonable compromise." I heard the relief in his voice.

With a newfound resolve, I sat up and drew in a deep breath. "What would I have to do?"

"I'll have my secretary call you to set up a time to come in, and we can hash out the details. How does next week sound?"

"Next week would be fine." My stomach twisted as reality sank in. One more week before the inevitable. I had no idea how I'd manage the life of a teenager when I couldn't even manage my own.

"Good. It's settled. I'll see you then."

CHAPTER 7

MADDIE

I SLUNG MY LOADED-DOWN BACKPACK OVER my shoulder. In addition to the two tests I needed to study for, I had enough homework to keep me busy for a month. At least I wouldn't have to worry about what I was going to do this weekend, when I'd usually be at my dad's house. No way would I be going over there to spend time with the stepmonster. Eventually, I'd have to go and get my stuff out of the house, but I'd avoid that as long as possible. I'd known from the first minute I'd met her that she was heartless.

Dad had called from the airport to say he was picking me up, but when he pulled into the driveway and *she* was in the car—in the front seat, where I usually sat when it was just me and Dad—I knew things would never be the same.

"Hey, sweetheart." Dad jumped out to give me a bear hug, but she stayed in her seat, staring through the glass at me as if she wanted to squish me like a bug for touching my own dad. "I've missed you. How about we go to the Silver Bullet? I have something I want to tell you."

The diner was my favorite place to eat, but I didn't want to go there if she was going. "Okay, Daddy."

He held the door open for me, and I climbed into the backseat, my eyes glued to the back of her perfect head. I lost my appetite watching them stealing glances at one another, having a silent conversation the whole way. As soon as he parked, Dad lifted her hand and squeezed it, the special way he'd squeezed mine before every recital. I clenched my fists until my fingernails bit into my palms but refused to scream. I wouldn't give her the satisfaction of knowing how much it hurt to see my dad sharing something so private with someone else. I climbed out of the car before they'd even unbuckled, grabbing our regular booth in the back. I kept telling myself it was just dinner. I could make it through one lousy damn meal with her. And if I were lucky, I'd never have to see her again. But I was never *that lucky.*

That was the day he told me he'd impregnated and married her. That I'd never be rid of her.

With a shudder, I forced myself into the present. I liked to think that with Dad gone, I'd never have to see her again. Unfortunately for me, that stupid baby would tie her to me forever.

"Let me carry that for you." Brody lifted the bag off my shoulder.

I glanced at his stupid smirk. "Trying to get back in my good graces?"

"Well, you have been avoiding me all week."

"And apparently, you didn't take the hint." If he hadn't grabbed my bag, I would have put as much distance between us as possible.

He waved at a couple of his friends then turned to walk backward down the hall, facing me. "I'm sorry, okay? I shouldn't have let you get that far gone on Saturday, and I should have stuck around to make sure you were all right. Forgive me?" He wasn't paying attention to where he was walking and almost smacked into a girl half his size. I reached out and grabbed his coat to pull him out of the way, but I ended up pulling him toward me. He smiled and wrapped his arms around me. "I'll take that as a *yes.*"

I knew I should have pushed him away, kept up the appearance of being angry a little longer. That was how the game was played, after all. But I couldn't deny how good it felt to have someone hold me like that. Even *him.* I rested my forehead on his chest, just under his chin. His coat smelled like snow with a hint of weed. Flocks of students walked around us to get out of the building. They were probably all staring, but I didn't care. "I'm still pissed at you."

"I know." He rubbed his hands up and down my back. Even through my thick winter jacket, I could feel the heat of his touch. "Let me make it up to you?"

I stepped back to look at him. "How?"

"I have a swim meet this weekend, but next weekend, Luke's parents are letting him use the camp. I'll pick you up and bring you home like a proper date. What happens in between is entirely up to you."

I narrowed my eyes. Somewhere in the back of my mind, I knew his plan was a bad idea. But to the new me—the me who wanted to feel something, *anything*, the more painful the better—it sounded perfect. "I'm staying at Haleigh's."

His expression said he misunderstood my hesitation, and that played right into my hand. "She doesn't have to know where we're going. It's a private party anyway."

I didn't like the idea of lying to the one person who actually gave a damn, but I had to admit, I really wanted to go. "Okay, I suppose," I said on a calculated sigh.

He looked over my shoulder then grinned down at me. Before I could stop him, he kissed me right there in the middle of the school's main lobby. "Later," he whispered in my ear then handed me my backpack and walked out of the building.

I told myself I was in control, but the kiss affected me. A moment after that—as I tried to steady my racing heart—Grey passed me. He looked so disappointed as he glanced back then rammed the front door open and stormed off toward the parking lot, a flurry of snow trailing behind him.

I shrugged my bag onto my shoulder and went to meet Haleigh at her car. Halfway down the front walk, I saw her talking to an old woman wearing way too much makeup, obviously trying to look years younger than she was.

"Hi, Grandma," I said. "What are you doing here?"

Grandma Rosie yanked me into her arms, suffocating me in her perfumed cleavage. "I was just telling your friend I thought you'd like to go home for a while. I could stay with you at the house."

My grandmother had never stayed at my house before. She lived in an apartment on the other side of town, and my mom didn't invite her over very often. I'd spent the night with her the day after the accident but then went to Haleigh's when her parents offered. I was pretty sure Grandma didn't want to be stuck with a teenager, but since she was my closest relative, I supposed she felt obligated. And for the moment, she didn't reek of alcohol.

"I'll have to check with Mrs. Thompson." I shot a glance at Haleigh.

Haleigh shrugged. "I'm sure my mom will be fine with it. You haven't been home all week."

"Yeah, okay." What choice did I really have?

"Wonderful." Grandma Rosie beamed. "We'll stop by later to pick up Maddie's things," she said to Haleigh then climbed in the driver's seat of her beat-up blue sedan.

Haleigh pulled me into a quick hug. "You know you can stay with me anytime, but it might be good to sleep in your own bed and stuff."

"Thanks. I'll call you later." I climbed into the passenger seat and reached for the seatbelt only to let it go just as quickly.

Grandma's little car traveled the slippery roads just fine, which gave me pause since Dad had had a much nicer car but somehow lost control of it. He'd clipped a guardrail and rolled it down a steep hill before it smashed into a tree. Everyone else avoided driving by the site of the accident when I was in the car, but Grandma slowed to just under the speed limit as we navigated the 'S' curve near the scene.

I picked at the cracked vinyl seat. I didn't want to see if the rail still showed signs of the accident or if it'd been fixed over the past week and a half. I didn't want to see where his flipping car had torn up the ground, and I didn't want to see the bare spot on the hill where the tree he'd hit used to be.

"I think our first order of business should be to get some food," Gram said. "We'll stop at the house to see what's there then go do a little shopping. How does that sound?"

"Sure." I thought of the last meal I'd had at home. Dad had come over for dinner on Wednesday before he and Mom went out. Dad didn't even mention Alex. He didn't seem to care she was out of town. Mom made meatloaf—his favorite—and it was as if we were a real family again. The leftovers were still in the refrigerator, probably spoiled by now.

"Grab a bag of Cheetos for later," Grandma called to me from the other end of the aisle.

Mom never let me have junk food. She'd said I'd thank her for it when I was older. I threw two bags of the cheesy puffs into the cart and caught up with Grandma near the frozen foods.

"All we have so far are Cheetos, Swiss Cake Rolls, Oreos, and Diet Coke. Don't you think we're forgetting something?" *Like real food.*

"Oh, yeah! Where's the liquor aisle? I need a bottle of Jim Beam."

"It's back the other way. I'll go. You stay here." It was already almost five, and I was starving. If I waited any longer for her, we wouldn't be eating until midnight.

I grabbed the biggest bottle I could find and headed to where I'd left my grandma picking out frozen burritos, pizzas, and fried chicken. I hadn't made it two steps before the doctor my mom had gone out with a couple times turned his cart down the aisle. Spinning around, I headed in the opposite direction. Hightailing it into the bread aisle, I collided with someone's chest and something soft.

"Sorry I—" *Crap!*

"You smooshed my bread." Grey scrunched up his face, puffing out his pillowy lips like a pouting little boy.

I rolled my eyes and clutched the bottle to my chest, trying to hide the label. "Go get another loaf."

I almost laughed at his horrified expression. "I can't do that."

"Why not? It's not technically *your* bread. It's the store's bread." I snatched the ruined package from his hands and put it on the shelf then took a new loaf down and handed it to him. "There. Now you don't have to worry about a guilty conscience."

His lips curved into a devilish grin. "Yeah, I guess *you'd* know all about having a guilty conscience."

"What the hell is that supposed to mean?"

He nodded toward the bottle in my hand. "I hope you're not planning to smuggle that out in your shirt. Tiny little thing like you couldn't hide a shot glass, let alone a whole bottle."

I glared at him. "Do you come up with this stuff on the fly, or do you spend all day thinking up ways to annoy me?"

"All day, all night, all the damn time..."

"Well, I'd wish you'd stop."

I shoved past him and thought I heard him mutter, "You and me both," before I stalked off to find Grandma loading our cart with Jell-O.

"Gram, what are you doing?"

"It's on sale." She waved a couple of boxes in the air as if she held a pair of winning lottery tickets.

"Why do we need so much?"

"Jell-O shots! Jim Beam puts the 'J' in J-E-L-L-O."

Can I crawl under the cart now? "Well, sale or not, we don't need *that* damn much Jell-O. We can get one." I pulled all but one box out of the cart, but Gram tossed in one more. "Fine. Two."

She flashed another one of her snaggle-toothed grins before something behind me drew her attention. "Who's this handsome thing?"

I spun around to see Grey taking a half a step back.

My cheeks burned as I struggled to define my weird relationship with Grey Daniels. "Oh, this is Grey. We go to—"

"So is this your young man?"

"No!" We shouted at the same time, and for once, Grey and I were in agreement about something. He was most definitely *not* my 'young man.'

"We go to school together," Grey clarified quickly, taking another step away from my Grandma's leering stare.

"Why don't you invite him to come over for dinner? We could have a party… just the three of us." She winked at him.

Oh. My. God.

"Uh, I'll have to catch you Monday, Maddie. I've gotta get this bread home before it gets cold, or stale, or whatever." And he bolted before I could even process what had just happened.

Grandma licked her chapped lips. "Too bad. That would have been fun."

I gripped the cart, white knuckled, remembering the story Mom told about Grandma trying to steal her prom date. I'd always thought she was kidding. "Gram, I don't know about you, but I could really use a drink."

"That's my girl."

CHAPTER 8

ALEX

The ringing phone jarred me awake, and I stared down at the same number that had been calling me for days. "Hello?" My voice cracked, and I cleared my throat.

"Mrs. Barrett?" The woman's stern voice was familiar, deep and authoritative, but I couldn't place it.

I scooted until my back rested against the headboard. "Alex Barrett, speaking."

"This is Joyce Walker. We met briefly at your husband's... *funeral.* I've left a few messages for you but haven't heard back."

"Oh, sorry." I blurted out the words despite not being the least bit sorry for missing her calls. "I haven't been checking my voicemail. Forgive me, Mrs. Walker, but what exactly can I do for you?"

"Well, I've been trying to get some paperwork signed, but specifically, this morning, Maddie didn't show up for school. I phoned the Thompsons and was told Maddie went to stay with her grandmother for the weekend, but I don't have any contact information for—"

"What do you mean she went to stay with her grandmother?" The blood rushed from my head as I shot up out of bed too quickly. "She's not supposed to be with Rose or her aunt Shannon. My husband left strict instructions to that effect. That should be on file at the school."

"You would be correct. But she didn't leave with her from school. She was staying with Haleigh's family when she was picked up." A long silence followed, and for a moment, I thought she'd hung up. "Forgive me for being rude, Mrs. Barrett, but Mr. and Mrs. Thompson had no way of knowing about the family restrictions Mr. Barrett had in place.

Shouldn't you have shared that with them before agreeing to leave Maddie in their care?"

"Of course, you're right, Mrs. Walker," I ground out her name, pushing back a surge of temper. "But my husband had just died. I wasn't even aware Maddie was my responsibility until a week ago. And for the past several days, I've been recovering from… *a personal illness.* So if you'll just give me a few minutes to get my bearings, I'll see what I can do to locate Rose and Maddie, and I'll call you back."

After hanging up on the clearly annoyed Mrs. Walker, I set out on a fact-finding mission to track down my errant stepdaughter.

The first place I could think of to search was David's personal effects. I hadn't touched the envelope since the coroner's office had given it to me after the accident.

The ghost of nausea past reared its ugly head again as I pulled open the dresser drawer where I'd stored his things that first day. The mere sight of the large manila envelope threatened to destroy the composure I'd finally managed after the nearly two weeks since… *that day.* I poured the contents onto the disheveled bed. His cell phone, wallet, and key ring taunted me from the sheets. They'd left his wedding ring on his finger, where it belonged. Where it would never come off again.

After too many days off the charger, his phone wouldn't power on, leaving me with no way to look up Rose's number, if she even had a cell phone. I dug through the cards and bits of paper in his overstuffed wallet, leaving a wad of folded money in the pile along with the other items I had no desire to see.

After staring at the bed for more than a few minutes, I picked up his key ring. The tarnished half-heart was the exact opposite of mine. We'd picked them up at a souvenir shop on Mackinac Island while on our honeymoon. Scratches and dings covered his half, and I couldn't help wondering how many of those were from the accident and how many were from David dropping it.

I recognized most of the keys—he had twice as many as I did—both my car and his, the house, the safe in his office, his locker key for the country club, another car key I didn't recognize, and a key I couldn't identify. It was similar to the one that unlocked our front door but not the same. I suspected this was the key to Sarah's house.

Digging through the things that had touched the last few moments of my husband's life had gotten me no closer to finding Maddie or her grandmother, but it did open up a Pandora's Box of emotions I wasn't sure how to deal with. Sarah had been in the car with David on that icy road. *Why?* Why was my husband with his ex-wife while he took his last few breaths? And would I find the answer if I went to her house?

After pulling my car into the driveway, I put it into park and sat, staring at the closed garage doors, willing the secrets within to reveal themselves to me. Was Sarah's car in the shop? Was David just doing a favor for the mother of his only child? My hands went to my flat stomach, and the empty spot inside me ached at the thought. Not his *only* child but the only child he would ever know.

The snow had stopped falling, but somehow, that made the air feel that much colder. No matter how long I spent in the desolate frozen wasteland that was Michigan, I would never get used to the weather.

Forcing myself to step out of the warmth of my vehicle, I lingered near the door, ready to escape if I lost the nerve. A thick layer of ice coated the sidewalk under my feet as I made my way to the front door. The unidentified key slid effortlessly into the lock and turned with ease.

The minute the door opened, I knew something was wrong. The pounding in my ears as I set out on this mission had masked the sound of the heavy bass thumping out of the speakers somewhere within the walls of the house.

I'd never smoked before, but I'd been around enough pothead video gamers in my day to recognize the smell the minute I stepped inside the small ranch. The distinctive scent of marijuana and overwhelming odor of cheap liquor permeated the house.

"Holy hell," I muttered under my breath as I strained to get my bearings straight. Pictures of Maddie in various stages of life were scattered along the walls and propped up on end tables. Christmases. Easters. Every first day of school from what looked like kindergarten to the most recent school year. And so many images of Maddie smiling in ballet costumes. Several included David with his arms wrapped around Maddie or Sarah, sometimes both. They seemed so *happy*. I didn't know why, but that disturbed me. "Hello?" I called out in a trembling voice. The house should have been vacant.

An over-processed blond head poked up from the sofa, facing away from the door. "Hey, come on in! Have a drink. We're celebrating."

Celebrating? "Rose?" I stared into her bloodshot eyes, confused as to why she was here. Why she was obviously drunk and celebrating in her daughter's—my husband's—house. "What are you celebrating?"

"We're celebrating Sarah's life, snuffed out far too soon but glorious while she lived it."

With his face everywhere around me, I felt as though David—and *Sarah*—were watching me. "Is that even appropriate? How did you get in? Did Sarah give you a key?"

"Hell no." Rose slapped the back of the sofa, sending up a cloud of dust. "She wouldn't let me keep a key, but Maddie had hers."

"Where is Maddie?" I looked around the room for signs that my stepdaughter was anywhere inside.

Rose waved me off. "Oh, she's around here somewhere. Kid can't hold her liquor."

I sucked in a breath, regretting it almost immediately, as the tastes and smells trapped in the house lodged in my lungs. "What! You gave her liquor? She's a teenager! She has no business drinking."

"It's not like she's out there driving around! Better to drink at home with supervision than to be out partying with a bunch of kids her age."

Unbelievable! "And who's been smoking pot? I should call the police."

"Pot? Shit. No one gave me any pot. Maddie!" She sat up further and bellowed for her granddaughter. "Maddie, get your ass out here. You've been bogarting the pot."

"Grandma Rosie?" Maddie's voice slurred from down the hall. "I'm lying on Mom's bed."

"Well, get out here. You've got company."

My skin bristled as David's barely recognizable sixteen-year-old daughter staggered down the hall, black mascara ringing her brown eyes like a raccoon's, her long honey-brown hair tangled in knots around her head, and uncharacteristically risqué clothing hanging from her lithe frame.

"You rang?" Even her voice sounded off.

"Maddie? What the hell are you wearing?"

She untucked the red satin slip from her panties and glared at me. "Well, if it isn't my wicked stepmother. What brings you to my humble abode this fine day? Here to bring me a shiny red apple?"

Under different circumstances, I might have laughed. Instead, I choked back my horror. "Your principal called. I guess I don't need to ask why you weren't at school today."

"Nope." Maddie turned on her heel, nearly slamming her head against the wall as she brushed past me, smelling like a homeless person, and made her way to the kitchen. "Hey, Grandma Rosie. Did you eat all the Cheetos?"

"You know I don't eat those damn things," Rosie barked in her smoker's voice as she pulled herself off the couch and brushed the orange dust from the front of her white shirt. "So what brings you here today… it's Alex, isn't it?"

My mouth hung open as I watched the scene unfold in front of me. "How could you sit back and allow this to happen? She's just a child! She's drunk and high and looks—*and smells*—like she hasn't bathed in days. And what in heaven's name is she wearing? Have you no morals whatsoever?"

Rose laughed in my face, and I held my breath to avoid a contact high.

"She's older than I was the first time I got lit. Her mama just died. She's allowed to grieve a little."

"Grieve? You call this grieving? This is just one step away from suicide. No wonder David didn't want you within two counties of his daughter. I've been to the lawyer. I know you're not supposed to be alone with Maddie."

The older woman's eyes grew hard, and she took a step closer to me. "Who the hell do you think you are? That's my granddaughter in there. *My* daughter died. If Maddie wants to go play dress-up in her mama's clothes to feel closer to her, who are you to say that's wrong? You're nothing. You're not family. Marrying her father doesn't give you a right to say what she can and cannot do."

I steeled myself against what I knew was coming next. "Oh, that's where you're wrong. According to David's attorney, *I'm* Maddie's legal guardian. You're the one who has no say in what she can and cannot do. And since this house now belongs to me, you're trespassing!"

"What?" Rose gaped at me, her stale liquor breath wafting across my face like the ghost of old garbage. "Sarah left the house to you? She wouldn't do that. We may not have had the best relationship, but my daughter loved me. I know she did. Just as much as I know she *hated* you."

I wrapped my hands around my midsection to hold myself together. Five minutes with Rose had ripped all those old wounds wide open again. "Well, she may have hated me, but David loved me. And he trusted me to take care of what mattered to him the most. So get out of my house."

"What the hell do you mean, *your* house? This is my mom's house!" Maddie stumbled out of the kitchen wielding an open bag of Oreos, leaving a trail of cookies in her wake. "*You* get out! I don't want you here. Just get the hell out. I hate you! I hate that stupid baby you're carrying. And I hate—" Before she could get the last word out of her mouth, Maddie vomited all over the front of herself, dropping down in a heap as she cried.

Part of me felt as if I should go to her. To comfort her. But I stood frozen in place as the last piece of the man I'd loved broke down in front of me, wondering how I would ever muster the compassion to do what he'd asked of me.

CHAPTER 9

MADDIE

STRUGGLING AGAINST THE WEIGHTS HOLDING my eyelids down, I managed to pop one then the other open. Even with hangover-induced blurred vision, I could tell I was in my room at home. My curtains blew wildly around the window, and the smell of Lysol was so strong I could taste it, right there on the tip of my tongue along with the bitterness of vomit and stale Cheetos.

It was too cold to get out of bed, but I had to pee, so I tugged on the heavy blankets until I had them wrapped around me like a toga, and made my way to the hall bathroom. As soon as I'd finished emptying my bladder, I heard voices carrying from the other room. I recognized Alex's sugary-sweet California accent.

Inching my way closer, I tried to make out what they were saying.

"I think I've finally managed to get the puke smell out of the carpet. I never would have thought I'd be giving a spit polish to my husband's ex-wife's house." Alex huffed as if she'd just finished running a marathon.

"You're doing the right thing here, you know." The man's soothing voice sounded vaguely familiar, but I couldn't place it.

Alex laughed, but she sounded anything but amused. "Right for who? For David? For Sarah? Certainly not for me. I just cleaned up from a drunken party my dead husband's former mother-in-law threw for his sixteen-year-old daughter. This isn't something people do on a regular basis. Maybe people on a Jerry Springer episode but not people where I'm from."

What a bitch!

"I thought you were from LA. Are you telling me you've never heard about crazy Hollywood parties or *Girls Gone Wild* in your neck of the woods?"

"Are you teasing me? At a time like this?"

"Come on, Alex. You need to relax. She just lost her parents. She's bound to act out. And as for the grandmother, from what I've heard, for a woman in her sixties, she's not exactly known for her maturity."

I rolled my eyes. I couldn't argue with what he'd said about my grandma. She wasn't very parental, but she did know a thing or two about helping me forget.

"You know, I called you in for a medical consult, not a psych evaluation."

Maybe the crazy bitch needed a psych eval.

"Well, in my expert medical opinion, what you did here today was a good thing."

"Thank you, Doctor."

"Now who's teasing?" His voice got all deep and sexy like Brody's when he was trying to get me to bend to his will.

Are you kidding me? I felt like I was a fly on the wall in a late-night, soft-core porn movie. My stepmom was flirting with some guy in my mother's living room. Thanks to Michigan winters and the stupid frozen ground, my dad hadn't even been buried yet, and she'd already replaced him. Acid clawed its way up my throat, and I swallowed it down. I hurried down the hall and back to my room before they caught me listening in on their romantic interlude. Not moments after I'd nestled under the warm covers, there was a soft knock against my door.

"Maddie? Are you awake?"

Would she never leave me alone? "Go. Away."

"I can't do that. We need to talk."

"I need to sleep. In case you didn't notice, I have a raging hangover. So unless you're bringing me a bag of White Castle, you can leave." I buried my face in my pillow.

The hinges creaked as the door eased open. "No, I don't have anything for your hangover. You should probably just suffer for a while. Maybe you won't be so willing to get drunk again anytime soon." The mattress dipped at the foot of the bed. "You know, you could have killed yourself drinking that much while smoking pot and whatever else you were taking."

"Ohh, reefer madness! Whatever shall we do?" I clapped my hands to my cheeks and lifted my face just enough to give her my best bitch brow. Her eyes seemed darker and sunken in, and her reddish hair had lost all its shine, as if she'd just finished a stretch in the local jail. *Good.* "Did you ever think maybe I was *trying* to off myself?"

Alex closed her eyes and muttered something under her breath. "You're not serious!" What little bit of color she had drained away until her face was the color of paper.

"You're so stupid. Of course I'm not serious." I wasn't trying, but if it happened naturally, no great loss. It was all I could do to keep from kicking her scrawny ass off the end of my bed. Instead, I pulled my feet away from where she sat and pressed my face deeper into the pillow with a groan. "Where's my grandmother?"

"She's gone."

I sat up faster than I should have, and my stomach gurgled. "What do you mean she's gone?"

"I called her a cab and sent her home." Alex stood and straightened her sweats—*Dad's* sweats. "She's lucky I didn't call the police."

I kicked at the blankets until I'd untangled myself enough to swing my legs over the side. "You sent her away? You have no right to do that! She's the only family I have left. You can't just dismiss her like the *help*."

She pulled her hands into her sleeves until they disappeared. "That's what your parents would have wanted."

"Why do you even care? Now that Dad's dead, you can do whatever you want. You won't be stuck with me anymore."

Alex barked out another cold laugh. "What I want isn't possible. What *he* wanted was for me to take care of you."

"He who? Who are you talking about? I know you're not talking about my dad, because he would've never wanted to leave me… especially not with *you*! He and my mom were getting back together." The minute the words were out of my mouth, I wished I could take them back. But since I was on a roll… "That's why they were together that day. They were making plans for the future. *Our* family's future." The line between what was real and what I wanted with all my heart blurred, and I let it.

Alex stood from the end of the bed and smoothed out the quilt before taking a few steps toward the door. "We can discuss this later—"

"There is no later. I'm going back to Haleigh's."

"No, you're not. I've already spoken to the Thompsons and the school. You're going to pack your things and come home with me."

"The hell I am!" I pounded my fists into the mattress. "I want nothing to do with you and your stupid baby. My dad only married you because you were pregnant. I mean, it's probably not even *his.*"

She tried to look cool, but I heard her gasp. "I'm not going to argue with you. You stink, you look like crap, and you don't get a say in this. I'll give you until dinnertime to grab a shower and a bag. We'll get pizza on the way back to the house."

My eyes burned into her, trying to set her on fire, but she just kept talking as she got closer and closer to the open door.

"I'm going to finish straightening things up out here. You have one hour." Then she left my room and shut the door behind her.

I looked down at the red slip I was wearing. After puking all down the front of it, it was completely ruined. I shivered as the cold air hit my exposed skin and ran to the bathroom.

No way I'd've ever admitted this to Alex, but I felt way better after taking a shower. I switched off the hairdryer and pulled a towel around myself when I realized I'd forgotten to grab clean clothes. I crept through the hall to my room, clutching the towel against me.

The guy's voice from before still rumbled in the living room, stopping me just short of my door. I held my breath, trying to overhear what they were saying.

"Alex, you need to rest. You've been on your feet for hours. Come sit."

"I'm fine."

"You're not fine. You look like you're going to pass out."

Good, maybe she'd die, and I'd finally be rid of her.

"Thank you again, for your expert medical opinion, but feel free to leave anytime you like."

He sounded shocked. "Are you kicking me out?"

"Don't you have a shift or something?"

"Let me worry about that. But no, I don't have a shift tonight. I switched with Dr. Adams. In your current state, you really shouldn't spend the night alone."

"Alone? As if that'll happen again with Sarah Jr. sleeping under the same roof as me."

She acted like I wanted *to sleep there.*

"Alex—"

"Don't."

"Did you tell her yet?" he asked.

"Who? Maddie? I will, but now is not the time."

Tell me what? That she'd already moved on? Like I could miss that. She was spending time alone with this guy, not even two weeks after my dad—her *husband*—had died? She was probably trying to find a new baby daddy for her evil spawn. I tiptoed back to my room. The last thing I wanted to do was to confront that lying bitch in my mom's house.

After closing my door as quietly as I could, I went straight to the folded pile of clean clothes stacked on my bed, the bed that had been made in the time it took me to shower. They were the same clothes I'd sifted through what seemed like days ago. "Don't touch my stuff," I muttered as I pulled a long-sleeved T-shirt and my favorite jeans from the pile and a clean pair of underwear from the basket beside it.

I picked my mom's things from the clean laundry and shoved mine into a duffel bag, tossing it against the wall by my backpack. *Ugh.* My backpack—where my homework still sat untouched. There was no way I'd have time to get it done before tomorrow. *Double ugh!* I'd missed a test.

"Maddie." Alex's voice carried through the closed door. "My car is leaving in ten minutes. You'd better be in it."

I'd rather you were under it. "Yeah, okay. Fantastic. Can't wait." As if my life wasn't already FUBAR—fucked up beyond all recognition—without adding Malibu Barbie to the mix. I grabbed my bags and reluctantly made my way to the stupid Porsche in the driveway.

On my way through, I glanced at the sofa and wondered if they'd had sex right there in my mom's house. *Bitch.*

"Where's the guy?" I looked around and only saw Alex sitting in the driver's seat of the car. Her boyfriend must have snuck out while I was packing.

"He did what he needed to do and left."

"I'll just bet he did," I muttered. "Hey, if I'm going to be stuck with you for more than a few days, I need to stop at Haleigh's and pick up the rest of my stuff."

"Days?" She turned to me and raised an eyebrow. "It's going to be a bit longer than that."

"Great." I huffed and folded my arms, sliding down in the seat until I could put my feet on the dash.

"My thoughts exactly." Alex kept her eyes on the road ahead of her. "Get your feet off the dash."

"I wish my dad was here."

"So do I," she muttered so low, I wasn't sure if I'd heard her right.

We pulled into Haleigh's drive, and I jumped out before the car had come to a complete stop. Being trapped in a vehicle with her was bad enough, and now I was faced with being trapped with her for the unforeseeable future.

Before I'd even raised my hand to knock, the door swung open, and Haleigh stood inside gaping at me, a piece of bubble gum dangling from her lips like drool. "I thought you'd died! What the h-e-double-hockey-sticks, Maddie? You scared the living poop out of me. Where have you been?"

I shrugged. "Just hanging with my grandma for a few days."

"Sure. That's why Mrs. Walker called here looking for you, and so did your stepmom. No one knew where you were."

"I was at my house. It's really no biggie. I'm fine. See?" I turned around as if I was modeling my jeans. "Now let me in. I'm freezing my nipples off out here."

She stepped to the side, her pigtails bouncing around her shoulders, and I brushed past her to go inside.

"Is that Alex's car? What's going on? Are you in trouble?"

"It's a long story. Basically, I'll be staying with her for a while. Or forever. Who the hell knows? Right now, I need to grab my stuff and go before she comes in here to talk to me again."

A few minutes and another duffel bag later, I was back in the Cayenne, and we were heading home. Well, my dad's home. I guessed it would be mine now too.

I followed Alex through the garage into the kitchen.

"What do you like on your pizza?" She pulled a wrinkled menu from a drawer.

"The usual."

"Pepperoni and sausage?"

"Eww, no." I gagged on my saliva. "Ham and pineapple."

She frowned. "We'll get two."

Alex called in the order while I dragged my stuff upstairs and stared at my homework for thirty minutes until the doorbell rang.

The smell of fresh pizza wafted up the stairs, so I abandoned my work and bounded down, suddenly ravenous. Alex had her cell phone attached to her ear with a stupid grin on her face, so I knew she was talking to *him* again.

"Hey, Maddie just came down to eat." She laughed. "Yes, I promise I'll call you later with all the details, but I've gotta go. Yes… I'll be fine. Coffee first thing in the morning. Okay. Bye."

I nearly lost my appetite but managed to force myself to eat three pieces anyway. The urge to ask her who she'd been talking to was almost overwhelming, but I resisted long enough to finish my meal and climb the stairs to bed. Tomorrow would be an interesting day, and as much as I knew I couldn't avoid it, I wasn't looking forward to it, at all.

CHAPTER 10

ALEX

"YOU'RE KIDDING! DRUNK?" NATALIE'S MOUTH hung open as she topped off my coffee.

I picked up the cup, blowing on it as I brought it to my lips. "Totally on her ass."

"And the grandmother knew?"

"Knew? Rose bought the booze." I lowered my voice as someone came through the door and stepped up to the counter. "I have no idea where Maddie got the drugs."

"Welcome to Bean There, Donut That. How can I help you?" Natalie immediately put on her public persona, greeting the customer and taking his order with practiced efficiency. The minute the door closed behind the man on his way out, the forced smile melted away, and her face morphed back into amused disbelief. "And you just waltzed in there and kicked the old bat out?"

"Basically. But not until I'd read her the riot act. I see why David was so adamant about keeping Maddie away from Sarah's family."

"Yeah." Natalie blew a chunk of blond hair out of her eyes and turned to check the coffee machine. "It would have been nice if he'd actually told you that. You would have known what you were dealing with."

I shifted my weight on the shiny red swivel stool. "There's a lot I wish he'd told me." *A lifetime of things I wished he'd told me.* "In two more years, it wouldn't have mattered. God, Nat, he wasn't even forty."

She took a step toward me with her arms out as if she might try to comfort me but changed her mind, forcing a smile as she wiped imaginary crumbs from the counter. "So… did Granny put up a fight?"

"No. When Maddie passed out in a pool of her own vomit, Rose freaked out, thinking I was going to call the police."

"Did you *tell* her you were calling the cops?"

"No, but I picked up the phone and called a cab, and I guess since she had no idea who I was talking to, she assumed the worst. She grabbed her stuff and got the hell out of there."

"She just took off in her car, drunk?"

"She bolted before I had a chance to stop her. I wouldn't have let her leave if I'd known she planned on driving drunk. I may not have wanted anything to do with her, but I sure as hell didn't want someone else's blood on my hands. Can you believe she actually had the audacity to ask me to repay her for the groceries she'd bought? If you could call any of it groceries. A bunch of junk is more like it."

"At least you tried to do the right thing."

"Except all the *right thing* got me was stuck with a bratty teenager who despises the very sight of me. This morning, I offered to drive her to school—I had to go there anyway to fill out paperwork for that crabby Mrs. Walker—and she said, and I quote, 'Haleigh's picking me up. The less I have to see you, the better.'" I took a final swig of my coffee then set it down with a thump on the counter. "I should have told her the feeling is mutual." The impulse might have been childish, but I couldn't seem to help myself.

"You can't really mean that. She's just a kid."

"I don't know. She was furious with David for marrying me. I had no idea someone so tiny could make so much noise. I thought David was going to have a stroke when she let loose with a blue streak that would have made a sailor blush. I often wonder if it would have been easier if we hadn't eloped, if Maddie and I'd had a chance to get to know one another before being thrown together as family. Every time I look at her, I see that angry girl her father introduced me to four months ago. Do you know what she said to me yesterday? She said her parents were getting back together. That's why David was with Sarah that night." The rest of Maddie's words from the other night rang out in my head. *He only married you because you were pregnant.*

"You don't actually think they were… you *know*?"

"No. Of course not. She's just trying to get under my skin." I shook off the thought of Sarah and David sneaking around behind my back from my overactive imagination. The man who married me would never do that. "I told the attorney I'd keep Maddie until the end of the school year. By then, I should be able to find someone more suitable, someone who might actually want her."

Natalie scowled. "Harsh much?"

"That's not what I meant, and you know it." I blew out a breath. "I'm not equipped to raise a teenager, and she obviously doesn't want me to either. For all I know, there's some long-lost family member who would fight me to take her. Someone who won't look at her face and see Sarah staring back at them. I just know that isn't me." We sat for a few minutes without saying anything until the quiet grew uncomfortable. I cleared my throat. "You know Mike Allen, don't you?"

"I've heard the name."

"He and David have been friends forever. He's Maddie's godfather. He has kids her age. Mr. Howard's going to approach him to see if he'd be willing to take Maddie."

Natalie's eyebrows shot up. "So you'd just pawn your husband's daughter off on the first name on the list?"

My mouth dropped open. I felt as if she'd stabbed me through the gut. "God, no, but what am I supposed to do? She'd rather live with her drunken old grandmother than me. She hates me. And not only that, but how the hell am I supposed to be someone's mother when I couldn't even—" A fresh stab of pain lanced through me.

"Stop." Natalie's hands came up in front her as if she could block my thoughts. "That had nothing to do with anything you did. Those things just happen—no one knows why— but certainly not because it was known throughout the cosmos that you'd be shitty mother material. I don't think even you could predict that, at this point."

"Yeah, well, whatever." I waved her off. "Regardless, I'm not exactly equipped to handle a troubled sixteen-year-old, who hates my guts, all on my own."

Natalie screwed up her face, wiping a hole in the clean counter.

"Hey… speaking of *all on your own,* what was it you were saying about a certain doctor showing up on his white horse the other night?"

Not this again. "Stop. I told you yesterday. I didn't know who else to call in this nosy little town, and his card just happened to be in my pocket."

"Just happened to be, huh?" Natalie bumped my shoulder. "That's awfully convenient."

I rolled my eyes. "It was a fortunate accident, nothing more. Stop reading things into it."

Natalie flashed a bright smile. "I'd say I'm not your only friend in this town anymore."

The woman seriously had no shame. I eyed her cautiously, wondering if she'd lied when she said she was twenty-eight. She didn't act much older than Maddie. "*I'd* say you'd better make yourself useful and pour me another cup of coffee before I find a new place to loiter in the mornings."

"In this town? It's me or Mitchell's Tavern, and trust me. I went to school with Scotty Mitchell. The conversation here is way more stimulating."

"While I'd love to stay here all day, partaking of your *stimulating* conversation… I've already had three cups of coffee, and I'll be hard pressed to concentrate on meeting my project deadline if I have a fourth."

"You heading out?" Surprise colored Natalie's expression.

"Yeah, I think my bereavement leave is up right about now. It's time I got back to work. Even before all of *this,* the suits were all over me, breathing down my neck to come up with a new concept. But hell, maybe diving into the creative process is just what I need to take my mind off of things."

"You mean those greedy bastards aren't living high off the hog from the last three games you came up with? The new kid working here was going on and on about how *Mystic Realms Three* is still on backorder from Christmas. Apparently that's what he's buying with his first paycheck."

My lips tipped up of their own accord. "See, that's why I do what I do. The absolute devotion of the players makes it all worthwhile."

"Well, don't work too hard. I'm sure Ben would agree with me when I say you need to take it easy."

I shook my head at her repeated attempts at playing matchmaker. I'd known Natalie long enough to know she dealt with grief in her own way. Her own highly inappropriate way, but who was I to judge? "See ya later, Nat."

"Later, 'gator."

The pulsing beat of death metal music threatened to make my eardrums bleed as my laptop curser blinked at me over and over again, taunting me from the screen. Like the constant ticking of a metronome… timing my inability to think of a single innovative game concept that would appeal to the ever-changing mind of a teenager. It had all been done before—if not by me, by someone else. And the idea that I could come up with something fresh and new just two weeks after my husband's funeral and a week after losing our baby was ridiculous. Even my old standby mood music wasn't helping.

I switched off the iPod and stood to stretch, tossing my headphones into my chair. David hated death metal, which was why we had separate offices—and I had the best pair of headphones on the market. But not even the most expensive, noise-dampening headset could drown out the voices screaming at me that he was gone.

After a moment, I switched the iPod on again and shuffled through the songs until I found my David playlist. I cued up "Unforgettable" and disconnected the headphones so the music could play through the speakers. Nat King Cole's velvety voice filled the room, and I closed my eyes, swaying to the melody. If I kept my eyes shut, I could almost feel David's presence in the room. Almost hear his voice singing along with the music. Almost feel his arms wrapped around me, pulling me close.

My phone buzzed with an incoming text, breaking the spell.

Unknown caller: Hey.

Me: Who is this?

Unknown caller: Oh, sorry. It's Ben. Checking in to see how Maddie's doing today.

Me: Oh hey. Well enough to drive me crazy from the moment she opened her eyes.

I debated saving his name in my contacts but decided against it. It wasn't as if I had a reason to talk to him that often.

Unknown caller: I'm familiar with the concept of being driven crazy. Perhaps you should take a nap while she's in school. You still need your rest.

Me: I was trying to work, but since that's not happening, perhaps I'll take your expert medical advice instead.

Me: You really seem to be going above and beyond the normal doctor/patient thing.

Unknown caller: You seem like you could use a friend.

Me: I'm definitely short on those around here.

Unknown caller: Problem solved. Sleep well.

I didn't know what to think about him yet. Part of me wanted to embrace the friendship he was offering. The other part wanted to hide in my fantasy where David had never left, and I wasn't alone. I stared at his text for a few minutes before grabbing my coat. There was no way I was going to be able to fall asleep with David so fresh in my mind. I didn't want the dreams to come. It was just that much worse when I woke up, and he was still gone. I only had one viable solution. I needed inspiration. I needed to shoot something. I only hoped the local laser tag facility was open on a school day.

CHAPTER 11

MADDIE

F*INALLY*. IT WAS SATURDAY NIGHT. I'd managed to avoid Alex as much as possible during the week. School kept us apart during the day, and homework gave me an excuse to lock myself in my room at night. Not that I was actually doing the homework. My teachers were surprisingly accommodating, all but giving me the semester off. Playing the dead parent card times two had worked out better than if I'd planned it.

Then again, my only plan was to steer clear of the stepmonster and get wasted… often. In less than thirty minutes, Brody would pick me up, and with any luck, I'd be able to stretch things out for the rest of the weekend. I had the expensive lingerie Mom never had a chance to wear tucked into my backpack, along with a change of clothes and the condom I'd swiped during health class.

"Maddie?" Alex's voice carried up the stairs. "Are you expecting someone?"

Brody!

"Yeah." I checked my reflection one last time, my bleak expression staring back at me. "Be right down!"

I hurried down the steps and yanked the door open as he was reaching out to knock. My tummy flipped at the sight of him dressed like he was heading into a debate club meeting or something, rather than what I knew he had planned for the evening. "Hey," I said to him, looking over my shoulder. Then I called out to Alex, lurking just around the corner. "I'm going with Brody."

"Wait!" Alex said.

The last thing I wanted was for her to give him the third degree. "We're going to be late."

"Late for what?" Alex jammed her fists into her hips and gawked at us. Her hair hung in strings around her face where it had fallen out of the messy ponytail. She was really starting to let herself go. "You didn't tell me you had plans."

"It's just Brody. We're going to his place to hang out. We need to pick up some people on the way."

"A party?" She snapped her mouth shut as if weighing the options.

"No, just hanging out with some friends." I resisted the urge to stomp my feet. Why, of all times, did she choose *this* one to get all maternal on me?

Alex turned her glare to Brody. "Your mom and dad will be there?"

I rolled my eyes. Right. Like I'd have sex with Brody in front of his parents.

Brody flashed his Hollywood smile. "Don't worry, Mrs. B, I'll take good care of Maddie."

Alex chewed on her chapped lower lip. "My attorney—well, *David's* attorney—tried to call your father earlier this week, but he hasn't returned the call."

Way to kill the mood. "What does Dad's lawyer want with Mr. Allen?"

"Just something about the will. Nothing you need to worry about." Alex took a step back, fidgeting with the buttons on the ugly orange sweater hanging off her body like a tarp. "It's really nothing. You two go on. Don't be out late."

"Dad was away on business all week. But I'm sure he'd love to talk to you. He's going to miss Mr. Barrett on the golf course come spring."

Alex sighed. "That's sweet of you to say, Brody. I'll check in with him sometime next week."

"Okay, well, we're leaving. Bye." I tugged on Brody's arm, dragging him out the front door. "God, I thought you were going to have us stuck there all freaking night long."

Once I'd buckled myself in, he pressed a white capsule into the palm of my hand. "Take this, princess. You'll forget all your problems in a matter of minutes."

I popped the pill into my mouth, swallowing it dry. "Thanks. I didn't know you could see my thoughts."

"I plan on seeing a lot of you tonight... and *this*"—he tapped my head—"is the last place I'm going to be looking."

Holy shit. Holy shit. Holy shit! As much as I thought I wanted this—and I did—I was terrified. But as the reality sank in, and the pill's effects kicked in, my inhibitions fell away. "And *this*—" I cupped him between his legs "—is where *I'm* going to start."

A bone-deep cold soaked into me. I rolled to my side and pulled the blankets around my naked body. My head hurt. My legs throbbed. And my insides ached in a way that left me emptier than I'd been before. Why had I thought sacrificing my body—giving up my V-card to the biggest douche in Michigan—would fill the void left when my parents died? *Because I'm a cutter who doesn't cut, that's why.* It took a lot of effort to be sure all my scars were where no one but me could see them.

"Thought maybe I'd have to dump this water all over you to wake you up." Brody jiggled an open water bottle in my face. A few drops splashed out and hit my arm.

My hand trembled as I reached out for it. "Thanks." I swallowed a few big gulps then handed it back. "What time is it?"

"Almost midnight. You need to finish the bottle and get dressed, so I can get you home."

"Home?" I didn't *have* a home anymore. I had two houses, and I didn't belong in either of them. I reached for him, wrapping my fingers around the hem of his shirt. "Can't I stay... with you?"

He laughed. "I'm glad you liked it that much, but we have to keep up appearances for the 'rents. Actually, I'm glad Alex is so lax about who you go out with. Your dad would never let me take you out."

I nodded.

"So you knew he told me to stay away from you?"

I shrugged. Dad never came out and said Brody was a bad guy, but he wasn't subtle whenever the topic came up. "Not in so many words." I slowly sat up, and the room spun for a second before he shoved the water bottle back in my hand.

"Finish this, and come out when you're dressed." Then he left me alone in the room.

I eased myself out of bed and found my clothes in a heap on the floor. My unopened backpack sat in the corner. "Looks like neither one of us will get a chance to wear that lingerie, Mom." It took me several tries to get my arms into my shirt. My legs were like jelly. Flashes of the previous few hours filled my head. Some of them were nice, like Brody leading me away from the rest of the party. But judging by the way I felt now, my brain had blocked out the not-so-pleasant memories.

"Maddie, we need to go," Brody called from the other side of the door.

I grabbed my bag, dragging it and myself across the room. The muscles between my legs ached and burned, and I sort of hoped I had the bruises to remind me. "I'm ready."

After a silent fifteen-minute car ride, he pulled into my driveway. "Thanks, babe. You were great." He leaned over and pressed his cool lips to mine. He didn't linger, didn't open his mouth, just a quick peck before pulling away.

I nodded then opened my car door and climbed out.

"See ya." He threw the car into reverse before I'd even shut the door.

The cold air filled my lungs and cleared my head just enough for me to slide my key into the lock and slip into the house as he drove away. I dropped my backpack and kicked off my snow-soaked shoes in front of the washing machine. As I shrugged off my coat, I noticed a dim light coming from the kitchen. I tossed my jacket on a hook and fluffed my hair in front of my bloodshot eyes. I didn't need Alex bitching at me tonight. But unlike Mom who would have waited up all night, she wasn't even in the kitchen. I flipped the light off and moved as quietly as I could toward the stairs, hoping she was in bed already.

"Maddie, is that you?" her sleepy voice came from the living room.

I stopped, trying to decide if I should answer or not. "Yeah, I'm going up to bed."

"Okay" was all I heard her say before I scurried up the stairs and locked myself in my room as fast as my sore body would let me. I flopped down on the bed and muffled my sobs in a pillow, crying myself to sleep.

"What the hell is this?" Alex screeched, jarring me awake. Her sunken eyes stretched wide as she stared down at me, making her look like some psycho rag doll or something.

I bolted up out of bed, still fully dressed from the night before, and grabbed the red silk and lace from her hands, causing the single condom to land on the plush cream carpet at my feet.

Alex's eyes stared at the foil square, and I almost laughed at the over-the-top expression on her face. If only I hadn't been twice as mortified as she looked. "I don't know what I should focus on first, the fact that you were smart enough to carry a condom or the fact that it's quite obviously unused."

"Obviously, there's a reason it's unused." I bent down and snatched the condom, tucking it into my pocket. I wasn't about to tell her Brody had a big enough stash to screw the whole cheer squad, so we didn't need mine. That info was on a need-to-know basis, and she most definitely didn't need to know.

"And if you didn't reek of *morning after*, I might take some small comfort in that." Alex folded her arms and locked her creepy doll eyes on my face, igniting my skin.

I swallowed back the sloshy contents of my stomach. "What are you doing with my stuff? You have no right going through my things!" I immediately regretted my fast movements and stumbled back onto my bed.

"I thought you wanted me to wash what was in your backpack since you left it right by the machine. And are you hungover again? I can't believe this, Maddie. I let you go out for one night with your godfather's son, and you come home like *this*. What would your dad have thought?"

"Well, unlike you, my dad would've wanted me to stay far from Brody Allen. So if you have to ask that, then you obviously didn't know Dad very well." I threw the lingerie behind me and stared up at her. "Maybe that's why he was getting back together with Mom. He probably never told you *anything* because he didn't really love you. Or because he knew you were sleeping around. He loved my mom, and they were happy. Happy with each other until you ruined it. This is all your fault! I wish you'd been the one in that car."

"You have no idea." She opened her mouth then closed it again, before walking out and slamming the door behind her.

Muffled sobs carried through the barrier between us, and I flinched back from the sound. I crawled back to the head of my bed and hugged my pillow.

CHAPTER 12

ALEX

MORE THAN A WEEK LATER, Maddie's words still played on an endless loop inside my head as I pulled into a parking spot outside of Mike Allen's office. I didn't want to think I was that person, the one who leveraged hurt feelings to make a decision—and she *had* hurt my feelings, cut me to the bone, and watched me bleed out—but nevertheless, there I sat, staring at the nondescript brick building, screwing up my courage to ask my husband's oldest friend to take his daughter off my hands.

What the hell are you thinking? She's sleeping with his son. Surely, they wouldn't allow that to continue under *their* roof. Douchebag kid aside, the Allens *had* to have been better parents than me. David and Sarah had picked Mike to be Maddie's godfather for a reason.

Hadn't they?

I checked my reflection in the rearview mirror one last time before climbing out of the car. It didn't matter that I'd showered and made an effort to look somewhat presentable for the first time since David's funeral. I couldn't seem to shake the vacant look in my eyes, as if my soul had deserted me the day he'd died. Maybe I'd lost a little bit of it when I'd decided to carry through with this horrible plan, but I didn't know how much more I could take. I tried to live up to the person David wanted me to be when he'd decided to leave his daughter to me, but I failed at every turn.

Maddie and I were no closer to finding common ground than before, and she'd made it perfectly clear how she felt about me. I needed to silence the chorus of disapproving voices inside my head just long enough to remind myself I had no other options. The Allens were the perfect solution for an imperfect situation. I only hoped Mike agreed.

A perky blonde in a pink pantsuit greeted me, leaving me to sit in the waiting area while she announced my arrival. My hands trembled, and I shoved them under my legs to keep them still. If only I could keep the rest of me from shaking. I felt as though my body was coming apart at the seams. *What am I doing here?* The question stung the tip of my tongue, waiting for me to come up with a valid response. David had thought enough of the man to make him Maddie's godfather, so why couldn't I get the words out? Why couldn't I convince myself, at least?

Because you're a terrible person, my conscience screamed at me. *His son took advantage of a young girl who'd just lost her parents. Oh my God, I can't do this!* No matter how I felt about her at that moment, Maddie deserved better from me.

I jumped up to leave just as Mike Allen stepped out of his office and pulled me into an awkward hug, like a long-lost relative, the kind you make small talk with at family gatherings then talk about behind their backs. "Alex. So good to see you."

"G-good to see you too." I stumbled over the words as I worked to keep the shock off my face. *The man barely acknowledged me at the funeral, and now he's hugging me?* As if red flags weren't already going up inside my brain.

Mike ushered me into his office and waved me toward a quartet of dark-brown leather club chairs facing a round coffee table. He waited until I'd taken a seat before sitting across from me. His perfect sandy, Ken-doll hair swooped to the left, defying gravity as he moved. "So what brings you to see me today?"

I said the first thing that came to mind. "I, uh, I just wanted to come talk to someone who knew David. I thought maybe you could help me understand what happened the day he died."

"Of course, I'll do what I can. I must admit, though, I didn't understand many of his decisions in recent months." Mike flashed a plastic smile. "When we spoke on the phone, you mentioned having questions about David's will. Alex, I've got to be honest with you. I'm a little shocked to find out he changed it to include you."

His words hit me like a sucker punch to the gut. But I must have been a glutton for punishment because, without taking a breath to think it through, I blurted out, "Why?"

I caught his eyes as they flicked from my chest to my face, where his gaze went from curiosity to pity. "Well—and I hope you don't take this the wrong way—it's just that Claudia and I always figured he and Sarah would get back together. We'd been friends for years. All the way back to high school, for Christ's sake. David and Sarah were the real deal. It came as a total shock when they split up, but for a while there, it seemed like they were well on their way to a reconciliation. And then—" He stopped and ran his hand along the back of his neck.

Since I'd already opened the slippery can of worms, I pushed for more. "And then…?"

"And then you happened." Mike shifted in his chair. "He mentioned he was dating someone. But I didn't realize your relationship had gotten so serious. From my perspective, *marriage* came out of left field. I was left scratching my head, trying to figure out how, or rather *why*, things progressed so quickly."

His words had me stunned into silence. My heart hammered behind my ribs. My fingers itched to rest over my empty womb. Obviously, David never mentioned the baby, and I had to wonder why. Why wouldn't he tell his best friend we were expecting? And Sarah had to have known. *Maddie* knew. And neither of them told anyone either? Did Sarah think it would just go away if she didn't talk about it? The familiar ache returned twofold.

When I didn't respond, he continued. "But as taken aback as Claudia and I were, it didn't compare to Sarah's reaction. She always thought he'd have his fun and come back. We all did. As you can imagine, we were… *stunned* to find out he'd gotten married. But even after that, I still expected him to come to his senses. I'm fairly certain Sarah felt the same way."

"Come to his senses?" It took everything in me to force myself to breathe, in and out, one measured breath at a time. *Why is he telling me this? What purpose does it serve?*

He waved his hand. "I didn't mean it like that."

"We'd been seeing each other for months."

Mike leaned forward, resting his elbows on his knees. "Forgive my bluntness. You're young and beautiful. I'm sure he loved you in his own way, but you can't compare a few months with the better part of two decades. Just be glad you still have your whole life ahead of you and nothing keeping you here. I'm sure Sarah's family will take good care of Maddie. You can go back to sunny southern California and, as Brody says, hit the reset button and start over fresh."

My defenses screamed at me to retreat, but his attack had left me too dazed to think straight, so instead, I went on the offensive. "Were you aware Brody has been seeing Madison?"

Something I said seemed to strike him as funny. A wide smile spread across his face, and he relaxed back into his chair. "She's a lovely girl. My son has good taste."

"She's just a kid—not even seventeen."

He winked, and I wanted to slap the smug smile from his lips. "She's above the age of consent."

I'd let myself believe he didn't know what his son was capable of, and here he was, gloating like a proud peacock. This time, I leaned in, pulling my hands from under my thighs to rest them on the table in front of me as I invaded his personal space. "He got her drunk and had sex with her while under the influence. Unprotected sex, I might add."

He made a choking sound. "I taught him better than that. The boy knows to use protection."

"Obviously not. And as far as I know, Michigan hasn't legalized underage drinking yet."

The muscle in his jaw flexed, and he spoke through his teeth. "No, of course not. I'm assuming you have some sort of proof?"

"I know what I saw. Maddie left with Brody and came home intoxicated, reeking of sex and liquor. Tell your son to stay away from her. If I see him anywhere near Maddie, I'll call the police."

He steepled his fingers in front of him. "Alex, did you actually *see* my son providing Madison with either drugs or alcohol? Did she accuse him of something?" I reluctantly shook my head, and he smiled. "Well, there you have it. No harm done. It makes me sad to hear that my goddaughter isn't holding it together since her parents passed. Another reason I wish David had come to his senses a bit sooner."

My muscles vibrated with tension. "Sooner?"

"Isn't it obvious? They had to have been together that day for a reason."

I buried my face in David's favorite sweatshirt, hoping to breathe in even the slightest trace of him, but after several weeks of wearing it, I could only detect my own scent. I dragged it over my head, letting the soft fleece envelope my body like a warm embrace. These little things—his clothes, his personal belongings—they were all I had left of him. And after the day I'd had, I wanted nothing more than to lose myself in those insignificant pieces.

I dug through the hamper, desperate to find something, anything, that still carried David's scent. With a plain white T-shirt pressed to my nose, I heard soft footfalls in the hallway, and my head snapped up. "Maddie?"

Even without seeing her, I could tell she'd frozen where she stood. "Yeah?"

"Can you come in here, please?" I dropped the shirt to the pile and sat on the edge of the bed. The unexpected need to defend her against the Allens swelled in me again, and I suddenly wanted to share this moment with the only other person who could possibly feel the same level of grief as me.

Maddie stepped into the open doorway but not all the way into the room. She wore the same bitter expression I'd come to expect from her. "What do you want?"

I poked at a pair of red plaid boxers. "I, uh, was going through your dad's stuff, and I thought maybe you'd like to help me."

"Yeah, okay." She kept her eyes on the floor as she made her way to the bed and sat on the opposite side. She stared down at the pile I'd created and scrunched up her nose. "Is this his dirty laundry?"

I couldn't help laughing. "Yeah. Gross, huh? I just couldn't bring myself to wash it... until now."

"I, um, I don't want his dirty boxers." She grinned. Not quite a full-blown smile, but I'd take it. "You can keep those."

"What about his watch? Or..." I pointed to the nightstand where his phone and iPod sat charging. "His iPod? I'm not quite ready to part with his phone but maybe after I have a chance to go through his pictures and stuff."

She hopped up, pulled the phone and the shiny silver MP3 player from their chargers, and climbed into his spot on the bed with them. I could almost imagine him sitting next to her, smiling over her shoulder like one of the pictures on Sarah's living room wall.

CHAPTER 13

MADDIE

I PRESSED THE POWER BUTTON ON Dad's phone and waited while it came to life. "Is it okay if I look through the pictures?"

"Just don't delete anything until I've had a chance to look." Alex picked up a navy sweater and brought it to her face.

Sitting in a pile of my dad's dirty laundry with my stepmonster wouldn't have made my list of "things to do before I die," but I missed him so much, surrounding myself in his scent—all cough drops and the expensive cologne that smelled like new leather—made spending time with Alex seem almost worth it. And flipping through the pictures on his phone added a bonus round to the weird game we were playing.

"Oh my God, I'd almost forgotten about this!" I highlighted the image of Mom and Dad from last Christmas—the one *before* Alex came into the metaphorical picture—and sent it to my phone. I'd been so sure they were one good kiss away from getting back together that day. The love in Mom's eyes jumped off the screen. Not long after that, Dad started dating Alex.

"What are you looking at?" Alex leaned over my shoulder, and I felt her stiffen. "Oh." She jumped back to her own side of the bed.

I almost said something snarky but held it. The woman had been sniffing my dad's dirty clothes. "That was from before he met you." I didn't know why I felt the need to explain it, but I did.

"It's okay." Her smile wobbled, but it almost felt normal sitting there with her.

A calendar reminder popped on the screen. *Sonogram appointment Tuesday 2pm. Get Alex flowers.*

All the shitty things I'd said about the baby came back to haunt me. Dad would have wanted me to get to know my new brother or sister. No one said I had to particularly like his or her mother to do it. "Oh, hey, do you still have the sonogram thing tomorrow? I could… I dunno, maybe I could go with you? I've never seen a bun *in* the oven before. It might be kinda cool."

Alex slid her eyes in my direction, and the frostiness from before came back. "No. I don't have the *thing* anymore."

Cryptic much? "Oh, okay. Well, maybe next time. I think I'd like to go next time you have a doctor thing. You know, take an interest in my new baby, whatever it is?"

"That's really not necessary." Unexpected hostility oozed out of her as she balled up a blue pinstripe dress shirt and tossed it into the whites she'd separated out of the laundry.

I kept my eyes trained on the phone. "I know it's not necessary, and I know what I said before, but I'd really like to."

"I said, no." She barely whispered the words, but it felt as if she'd slapped me. We sat quietly on opposite sides of the mattress with a dwindling pile of laundry between us. Then she blew out a breath. "But it's nice of you to offer."

A sudden urge to understand what my dad saw in her hit me, and I clicked the calendar, bringing up the entire month. Just about every day had some sort of entry, mostly work stuff, but there were a few personal things scattered in between. And then I saw it. Well, more than one actually. In fact, Dad had marked off several blocks as *Sarah.* I paged back to January—to the day they'd both gotten into Dad's car and driven off together—and there it was in bold letters. Mom's name. My eyes snapped up to Alex's face as the realization sank in. She had no idea.

"What is it, Maddie? Are you okay? You look like you're gonna be sick."

Guilt stole my voice, and I shook my head, tucking the phone against my chest and holding it tight.

"What's wrong? Let me see." She reached for the phone, but I wouldn't let go.

I'd done this. I'd wanted my family back so badly, I didn't care who

I'd hurt. If I hadn't pushed them back together, they wouldn't have been in the car that day.

"Come on, lemme see." She shook her hand at me, waiting for me to place the phone in her palm, but I held tight.

I swallowed down the lump in my throat. "It's just the pictures. They make me sad, but I still want to look through them."

"Oh." Her hand dropped to her side. "Okay."

The phone chimed with a message, and both Alex and I froze. It took a moment for me to realize it had been my phone, not Dad's. "Uh, that's me." I pulled my phone from my pocket and opened the new message from Brody.

Brody: WTF, Maddie?

I stared at the message before tapping out a reply.

Maddie: What?

Brody: You snitched.

Shit! Brody was clearly pissed. He'd managed to avoid me the whole day at school, so I couldn't imagine what he meant.

Maddie: When?

Brody: Think about it.

"Everything okay?" I felt Alex watching me like a zoo exhibit.

"Uh, I need to make a phone call. Be right back." I scooted out of her room and down the hall into mine. As soon as I'd closed the door behind me, I hit the autodial for Brody. He answered on the first ring.

His voice startled me as he shouted through the line. "You fucking told your stepmom about Saturday night?"

Shit, shit, shit. "No."

"No? Then how'd she find out?"

"I woke up Sunday morning with her standing over me." I left out the part about her finding the unused condom and Mom's lingerie. "It's not like she couldn't tell by smelling me."

"Well, thanks to you, my dad's on my ass about… fuck, about *everything*." I could practically hear him pulling out his perfect hair as he paced. "I should have known better than to get involved with a little girl. Jesus, Maddie, you couldn't have been more careful?"

"I'm *not* a little girl. And how did your dad find out, anyway?"

"Your stepmom went to see my dad today. She fucking threatened to have me arrested if I came near you again. Can you believe that shit? As if I'd go anywhere near you now."

"She did what? And what do you mean you wouldn't go near me now? I didn't do anything wrong."

He laughed, but the empty sound of it gave me chills. "You didn't do anything right, either. Maybe I just need to stick to my own crowd for a while. It was fun, but we're done."

"Brody, wait! Is this your bullshit way of dumping me and blaming me for it?" My voice echoed against my bare walls, but he'd already hung up. "Are you kidding me? Seriously. Are. You. Kidding. Me?" I stared at the blank screen on my phone before tucking it back into my pocket and storming down the hall to my dad's room.

Alex had curled into a ball on top of his clothes clutching his phone the same way I had before I'd abandoned it for Brody's tirade. "Did you see this?" She held out the phone to me, but I couldn't care less about whatever it was she wanted to show me.

"Did you talk to Mr. Allen about me?"

"What?" She lifted her head and wiped at the tears streaking her face. "What are you talking about?"

"Did you tell Mr. Allen about me and Brody?" I enunciated each word clearly, so she wouldn't misunderstand me.

"I... yes. I did." She sat all the way up, still clutching Dad's phone. "I don't like him. Or his dad for that matter. I don't want you seeing him anymore."

"You're not my mom. You can't tell me who I can and can't see! And who gave you the right to tell Brody's dad about my personal business? I'm like, horrified and embarrassed that he knows."

"He's Brody's dad. He has every right to hear what Brody's been up to, particularly if it's illegal, and giving liquor to a minor is definitely illegal."

"Oh. My. God!" I wanted to break something, preferably over her head. "Do you not get it?"

The sad Alex I'd walked in on disappeared, and the bitch I remembered took her place. "Oh, I think I get it just fine. It's *you* who seem to be confused. You're grounded until the weekend, and after that,

I don't want you anywhere near Brody Allen. He's a disrespectful little shit."

I wanted to strangle her with my dad's dirty boxers. "Well, thanks to you, that *shit* wants nothing to do with me."

"Good. Problem solved."

"I hate you!" An animal scream forced its way out of my throat, and I turned on my heels and stormed out, slamming the door behind me.

Truce officially over.

CHAPTER 14

ALEX

I SPENT THE REST OF THE week failing as a parental figure while Maddie singed holes through my soul with her blistering stare. She despised everything about me, from the way I scrambled eggs to the way I drew breath in her airspace. Exhaustion, both physical and mental, weighed me down. While it had been comforting to know I wasn't the only one in the house anymore, I couldn't relax until I knew she'd fallen asleep. Visions of her sneaking out plagued my thoughts each night until I drifted off into fitful pockets of sleep well after two a.m.

By the time Saturday morning rolled around, I felt as if it were *my* sentence being lifted, not hers. After giving the Thompsons a quick rundown of the rules of the new regime, I left Maddie in their care for the weekend and headed straight for my own personal oasis and the biggest damn cup of caffeine Natalie could pour.

"Well, just so you know, I wouldn't put much stock in what Mike Allen has to say. He's obviously an asshole, and apparently, the apple doesn't fall far from the tree." Natalie leaned against the counter and brushed muffin crumbs from her apron.

"I guess. I can't help wondering, though. Maddie has all but beaten me over the head with the idea that her parents were sneaking around behind my back." After everything that had happened, my unwavering belief in David had begun to falter. Bits of circumstantial evidence against him that had started out like microscopic holes in the ice were suddenly branching out like spidery cracks along the surface. I wanted to ignore the voices in my head, but over the past week, they'd gotten louder.

"She's a kid. Of course she wanted her parents to get back together. That's practically the universal wish of all kids with divorced parents. She wouldn't exactly have the fast track to the truth, though. And you're both too close to the situation. You're still grieving."

I grabbed onto Natalie's line of reasoning like a life raft. "Yeah, you're probably right. It's just..." As badly as I wanted to tell her, I couldn't get the words out. As long as I kept the secret to myself, didn't say it out loud, it didn't feel real.

"What?"

I shook my head, hoping to dispel the images from my brain. I'd hidden the evidence under a pile of folded laundry, but out of sight was most definitely *not* out of mind. Some things couldn't be unseen. "I just wish going to see that jerk had been the low point in my day."

"What could be worse than spending an afternoon talking to Mike 'asshat' Allen?"

I barked out a hollow laugh.

"Well? Don't keep me in suspense."

I nodded, giving myself permission to rip the proverbial Band-Aid off the open wound in my heart. If anyone could help me make sense of everything, it would be Natalie. I knew I might not like her methods, but in the end, she was the unlikely voice of reason keeping me somewhat sane. "I was doing what you said, going through David's things. I cleaned out the hamper. Sorted and washed his laundry." I didn't tell her about practically huffing his dirty clothes. She'd never let me live that down. I certainly couldn't tell her about the hours spent searching through the pictures of him and Sarah from before we'd even met like some sort of schoolgirl stalker. "Maddie had been looking through his phone and, well, I don't know if she did it on purpose or not, but when she gave it back to me, his calendar was up. I figured I should see if he'd made plans for Valentine's Day—reservations I needed to cancel, you know?"

A fresh wave of sadness swept over Natalie's features, and she pulled me into an awkward one-armed hug with the counter between us painfully digging into my ribs. "Oh, sweetie. I'm sorry. I know this must be hard. This would have been your first Valentine's Day as a married couple."

"There wasn't anything there—no Valentine's plans. I guess he never had time to..." I wiped away a few stray tears. "I did find an interesting entry for today's date. He'd blocked out several hours for Sarah."

Natalie gasped, and her hand flew to her mouth.

"I know. I was scheduled to be out of town this week. I cancelled all my travel dates when... well, I cancelled everything, but when I searched through his phone..." Everything about the memory made me feel as though I'd somehow invaded his privacy and stumbled upon some seedy secret my new husband had kept from me. I wanted to be sick. "He was planning to meet her, Natalie. On the Saturday before Valentine's Day, my husband had a *date* with his ex-wife."

"Holy shit!" Natalie swore through the hand covering her mouth. Then she dropped it and waved it as if doing so would scatter the truth like dust motes through the air. "But... maybe it was innocent. I mean, they did have a kid together. It could have been something totally harmless, right?"

"I thought of that too, so I checked the rest of his calendar. I found several hours blocked out on the day they died, of course, but Natalie, there were more. And almost all of them fell on days I was out of town. It's like he had this whole other life going on right under my nose, and I had no idea." A cracking sensation spread out from my sternum and through my limbs. I was Humpty Dumpty, and David's iPhone was the wall. All it took was one push to break me.

She stepped around the counter and pulled me into a tight hug as if she knew I needed someone to hold me together. "I'm so sorry, sweetie. I-I don't even know what to say."

After several moments of standing there wordlessly, Natalie released her stranglehold on me and managed to elbow my cup as she stepped back. Lukewarm coffee splattered the front of my sweater. "Oh, shit. Sorry." She grabbed a damp rag and started toweling off my boobs.

The absurdity of the situation hit me as I wiped the trail of tears from my face. A bout of unexpected laughter caught me off guard. "Step away from the goods before you start something you can't finish. I *am* a lonely widow woman, after all."

Natalie froze with her hands still fondling my breasts, and her mouth dropped open—as if she'd forgotten I knew how to make a joke—then she yanked her hands away and threw her head back and laughed. "Sorry. I got carried away there for a minute."

Another shift in mood passed over me like an eclipse, sucking the lightness out of everything again. "I don't know what to think." My voice came out as barely a whisper, and I jumped back onto my stool. The air around us had grown heavy as my predicament pressed down on me like a lead blanket. "Was my husband cheating on me? With his ex-wife?"

Natalie hopped onto the stool next to me. "If he was, he was the biggest idiot on the planet. You're beautiful, and smart, and he was damn lucky to have you. Hell, I've already groped your boobs. I'd sleep with you if I swung that way."

I knew she was trying to make me smile, and I wanted to. I really did. But I couldn't help wondering if people told Sarah the same thing when he'd left her.

"Okay, that's enough sadness for one day." Natalie snapped her fingers as if she had the power to change moods with her will. "You know what… I have just the thing to cheer you up, and forget about saying no."

"I'm afraid to ask." I wiped more unshed tears from my eyes.

"You should be." She laughed. "But after the week you've had, I think it's high time we went out and got shitfaced."

"Drunk?" I could only imagine the horrified expression on my face. "You want *me* to go out and get drunk?"

"Sure." She shrugged. "I'm sure you've done it before. You went to college, right? Isn't that typical Saturday night stuff for the university crowd?"

Had I ever gotten drunk in college? I didn't remember a single time I'd done anything so reckless. At least, not back then. I wasn't that girl. I didn't *do* reckless. I didn't drown my sorrows in booze. "I wouldn't know. I spend my Saturday nights glued to a screen playing video games with computer nerds on either side of me."

"Oh, sweetheart… you've been deprived. We are *definitely* gonna get smashed tonight. I'm even closing early, so we can get a head start. You know what they say… a night out is good for the soul." She had a strange way of looking at things, but desperation wasn't a good look on me. Maybe Natalie was right.

"What will people think? It's only been a month since my husband died. What about Maddie?" No matter how hard I tried, I couldn't stop thinking about her, and about the moment we'd *almost* had. In the midst of our intertwined tragedies, we'd finally clicked. And then the whole Brody thing had come to a head, and she'd gone off on me again.

A glimmer of anger flashed in Natalie's eyes. "I think people can mind their own damn business. If your husband had been where he belonged, he might still be alive."

I opened my mouth, but she put up a finger to stop me. Was I the only person out of the loop? The only one who didn't know David and Sarah were destined to be together for eternity. *'Til death do they part?* Maddie had been so *sure* they were getting back together.

She turned her heated stare on me. "Don't even go there. You already said this was the first weekend she's off grounding, and the kid is spending it with her friend. And before you come up with another weak excuse, I know you, Alex. You made sure they'd watch her like a road crew convict, right?" I nodded, and she went on. "So you have no excuse. We're going. And that's final."

"I can't believe you talked me into wearing this." I looked down at the shimmering blue minidress clinging to my every curve as I tottered on a pair of dangerous, strappy heels. A woman I recognized but couldn't place did a double take as she passed by me in her simple black sheath and pearls, and a wave of guilt threatened to knock me off my feet. "I look ridiculous. I should be wearing black." Preferably black sweats and fuzzy socks while curled up on my very own sofa watching Lifetime TV for women.

Natalie scoffed. I wanted to believe she cared about my feelings, and I knew she did in her own weird way, even if it didn't seem like it sometimes. And yet I only had myself to blame. I'd let her drag me out without the giant W stitched across my chest. "Wearing black is so two centuries ago. You look *hot*."

"It's February. I'm dressed for summer… in *Paris*." I glanced around the room, hoping I wouldn't see anyone else I recognized. Or more importantly, I prayed they wouldn't see me.

"We'd be all the rage in Paris. Let's pretend we're there." Natalie fiddled with her blond updo and danced off toward the bar, muttering in a pathetic French accent. "Come on, *mon cheri*... let's get our drink on!"

A plate of greasy onion rings and two drinks later, I no longer cared what I was wearing. As inappropriate as her methods were, I appreciated the effort. Wallowing in self-pity was almost impossible with Natalie around.

"*Holy shit!*" Natalie grabbed ahold of the back of my dress, tugging me until she had her lips at my ear. "Don't look now, but there's a hot doctor in the house."

I spun around to see Ben striding in our direction.

"Ben..." My jaw dropped open, and I quickly closed it. He looked different—*good*—dressed in dark denim and a slightly rumpled navy button-down. And he seemed as surprised to see me as I was to see him.

"Alex?" His eyes flitted between Natalie and me.

"Funny running into you here." I snuck a glance at Natalie's not-so-angelic face before giving her a full-on glare. I knew what game she was playing, and I did my best not to buy into it.

"You look dashing, Doc. Glad you could make it," Natalie stage-whispered, directing her mischievous grin from me to Ben.

Ben fidgeted. "Yeah, uh, thanks for the heads-up there, Nat."

After Ben's comment, she dropped the pretense and laughed. "Hey, whatever works, right?"

I gave up trying to melt Natalie with my stare and turned to face Ben, a forced smile stretching my lips. I could do this. We were friends. Friends hung out together all the time. "We might as well make the best of it. Right, *friend*?"

Ben reached up to grip the back of his neck. He didn't seem all that enthusiastic about the whole *friend* thing. "Sounds like a plan. Can I, uh, buy you a drink?" Natalie cleared her throat, and Ben blushed. "Both of you, I mean."

"Hell yeah, you can buy us a drink. It's about time you asked."

Natalie slapped him on the shoulder and scooted over so there was an empty stool between us. "Hop on." She patted the seat.

Ben's sweet mint and hospital sanitizer scent surrounded me as he slid between us, careful not to brush against me. He took his seat and waved the bartender over to order a round of appletinis for us and an imported beer for himself.

Natalie raised an eyebrow. "Appletinis?"

"It's a girlie drink, isn't it?" He shrugged.

"That it is…" Natalie lifted her drink in a salute before bringing it to her lips. "Bottoms up!"

After another round, Natalie wandered off under the guise of saying hi to an old friend, leaving Ben and me alone at the bar.

"So, Doctor…" I swirled my drink, watching the thin layer of ice crackle along the top.

He leaned in slightly, keeping his body just outside of my personal bubble. "So… Mrs. Barrett…"

I cringed. "Please, call me Alex."

"Then no more 'doctor.' It's just Ben."

With a simple nod, I agreed. "Okay, Ben."

"So…" He took a swig of his beer, glancing toward the end of the bar where Natalie shamelessly flirted with the bartender. "Tell me how she managed to drag you out to a pub on the weekend before Valentine's Day."

"You *have* met Natalie, haven't you?" I barked out a laugh. "She's not exactly subtle."

He let out a long sigh, leaving me with more questions than answers. How upset had he been to find out she'd duped him into an evening with me? Not that he disliked me. I knew he didn't. But the awkward tension between us was more than obvious. We'd agreed to be friends. Surely, I could be friends with a guy. "That's true… but she means well."

"I know." I brought the glass to my lips, breathing in the tart Granny Smith flavor before taking a sip. "That's probably the only reason I haven't tied concrete blocks to her feet and pushed her into the lake."

He bumped my shoulder in that way guys did—as though we were drinking buddies. Nothing more. "That and it's frozen solid."

"There's always that." The ramifications of the frozen Michigan landscape hit me, and I downed the rest of my drink in an attempt to contain my emotions. I couldn't let myself forget for one minute.

Ben watched me with a curious expression. "You okay, over there?"

"Never better." I wiped my lips with the back of my hand, caught the bartender's eye, and signaled for another round. "What about you? How'd she manage to drag you into her little scheme?"

He laughed—a deep, throaty sound that warmed me like the sunny beaches of southern California, more than even the liquor I'd consumed. "She just said to meet her here for a quick drink. I told myself one drink with Nat would be harmless. I suppose I should have known better."

"Well, I'm sorry you got stuck babysitting me tonight. I'm sure you have women lining up to date you." Women who had a right to date him. Women who weren't inextricably in love with dead men.

He took a swig of his fresh beer and licked the foam from his upper lip. "No one lately."

"No one?" That surprised me. Even *I* wasn't blind enough to miss how attractive Ben was. No matter how hard I'd tried not to notice. "How is that even possible?"

"I've had other things on my mind." He didn't elaborate. Instead, he focused on scrawling his name in the condensation collecting on the outside of his glass.

"Yes, well, I suppose, with Sarah gone…" I must have done something horrible in a past life to find myself surrounded by men who'd loved Sarah Barrett. I felt as if my destiny had so intertwined with hers that even death couldn't break me free of it. Thinking about Sarah brought back images of her and David together. My imagination twisted the old photos I'd seen into grotesque visions of them writhing around together on my bed while I watched as if my subconscious enjoyed torturing me for finding Ben even the slightest bit attractive.

"Sarah and I weren't meant to be." Ben's voice brought me out of my self-imposed nightmare. "Besides, it would have never worked out."

"Why?" I didn't know why I asked. Maybe my morbid curiosity just got the best of me.

He scooped up some peanuts from the bowl in front of us and popped a few into his mouth. "I don't know if ever I told you about the time I met David."

I shook my head and waited.

"Sarah and I had just come back from dinner—our third date—and I'd walked her to the front door. We'd had a nice time. Not spectacular. Not life changing. Just *nice.* But we'd been out three times, and we hadn't even kissed yet, so I was ready to go for it, you know? Make my move." He flashed a quick grin before his lips turned down again. "So there I am, ready to take the next step when David pulled into the driveway to drop Maddie off. Jesus, it was as if I'd never met the real Sarah Barrett. She took one look at the guy and lit up like a kid on Christmas morning. She never looked at me that way, that's for damn sure."

I scooted forward. "So what happened?"

"Nothing." He laughed. "Absolutely nothing. I said good night and went home."

"Just like that?" I wanted him to lie to me, to change the way the story ended so we could all live happily ever after, but I knew better.

"Just like that." He ate the last peanut and brushed his hands off. "She was a great lady, but she had one tragic flaw."

"What?" Time seemed to stand still as shallow puffs of breath passed my open lips. Part of me knew what he was about to say, and I tensed up, waiting to hear the words.

"Isn't it obvious? She was still in love with her ex-husband." He scratched his head and mumbled something that sounded like, "story of my life," but I couldn't get past the first thing he'd said. *She was still in love with her ex-husband.*

All the anger I'd thought I'd locked away came rushing out as if a dam had broken. Maddie's words, Mike Allen's words, Ben's words, the calendar… all flooded my consciousness until my thoughts screamed. Sarah was still in love with David. And David was still in love with her. That was the only conclusion I could draw. My husband had been in love with someone else when he died. And there I was, still mourning a man who'd been about to leave me.

I choked back a sob when what I really wanted to do was scream. David's death had taken so much away from me, including robbing me of the right to be angry. The "death" card trumped the "scorned" card every damn day of the week.

Ben dragged out the doctor face, eyeing me like an emergency room patient. "Hey, are you okay? You know just because she loved him, it doesn't mean he still loved her." I felt as if he'd read my mind, hitting the bull's-eye on my deepest, darkest fear. "You look like you're going to be sick. How many have you had?"

"I'm fine," I spat, downing the fresh drink in front of me. "I haven't had nearly *enough*."

"Alex, I'm serious. You need to slow down." Ben put a hand on my knee, giving it a gentle squeeze as he leaned in. "Do you need some air?"

I closed my eyes and let myself imagine David sitting across from me. For one, all too brief, moment I felt *David's* warm hand resting on my knee, *his* strong pulse beating against my bare skin. *His* Heineken-flavored breath washing over my lips. *David's*, not *Ben's*.

A cross between a laugh and a sob burst out of my throat. Then it hit me. Why had I worked so hard to stay faithful to the memory of a man who'd betrayed me? Did I ever really know him at all? "Oh, I need something all right." I gripped the front of his shirt, tugging him the short distance between us until his mouth was right there. Tears clouded my vision, but I didn't care. "I need you to kiss me until it doesn't hurt anymore."

Ben's eyes flashed to my lips for an instant before locking on mine again, pain etched across his features. "You're drunk."

"Not that drunk. Even if I am, so what? It's just a kiss." I begged with my eyes, desperate for him to press his lips to mine, desperate to feel something other than pain for one damn minute.

He shoved a hand into his hair. "Jesus, Alex. No, I'm not going to kiss you."

"Fine. I'll kiss *you*." I smashed my lips against his, shutting out the voices, the sounds around us, and very nearly the pain. Despite his reluctance, he kissed me back, and I let myself drown in it until he broke away, panting.

"Alex, no." His eyes went wide, as if he'd seen a ghost. "Not like this."

My lips tingled, and I pressed my fingers to them, still feeling his warmth, still tasting him on my tongue. "I thought you wanted to kiss me."

"I do." He shifted in his seat then glanced down at his lap. "God knows I do. But it's too soon. You've been through a lot—*too much*—in a short amount of time. And when I imagine kissing you, I always imagine you kissing *me*. Not you trying to punish a ghost."

"I'm ready to forget. I *need* to forget. Even if just for tonight. If you're not interested, I know at least a dozen guys in here will be." I slid off my stool to stand between his legs.

"You're drunk." He growled. "And you're not exactly making this easy for me."

In the back of my mind, I think I realized I was being unfair. Cruel even. I knew I'd taken advantage of his inherent need to help people and his obvious attraction to me. But in that moment, I'd had too much to drink, and too many emotions dragged me under. I pressed myself against him with a snarl. "I hope I'm making it very hard. Now are we leaving or what?"

Ben swallowed then cleared his throat, averting his eyes from mine. "Let's find Natalie. I think she should take you home."

I pushed away from him with a growl of my own. "I. Don't. Want. To. Go. Home. There's nothing there for me. Don't you get it? Every memory I have is a lie. I feel like I'm as dead as he is when I'm there." I swiped at a stray tear, grabbing his chin and forcing him to face me. "I want... no, I *need* to feel alive again."

"Fine. Come on, come home with me."

"I thought you'd never ask."

CHAPTER 15

MADDIE

HALEIGH TWISTED HER LAST PERFECT ringlet into place and spritzed it with hair spray. She reminded me of a Disney princess in her glittering blue gown and fancy hair. "I'm so glad Alex paroled you so you could come over this weekend. The past two weeks must have felt like a century to you. You never did tell me why she was so pissed."

Pissed? Understatement. But on the plus side, Alex seemed to hate having me stuck at home as much as I did, which gave me some satisfaction. I had a feeling that's why she'd let me stay over at Haleigh's this weekend, only *after* she'd confirmed the plans with Mrs. Thompson. "It was stupid, and she overreacted, as usual."

I could never admit the truth to Haleigh. She'd have freaked out, and I needed *that* like I needed another thrilling evening at Casa Alex. If only my bitch stepmonster hadn't searched my bag. Then I wouldn't have been grounded until the end of time—or two weeks, whichever came first—since it was apparently hell on earth to deal with me on a daily basis. I missed my mom so much I could barely breathe, and the only other person I'd even considered talking to had been ignoring me.

"Earth to Maddie." Haleigh waved her hand in front of my face. "You still need to do your makeup."

"I don't understand why you're making such a big deal out of this stupid dance." I glanced at my reflection and groaned. The floor-length dress was stunning. I couldn't even pretend it wasn't—giant black embroidered roses scattered across a snowy white background—but despite feeling as if I'd been crowned snow queen, I wasn't up for the festivities. I almost wished Alex had refused to let me go. But after Mrs. Thompson swore on a stack of Harlequin Romances or some damn thing, Alex had agreed to allow it. *To the dance and back to the Thompsons, no boys, no booze, and no drugs.* And since Mrs. Thompson had promised to take full responsibility for me, I couldn't even think about breaking the rules.

Haleigh shoved my recital makeup bag into my lap and motioned me toward the mirror. "You're just pissed because Brody has a date, and it isn't you."

"I couldn't care less who he takes," I lied, digging through several tubes of hooker-red lipstick until I found the pale pink I was looking for. Brody had barely spoken to me at all since *that* night. As much as I wanted to hate the guy, a big part of me still wanted him. I missed his hands gripping my waist like he owned me. God, I missed his weed-flavored kisses and even his stupid wink and shitty smirk. And that made me hate him even more. I knew when I'd gotten involved with him he would end up cutting me open, but that hadn't prepared me for how much it would actually hurt.

"Don't worry, there'll be plenty of hot guys just dying to dance with you." Her icy fingers squeezed my bare shoulders.

My best friend, always the optimist, even when it came to things she knew nothing about. Not telling her why Alex grounded me was just the tip of the very cold and lonely iceberg keeping me afloat. I'd lost my virginity while high, and he'd treated me like crap ever since. Now, and for the rest of my life, when I thought about my first time, I'd see Brody 'jerkface' Allen's face. *Why am I doing this to myself?*

"What's with all the red lipstick?" Haleigh held up a tube of CoverGirl's Paint the Town. "Did you actually wear this for recitals?"

"Oh, yeah. I don't know if you noticed, but the ballet world isn't exactly known for class." Another lie. I'd long since pitched the nasty lipsticks I'd used in my dance days, so I'd shoplifted those from the drug store while on a tampon run with Alex earlier that day. But I wasn't about to tell Haleigh my plan. Part of me hoped I'd get caught, if for no other reason than to see the horrified look on Alex's face, but I'd had no such luck.

Her lips twisted to the side, and I could tell she held back a rude comment. "Why didn't you ask Grey to go to the dance? He's hot, and I don't really believe what people say about him. I think he's just shy. And don't you two have a class together this semester?" *Again, the optimist, and this time, changing the subject, too.*

"He's not my type." My hand shook as I applied a coat of mascara. Allowing Grey to invade my thoughts would be dangerous. The wrong kind of dangerous. The kind that could actually devastate me.

"Oh, well. I do wonder what he's always writing in those notebooks of his. Some kids say it's crazy scary stuff like planning mass murders, but I bet it's just poetry or something he doesn't want anyone reading."

I threw the mascara back in the bag then turned to smile at her. "I'm ready. Let's go, and for fuck sake, I hope someone spiked the punch."

"Are you serious?" Haleigh stopped rifling around in her purse and looked at me.

And for the third time that night, I lied. "No."

Brody wrapped Kelsey in his arms and kissed her right there on the dance floor, just as he'd done with me only a few weeks ago. Knowing he'd be there with someone else was one thing, but seeing him kiss her left a sour taste in my mouth. Something brushed my shoulder, and I glanced over to see Grey standing next to me. I almost didn't recognize him all dressed up in dark jeans and black suit jacket. He'd even styled his hair a little.

He leaned over me until his breath tickled my ear. "You know, you can't actually burn someone that way. You'll just end up with a wicked headache if you try."

I continued to stare at Brody with a bad case of tunnel vision. I barely noticed the elaborate snowflake decorations scattered around the gym, turning the room into some sort of grown-up version of *Frozen*. "Thanks for the advice."

"Advice you choose to ignore?"

"What's your problem?" I turned to him. "I didn't ask for your advice, and I don't want it. Yet you continue to pass it out like some sort of know-it-all on how I should live *my* life. It's my fucking life, so why don't you do what you've been doing all week and stay the hell out of it?" My heart threatened to beat out of my chest, and I had to take a steadying breath.

His eyebrows knitted together. "Is that what you're going to do? You're going to push away everyone who wants to help you and only let people in who don't give a rat's ass about you? Brody is a douche and a player, and the only girl he'll ever give a fuck about is the one he's with right now."

"Screw you, Grey. I was done with him anyhow. And don't tell me it doesn't bother you to see Kelsey with him. Everyone knows you two had a thing, and she dumped you like yesterday's trash." I looked away and took another deep breath, willing myself not to cry, and trying to ignore the way I felt when Grey was close to me.

"Great. That's just great, Maddie. Keep pushing." He stepped closer and lowered his voice. "Just so we're clear, I don't think I'm some all-knowing expert. I just—God, I like you, okay? And I don't like seeing you like this. I don't want your grief to get the best of you. Trust me. Brody's not worth it. Neither is Kelsey, for that matter, and for the record, I haven't thought about her in I don't know how long. They're both a waste of time and energy." He shoved his hands into his pockets as if suddenly nervous. Then he mumbled something I couldn't hear.

"You know what? You're right. They're all just a big waste of time." I left to grab my coat and headed toward the exit. As soon as I hit the parking lot, I made a beeline for Brody's car.

The shiny silver Dodge Charger took up two spaces, parked diagonally to avoid getting scratched—as if that would stop me from what I had in mind. I reached into my purse and fumbled around for the stolen tubes of lipstick. I pulled my glove off with my teeth to twist up the first one and proceeded to attack the windshield with glee.

As if working inside the lines of a giant coloring book, I smeared the glossy red lipstick over the glass. Not an easy task in the bitter cold. Once I'd killed each tube, I repeated the process, pulling a fresh one from my bag until only a few hard-to-reach spots remained. Then I moved to the rear window and started the process again.

"What the *hell* are you doing?" Grey's anxious voice startled me.

"Ever see the movie *Carrie*?" I stopped long enough to peek over at him before going back to my task. "Brody can consider himself lucky I didn't have access to a bucket of pig's blood."

"Maddie." Grey wrapped his hand around my wrist but didn't pull. The light was dim in the parking lot, but for the first time that night, I actually *saw* him. He looked... *scared*?

I shook his hand off. "Don't worry. I'm not planning to blow up the school. I just wanted to give him something to remember me by."

"Fine. But is this"—he waved his hand over the shark-attack red windshield—"really going to leave the lasting impression he's obviously left on you?"

"No, but why should that stop me?" I went back to scribbling on the rear window.

"What's next? Vandalizing his house?"

I stared at him with a straight face. "Thanks for the idea. What are you doing tomorrow? I'm pretty sure Alex bought enough truck stop toilet paper to last 'til the next century."

He gaped at me. "Really, Maddie?"

"Gah, Grey! I don't know what comes next. I don't know what's happening right now half the time. I'm just trying to make it from one moment to the next without completely breaking down. So you can either help me get back at the douchebag who punched my v-card, or leave me the fuck alone. Your choice."

He was silent for two full beats. "You... let him...?"

I huffed out a white cloud. "Yes. I had sex for the first time with Brody Allen, and he's gone right back to pretending I don't exist. And now I feel like shit because you're the first person I've told and the last person I'd want to admit that to. Are you happy now?" I leaned against the rear bumper, careful not to mess up my—or rather Haleigh's—coat.

Grey stood directly in front of me and pushed the heels of his hands into his eyes. "No. I'm like three *kingdoms* from happy right now." Then he sucked in a breath and stepped back, holding his hand out to me. "Come with me?"

"Are you kidding?" I almost laughed at the absurdity. I'd never wanted to go to the dance in the first place. I definitely didn't want to go back and pretend I hadn't just defiled Brody's precious while he dry-humped his girlfriend on the dance floor. "I'm not going back in there."

His lips curved up in a shy smile. "No, I was thinking you might like to get out of here."

"With you? I can't. I have to go home with Haleigh. And besides, I'm not exactly sure I trust you."

"I promise I'll take you to the safest place on Earth and bring you back in time to go with Haleigh." His ocean-blue eyes froze me in place. I couldn't turn away if I'd wanted to.

Something unfamiliar sparked in me. It reminded me a little of the time I'd plugged in my phone charger and accidentally touched the prong while inserting it. Only this time, it wasn't at all uncomfortable. In fact, I thought I might like to do it again.

I contemplated his offer for about thirty seconds before grabbing his hand. "This safe place isn't some shanty in the middle of Lake Michigan, is it?"

"No." He laughed. "I'm going to take you to my house."

We pulled in beside his stepdad's snowplow parked in the driveway, and he turned off the engine. "Grey, I'm not so sure about this. I don't know your dad, and I'm already in trouble with Alex."

"I promised, right?" He put his hand over mine in my lap and let his stupid blue eyes plead with me.

"But I don't really know you." He had no idea how close I was to caving and doing anything he asked me to do. And if I had my way, he'd never know.

He sat back and sighed. "Well, this is your chance to get to know me. Or I can take you back to the dance."

"No." I snatched the keys from his fingers before he had a chance to start the car again. "Let's just go in."

I pulled my coat tight around me as we went into the house through a side door. The darkened kitchen smelled like my mom's spaghetti and meatballs, making my mouth water. The clock on the microwave said ten, but there were lights on. Voices came from another room. I slipped off my heels, and Grey took my coat and purse from me to hang them in a small closet. I followed him toward the sound.

"My parents are through here."

I grabbed his sleeve to stop him. "Wait, I thought you said your mom died."

He smiled and took my hand. "She did. My stepdad remarried two years ago."

"Oh." What did it mean that he considered his stepmom his parent? Was I a mutant to hate mine?

"Come on." He tugged on my hand and led me to a small family room near the front of the house. "Hi, guys." Grey waved to a man, woman, and infant sitting on the floor together. The soft melody of classical piano music played from somewhere in the distance as the adults stared up at us. "This is Maddie Barrett. The dance was lame, so we decided to come back here for a while."

Grey hadn't let go of my hand, and I noticed the woman's eyes drop to our laced fingers. I would have let go, but the security of his grip held me in place for the moment.

"Maddie, these are my parents, Jeff and Marissa Daniels." Grey let go of me and bent down to pick up the chubby baby rolling around on a blanket. "And this is my brother, Chase."

Chase made a gurgling noise and smiled up at Grey.

"It's nice to meet you, Maddie," Mrs. Daniels said as she and Mr. Daniels got up off the floor. "We were just about to put Chase down. And now that Grey's home, I know he'll sleep better."

Grey kissed his brother's forehead and handed the squirmy infant back to his mother.

"Make yourself at home, Maddie," Mr. Daniels said. "And Grey, why don't you get this young lady a sweatshirt? The dress is lovely, but she might be more comfortable in something warmer." Grey's dad smiled at me, making me feel more welcome in the two minutes I'd been there than in all the time I'd spent with Alex.

"It was nice meeting you." I watched them leave the room with tears in my eyes then blinked them back before turning to Grey. "They seem great."

"Yeah, they are. A little overprotective. I wasn't kidding about this being the safest place on Earth. They've baby-proofed every square inch of the house." He rolled his eyes, and I laughed. "I'll go get you that sweatshirt."

"Okay. May I use your bathroom?"

"Sure. It's right off the kitchen where we came in."

I went toward the bathroom, stopping by the closet to grab my phone from my purse and sent a text to Haleigh. *"At Grey's house. Be back by midnight."* I wasn't sure how soon she'd check her messages, so I didn't wait for a response. I slipped my phone back into my purse then fixed my makeup in the mirror before looking for Grey.

When I got back to the den, he'd taken off his suit jacket and tie and rolled the sleeves of his white dress shirt to his elbows. He sat on the couch, holding a black game controller in one hand and a dark gray sweatshirt in the other. "Hope you don't mind Michigan State."

I shook my head and took the sweatshirt from him. It was two sizes too big, but it was also the softest thing I'd ever put on. "That's where my dad went." I sat down beside him and curled the ends of the sleeves around my fingers then brought them to my face. The shirt smelled like sweet lemons and pencils. I cringed when I realized I was almost as bad as Alex. I dropped my hands and caught Grey staring at me. My cheeks turned hot. "Sorry. It smells good. I like whatever detergent your stepmom uses."

He cleared his throat. "It's, um, not clean. I mean it is, but I wore it... earlier today."

"Oh." The heat trickled from my cheeks, down my neck, and across my shoulders.

"Do you like video games?" he blurted, and I was glad for the change in subject.

"Not really. My dad really liked video games. I think Alex got him into playing them. You'd think she owned a GameStop with her love of video games." I rolled my eyes as I imagined my juvenile stepmom dragging my dad to gaming stores on dates.

His face fell. "I guess we could just watch TV." He started to get up.

I put my hand on his arm. "I didn't mean it like that. You can play if you want. I'm just not that good."

"Okay. I got this new one, and there's a bunch of hidden treasures and puzzles you have to solve. You can help with that stuff." The smile on Grey's face was contagious.

"Sounds great."

For a little over an hour, we didn't talk about anything other than the game. I helped guide his character through passageways filled with booby traps and magical elements and solved puzzles out of ancient ruins. At eleven thirty, he turned off the game.

"I should get you back so you can go home with Haleigh." He fidgeted with the controller before placing it on the side table.

"Thanks for tonight. I'd still like to slash Brody's tires, but there's always next time." I'd meant it as a joke, but Grey looked anything but amused.

"If you really want to get back at him, then instead of slashing his tires or keying his car, do something more lasting, more permanent. Turn him in. He's eighteen, and he's been slipping you drugs and shit. He'll lose all his scholarships and possibly even serve time."

I thought about Grey's suggestion. What Brody did hurt, but not only had I done nothing to prevent it, I'd pursued *him*. Brody might have been an asshole, but deep down, I'd wanted him to hurt me. *Cutter who doesn't cut.* "I'll think about it."

A few minutes later, we were headed back to the school. When we pulled up at the school, students were exiting the dance in a small cluster. Haleigh walked out, scanning the parking lot. When she saw us, her eyes bugged out, and she mouthed, *OMG,* and I had to choke back a laugh. Her curls had all fallen out, and her dress wasn't as crisp as when I'd left her, but she looked like she'd had fun.

"Thanks again," I said to Grey, reaching for the door handle.

"Anytime." He shrugged.

I opened my car door then stopped. "What are you always writing in your notebooks?"

He scrunched up his face. "What?"

"The notebooks you always carry around. What are you writing?"

"Oh, I'm not writing. I'm drawing."

I gripped the handle tighter, wishing I didn't have to get out of his warm car. "They're not like psycho mass murder type drawings, are they?"

He threw his head back and cracked up, lighting up his whole face. "No. Nothing like that. I'll show you sometime, okay?"

"Okay." I climbed out.

He waved as he drove off. It wasn't until later, when I got back to Haleigh's house, that I realized I still wore his sweatshirt.

CHAPTER 16

ALEX

Light seeped in through my closed eyelids, bathing my brain in a red glow. *My first clue.* I was conscious enough to know my room faced the opposite direction, and the morning sun should definitely *not* be pouring in through the glass.

I wasn't in my own bed.

The second clue was Ben's arm wrapped around my waist, pulling me flush against him. "Mmm… so warm."

I froze as he nuzzled his chilled nose into my neck, and the night before flooded back in a rush. The bar. The kiss. I'd begged him to take me home with him. *Oh my God. Did we have sex?* "Ben?" I whispered, poking his arm. "Ben, I need to, umm, I need to pee." Any excuse to get out of his bed before he fully woke up and tried to stop me. If that didn't work, I'd have to resort to gnawing off my own arm.

"Yeah, okay." He rolled just far enough away for me to make my escape.

Tiptoeing across the floor, I collected my clothes, wondered how I'd ended up wearing a pair of Ben's boxers and his T-shirt, and hurried into the bathroom. "What the hell did I do? How much did I drink last night?" I mumbled, catching my horrified reflection in the mirror. Black splotches under my eyes, red lipstick like a Kool-Aid stain around my mouth, skin as white as a ghost. I splashed cold water on my face, wiping traces of mascara from around my eyes as I tried to figure out how I was going to talk myself out of this one. Apparently, I'd contemplated for too long because the next thing I knew, a knock rattled the door.

"Hey, are you okay?"

I flushed the toilet before opening the door to Ben's concerned face. My mouth fell open as I stared at him, standing there in a pair of black pajama bottoms that left nothing to the imagination. Who would have guessed the guy was packing a whole six under that doctor coat? "I'm fine."

He raised his eyebrows as if he wanted to say, "Liar, liar pants on fire," but instead, he tossed out the words no one wanted to hear the morning after. "We need to talk about last night."

I glanced down at his T-shirt covering my body, and a jolt of raw panic welled up in me, sending my heart up my throat. I had to get out of there, the faster the better. "Uh, yeah... sure, later. I need to get home before Maddie does."

"Then I guess it's convenient she won't be home until this evening." The bastard smiled at me. *Smiled. At. Me.*

"Who told you that?" *Deep breaths. In and out.*

"You did." Why did he have to sound so... so... *understanding*? "Right before you—"

"Right! Of course, I did." I stopped him before the mere idea of what I might have done overwhelmed my already strained senses. What the hell had I been thinking? *Nothing. That's what.* I never should have allowed Natalie to drag me out. I wasn't ready—would probably *never* be ready—for what had happened.

Ben leaned against the doorframe, blocking my escape. He had me trapped like a feral kitten. "So... I imagine you're pretty hungry. How do you like your eggs?"

"Why does that sound like a pick-up line?" I fidgeted with the hem of the red flannel boxers hanging off my hips and wished the floor would just swallow me up.

"It's more like a, '*I know you'd rather be anywhere but here, but we need to talk before you leave, so we may as well eat*' line."

"You caught me."

"Sneaking out? Yeah, but since the jig is up, why don't you at least have breakfast with me?"

I blew out a breath. Time to face the firing squad. "Fine. But just breakfast."

"Just breakfast." He tossed me a pair of hospital scrubs. "These will be much more comfortable than your dress." He averted his eyes from my exposed body, making me uncomfortable. The man had obviously seen me naked. Then, leaving me standing in the doorway, he left the room and presumably headed toward the kitchen. I fought to collect myself. My memories of last night were spotty at best. I swore that would be the last time I let Natalie talk me into anything.

I didn't know what I'd expected when I'd wandered out of the bedroom, but a cozy house wasn't even close. The warm, buttery walls and honey oak floors enveloped me like a hug. And for a single guy, he kept the place neat and tidy but not excessively so—certainly not the cold bachelor pad I imagined most young doctors preferred.

"Nice place." I sat down at the little round table.

"Yeah, my sister helped pick it out. She also did most of the decorating. It's not much, but I don't need much."

He flipped an omelet onto a blue transferware plate and set it in front of me. "This is fabulous," I said between bites. "ER doctor by day, gourmet chef by night?"

Ben set his plate down and slid into the chair across from me. "I wouldn't go so far as to say gourmet, but I do all right."

"Are you kidding me? This is, hands down, the best omelet I've ever tasted."

"Well, thank you. But I was serious about what I said earlier. We need to talk, and I think you've stalled long enough."

"Fine." I held my fork in front of me like a weapon. "But I think you should know, I don't remember anything after we left the bar, so I don't know if I should compliment you or make jokes."

He grinned. "So you don't remember coming back here? Or our night of unprecedented passion?"

"Oh my God." I dropped my utensils to the plate with a loud clatter and hid behind my hands. Once I'd managed to compose myself, I pulled my hands away. I was as bad as David. I'd cheated. "I'm so sorry. I-I'm really not that girl. I don't do things like... It's just that so many things had happened and—"

"I'm kidding," he said with more compassion than I deserved. "You passed out in my truck on the way home. Then once we got here, you turned your stomach inside out. Twice. After I helped you clean up, you asked me to rub your back while you fell asleep."

"That's it?" As horrifying as the truth was, it wasn't nearly as bad as what I'd imagined.

Ben played with his food for a minute before answering. "That's it."

"So... no night of...?" I swallowed the lump in my throat.

"Passion?" He laughed then pulled his face into a serious expression. "Sadly, no."

I blew out a breath, my shoulders slumping against the back of the chair.

"Should I be offended that you're so relieved?" He blushed as he picked at his eggs.

"It's not that. I don't know what to say. I like you. You're a great guy, but I'm not... I don't know if I'll ever be—" The picture of David and Sarah embracing popped up unbidden in my mind, and I shook my head to clear it.

"Hey, it's okay. I understand. I didn't expect... Alex, despite what you said last night, I know you're not ready." Ben reached across the table. His warm hand rested over mine, and for an instant, I wanted to latch onto him and hold on. But before I could consider what that meant, he pulled it away again. "But if you change your mind in the future... well, you know where to find me."

I nodded. "I do."

"And I wanted to apologize for what I said at the bar. I should never have told you Sarah was still in love with David."

The reminder was like a sucker punch to the stomach.

"That was unbelievably callous. I have no excuse. I hope you can forgive me."

"Of course. It's not as if I haven't heard the same thing from countless others lately. I have to learn to face the reality that my husband was very likely cheating on me with his ex-wife. If they hadn't... if it wasn't for the accident... even if I hadn't lost the baby, he would have probably left me eventually." Tears pricked at my eyes, and I picked up my fork to stab a piece of omelet. "I guess we'll never know for sure."

"Only an idiot would walk away from you."

I kept my eyes on my plate. "I'm not easy to live with. Just ask my stepdaughter."

"Hey..." He grabbed my chin, lifting my face to his. "Just for today, let's not think about anyone else. The rest of the world doesn't exist." He took my hand, tugged me out of my chair, and enveloped me into his outstretched arms.

"What are we doing?" His chest muffled my voice.

"I'm giving a much-needed hug to my friend."

I slowly melted into him. "Okay."

He rocked me back and forth, humming a song I didn't know. "As long as we're clear."

Natalie pushed open the door and glared at me. "You can come out now. He's gone. Or were you shooting for the whole Disney princess thing? You do know that mop isn't likely to whisk you off to the ball, right?"

I forced my lips to tip up in a smile as I stepped over the smelly mop bucket to exit the small space. "Thanks, Nat."

She shook her head. "I really don't get you."

"What do you mean?" I played dumb as I followed her back to the front and plopped back down on my stool to drink my now cold coffee.

"I *mean...*" Natalie snatched the cup out of my hand and replaced it with a fresh one. "The guy is a sweetheart. He spent an entire weekend taking care of your drunken ass, and now you're hiding from him in my storage closet."

"You don't understand." Hell, *I* didn't even understand.

My emotions were so twisted up *I* could barely stand being around me. In fact, I'd compounded my grief with at least a dozen lies I'd told myself, starting with the one about Ben being nothing but a friend. The traitorous ways my body reacted when he was around terrified me. Not that it mattered. I simply didn't have the luxury of feeling anything more than friendship for him. Even that was a stretch.

Somewhere along the way, I'd forgotten how to tell the truth—even to myself. Hiding behind the pain took up way too much of my energy. And to make matters worse, Maddie continued to ask me about my next doctor's appointment, and instead of coming clean with her about the baby, I ignored her like the psycho bitch she claimed I was. My life was an utter and complete mess, and I had no one but myself to blame.

"You're damn right I don't understand. It's been two weeks... *two weeks* since you've spoken to him. You ignore his calls, keep your lights off at the house, and hide in closets. And I'm pretty sure the man knows you were here, since you're the only one in town with a Porsche Cayenne."

"That's why I parked around back." I cringed. She was right. I'd completely lost it.

"Are you kidding me?" Natalie's eyes widened. "You parked in the damn alley just so you wouldn't run into Ben? You need therapy."

I sagged against the counter. "Why the hell do you think I come here?"

"Save the flattery. We both know you come for the coffee."

We both laughed, but it didn't hold any of the usual humor. I felt the disappointment coming off her in waves. And I didn't blame her.

Natalie was right about another thing. I *was* avoiding Ben. I wasn't even sure why. I just didn't know how to face him. I knew he wanted more from me than friendship, and if I had the capacity to be honest, I'd have to admit I wanted the same thing. How could I possibly go back to being just friends when just being near him made my heart race? My stupid, traitorous heart. David hadn't even wanted me, so why did I still mourn him?

"It's okay to feel something for Ben, you know. It's not like you planned it. It's not like you were running around behind David's back." The icy look she gave me sent chills up my spine. "Surely David would've wanted you to be happy if he already had one foot out the door before the accident."

Her words cut me. But more than that, they made me think. "Is that what I am? Happy? I certainly don't feel happy."

"Well, maybe if you'd stop playing cat and mouse and started playing house, you would be." She stared me down as if to challenge me, but how was I supposed to respond?

"He hasn't even been gone two months. Shouldn't I still be grieving? Not out having revenge sex with hot doctors? Ben deserves more than that."

"Revenge sex? Come on. You know better than that." She waved her hand through the air. "He likes you. You like him. This has nothing to do with revenge, or grief, or anything other than biology. I know the timing sucks, but you can't help how you feel. You're still alive... and young, Alex. Let the guy in. Your heart has room for more than one person."

I scoffed. "It wasn't exactly my heart driving the bus."

"Well, your heart just needs a little time to catch up. Besides, you didn't even *do* anything. Just talk to him, okay? What he doesn't deserve is the silent treatment. Trust me, this guy's a keeper." She gave my hand a squeeze. "And if he keeps moping the way he has been, he'll end up in his own emergency room with a broken heart."

"I just can't think about it right now." I needed to stay away from Ben before *both* of us ended up irrevocably broken. One of us was quite enough.

"Well, as long as we're avoiding delicious men..." Natalie changed the subject. "I can't believe you haven't met my new coffee boy. I swear to jeebus, he's going to get me arrested for the things I've been thinking. That boy is offensively attractive. And I'll tell you this: I'd fire him on those grounds alone if he wasn't ridiculously respectful, not to mention a damn good worker. And you wouldn't believe all the new business I'm getting. He has a freaking fan club. Oh, to be a teenage girl again, when gobbling chocolate chip muffins and chasing them down with caramel brûlée lattes wasn't a death sentence for my hips. And it's not just the teenyboppers. I saw my fifth-grade teacher flirting with him the other day! But I swear on a stack of *US Weeklies*, if he calls me ma'am one more time, I'll be putting up that *Now Hiring* sign again, and he'll be picking coffee grounds out of his ass for the next year."

"So why *haven't* I seen him yet?"

"He's at school during the day, and you're too busy hiding from Ben in the afternoon."

"Maybe I'll meet him this weekend."

"If you can drag yourself out of the closet long enough."

"I think Ben works all weekend."

Natalie dropped her head to stare at the floor. "You know his schedule *just* so you know how to avoid him?"

I shrugged. I'd called the hospital with assorted excuses, and at least one fake accent, to find out when he was scheduled. The last thing I needed was to run into him accidentally.

Natalie pulled a pan out of the oven with a loud sigh. "If we're going to start this therapy session, I'm going to need a double espresso, and you're going to need a muffin."

CHAPTER 17

MADDIE

"MADISON?" MR. WELLS'S GRUFF VOICE startled me awake, and I jerked my head up from my desk.

"What?"

He narrowed his judgmental eyes at me. "I asked who the Allies were in World War Two."

"Uh, us, Britain, and Russia?" I crossed my fingers that I'd remembered correctly from U.S. History last year.

He scowled as if it pissed him off that I knew the answer. "Russia was known as the Soviet Union at the time. But yes, those were the big three."

He moved on to something else, but he continued to throw looks at me for the rest of the class, probably to make sure I hadn't gone back to napping during his lecture. History wasn't the only class I couldn't concentrate in or the only one I was failing. The bell rang, and I scurried out of the room, eager to get out from under Mr. Wells's watchful eye and to get to my next class. Third-hour Earth Science was my favorite part of the day.

"Hey." I slid into my seat next to Grey. He looked too good for high school in his worn jeans and the icy-blue V-neck sweater that matched his eyes perfectly. We hadn't really hung out at all since the winter dance a few weeks ago, but we talked every day in class and before and after school. He'd even given me a ride home a couple times when he didn't have swim practice, and I knew Alex wouldn't be there to ask questions.

"Hi." He flipped his notebook closed before I could see what he was drawing. I'd tried several times to look over his shoulder, but he had some sort of sixth sense.

"You know I'm going to see them one of these days. You might as well show me now."

He flashed a devilish smile. "I'll make a deal with you. If you bring your English and History grades up, I'll let you see one of my notebooks."

"That is so not fair. I should have never told you about my grades." I threw myself back into my seat and forced a scowl onto my lips. "And do not give me the 'life isn't fair' speech. I know it isn't. If it were, I wouldn't be an orphan."

"You're crabby today, but you're not an orphan. You have Alex." He put his notebook in his backpack and pulled out his science book.

I glared at him then took out my things for class. "Please tell me you were trying to make a joke. Alex hates me and can't wait to get rid of me. I'm lucky she hasn't tried to feed me a poisoned apple."

He cough-laughed then shook his head. "Now look who's not being fair."

"Why should I be?" I snapped, a fresh wave of anger bursting out of nowhere. "And whose side are you on anyway?"

The tardy bell rang, and Mrs. Shoeman called the class to attention. I fumed for a few minutes, thinking maybe I'd been wrong about third hour being my favorite after all. Life *wasn't* fair. That was the point. So how could he expect me to be fair back?

Grey's knee nudged mine, and I scooted as far away from him as I could at our little table. He sighed, loudly, and when Mrs. Shoeman's back was turned, he reached under the table, put his hand on my thigh, and pulled me next to him again. Other than a brush here and there, and the two times he'd briefly held my hand, it was the first deliberate physical contact we'd had. My whole body flooded with heat and annoying excitement. I wanted to be mad at him, but he made it very difficult.

I dared a glance at him. His blue eyes stared back at me. Mrs. Shoeman turned toward the class, and Grey looked away. He kept his hand on my leg for a moment longer though, as if to say he wanted me there, next to him. *Close.*

When class ended, I took my time packing up, waiting for the room to clear a little. "What was that?" I asked him in a hushed tone.

"What was *what*?" His full lips quirked.

I rolled my eyes. "You *know* what."

"I'm a guy, Maddie. I don't read between the lines." He slung his backpack over his shoulder.

"Fine. Never mind." I spun around and headed for the door. A few steps into the busy hall, Grey grabbed my hand and spun me around to face him.

His beautiful face had turned to stone as he stared down at me. "Would you please stop doing that?"

"No. I have to get to fourth hour, and since it's English, I can't afford to lose any points for being late."

He pulled me closer, so close my toes touched his. "You don't get it, do you?"

"Get what? You are so frustrating." I wanted to push him out of my personal space, but at the same time, I wanted to hold him there and never let him go.

"*I'm* frustrating? For weeks, I've been trying to decide if I should ask you out or not, and every time I work up the nerve, you push me away again. I'm about ready to give up, but I figured I'd try one more tactic. So instead of *letting* you push me away, I'm pulling you closer." He tugged on me again for emphasis, and my nose nearly bumped his chin.

I struggled to respond. "Like… a date?"

"Yes. A date. And not some party. I'd like to take you to dinner and a movie."

The one-minute warning bell rang, and if I didn't hurry, I'd definitely be late for English. "All right, um, I have to go." I released his hand and stepped back.

He hiked his backpack up on his shoulder. "Yeah, sure."

For the first time in weeks, hope bloomed in my chest. I knew I should steer as far away from him as possible. Grey Daniels was way more dangerous to me than Brody ever was. Grey ruined every plan I had to punish myself. He made me smile when I had no right to be happy. And yet I couldn't force myself to walk away from him. "Meet me after school?"

"Okay." He shrugged, and I hurried off to English, making it through the door just before the tardy bell rang.

The promise of getting to see his drawings had me determined to turn my grades around.

"Are you honestly going to sit here without saying a word to me?" Haleigh's voice cut through my daydream. I'd spent most of lunch thinking about Gray taking me on an actual, honest-to-goodness *date.* Would he hold my hand? Would he insist on paying for everything? Would he—?

"Really, Maddie?" Haleigh's death glare hit me like a slap to the face, and I flinched.

"I'm sorry, Hale. Why don't you tell me about Todd? You guys are still going out, right?" I tried to remember what she'd said about Todd Harrison asking her out. I hoped I hadn't already missed something important, but that might explain why she seemed so annoyed with me.

"I feel like I don't even know you anymore. Seriously," she hissed under her breath. "Were you ever going to tell me you'd slept with Brody?"

I took a bite of my pear and immediately regretted not chewing it before swallowing as I choked out the words. "Wait, what?" The force of my jaw falling open almost hurt but not nearly as much as the scathing look she gave me. "H-how did you find out?" I whispered.

Tears filled her eyes, and I knew she didn't want to tell me. "Luke's sister. She's in my geometry class. She overheard Luke and Brody talking about it, and she said to tell you to watch out for Brody. She kind of sounded like she was speaking from experience, and she only told me because she knew we were friends."

"We *are* friends. I just… it wasn't what I expected. And yeah, Brody's an asshole."

"Is that why you've been ignoring me? I mean, I know things are hard for you with your parents and all, but I want my friend back." Haleigh blinked back tears, making me feel even guiltier.

My eyes burned, and I had to look away. "I'm sorry. I don't know what to say. I'll try, okay? I really will."

We spent the rest of the lunch period gossiping about Grey and Todd, and I almost felt like we were getting back to being us.

After school, I scanned the halls for Grey, thinking he'd meet me at my locker, but I didn't see him. Instead, I saw Brody heading right for me.

"What do you want?" I rushed to get my coat on. But hurrying actually slowed me down since I tangled my arm got in the sleeve, and he had to help me get it untwisted before I dislocated my shoulder. "I thought you wanted nothing to do with me?"

"Maybe I do, maybe I don't." He stared into my eyes while rubbing both my arms. "I really just want to know, what's up with you and Daniels?" he asked without letting me go.

"Don't touch me." I put my hands on his chest to shove him away. "And why do you care about me and Grey?"

He shrugged and pulled me a little closer. Close enough for his breath to wash over my face. "I'm looking out for you. I told you before, dude's a freak. And hey, I wouldn't want you dating any *creeps*."

I scoffed. "Don't you think that's a little hypocritical considering what you did to me and however many *other* girls you've slept with?"

"I never promised you anything, Maddie, so don't go being all judgmental. Let's not forget you wanted it as much as I did. I just wanted to know where you and Grey stand. I've heard some rumors."

"We're friends." Grey appeared out of nowhere to stand next to us. His hands tightened into fists at his sides, and the muscle in his jaw flexed, making my stomach flutter.

I'd never been so happy to see him.

"*Friends*. Huh." Brody smirked as he bent down and whispered in my ear. "Not as good a friend as me." He slid one hand down and put something in my pocket.

A shudder ran through me at his uninvited touch. Aside from being a means to an end, what had I ever seen in him?

Brody let go of me and stood back to smirk at Grey. Some sort of silent exchange happened between them, but since I had no idea how to read non-verbal guy-talk, I stood there as if I had no place better to be.

Grey's eyes shifted to me, and the blue seemed darker—*colder*—as if *I'd* done something wrong. "I have to work this afternoon, so I need to get going. You still need a ride?" he asked, but it didn't sound like he wanted me to say yes. In fact, it sounded more like he wanted to be as far away from me as possible.

"I can take you home, Mads." Brody offered with a wink, but I had no intention of getting in his car, the same car he'd spent a week ranting about how much money it cost to get it detailed after *someone* painted the windows in lipstick.

"No..." I glanced between them then took a quick step away. "I, uh, forgot I told Haleigh I'd come over for a little while. She's probably waiting for me." I waved then took off down the hall, hoping Haleigh hadn't left the parking lot yet.

"Holy fudge!" Haleigh yelped when I pulled the passenger door open and plopped into the seat next to her. "You scared the poop out of me. What are you doing? I thought you were going with Grey."

"You know, you might actually feel better if you used real swear words." I panted, still out of breath from running through the parking lot in the cold, trying to catch up to her.

"I don't need to litter the air with filth. Now will you *please* tell me what you're doing here?"

I took a few deep breaths then told her what happened with Brody and how Grey looked pissed off about something.

"Well, boys can be really stupid sometimes. So do you want to come over for a little while?"

"Nah, not today. Alex has been pretty decent lately, so I figure maybe I shouldn't rock the boat."

CHAPTER 18

ALEX

I STOOD ACROSS FROM A SHIRTLESS David with the wide expanse of king-sized bed looming between us, as if facing off on the battlefield. He stood his ground, eyes locked on mine, staring me down. His red flannel pajama pants rode low on his hips, drawing my eye to the loose drawstring. I might have been angry with him, but that could never lessen the pull I felt toward him. "Why are you so adamant that I go?"

He scrubbed a hand over a weekend's worth of scruff on his face—a sure sign he was getting frustrated. "Baby, opportunities like this don't come along every day. You need to grab it while it's still out there. I already feel like a world-class jerk for dragging you so far away from your family and a job you love. I can't sit back and watch you pass on something that could put you ahead of the pack. And yeah, you could wait. But if you put it off too long, you'll be too far along to travel." He continued to circle back to the same argument I'd already grown tired of.

I didn't want to go. Pregnancy hormones didn't agree with me, and I felt like shit. I just wanted to stay home and enjoy what would have been the first quiet moments in our short marriage.

"Listen, babe." I leaned across the mattress, pleading with my eyes. "There'll be plenty of chances for me to go to LA before I'm too pregnant to travel. I'm not even due until June. I'd rather stay here with you. It's not like I don't have several other back-to-back trips coming up that I can't *get out of. I deserve a few days alone with my husband—time to prepare my nest, so to speak—before getting back to the grind. I can help you pack up the Christmas tree, finish off the last of the molasses cookies."*

He shook his head, and my smile wavered. "I have meetings planned that I *can't get out of. It would be better for both of us if you go now. Get it out of the way, and we'll have the rest of January to do whatever you like."* *David crawled across the bed to meet me in the middle. He pulled me into his arms and collapsed against the pillows. "Admit it. You know I'm right."*

"Fine. I'll go, but I don't like it." My stomach twisted, and for a change, it had nothing to do with morning sickness. "It just feels wrong."

"Hey..." He grabbed my chin in his thick fingers and turned my face to his. "You and me? We're magic. What could possibly go wrong?"

I shot upright in bed, blood rushing in my ears as I clutched the blanket to my chest. The dream—*the memory*—had been so vivid. So real. I swore I could even smell him. The next day, we'd said goodbye like every other day. And the day after that, I'd gotten the call that he'd died. Just like that. I couldn't help wondering what would have happened if I'd stayed. Would he have cancelled his *meeting* with Sarah? Would he have gone anyway? Could I have done anything to change his destiny? Or was I simply deluding myself, and my time with David wasn't meant to last forever.

I climbed out of bed and set to work shoving the last of David's things into boxes then lugged each one down the stairs, creating a pile in front of the basement door. Taking charge of my life again gave me a weird sense of accomplishment, like maybe I'd taken a huge step toward healing, but I still wasn't ready to cart my husband's memories away. I knew I'd eventually have to come up with a more permanent solution, but until then, I'd settle for out of sight, out of mind.

I flicked on the light and peered into the shadows.

"What are you doing?" Maddie's voice startled me, and I spun around to face her.

I scanned her jeans and fuzzy red sweater. "Don't you have school?"

"I don't have to leave for like thirty more minutes. What's your excuse for loitering in the hall like a creeper?"

I nodded toward the boxes. "Taking these to the basement."

Maddie leaned against the wall and smirked. "How's that working out for you so far?"

"Well, I haven't actually taken any yet. I don't really *do* basements. As a native Californian, I object to the whole concept. I've been trying to work up the courage to go down. Your dad didn't happen to keep bodies or anything down there, did he?"

"So you've lived here for how long now, and you've never gone into the basement before?"

I shook my head.

Maddie rolled her eyes and scooped up one of the boxes. "Come on. I'll help. You probably shouldn't be carrying heavy things anyway, right?"

Guilt twisted my insides. Why hadn't I told her about the baby? What was I waiting for?

After helping me stack all five boxes in the storage room, Maddie switched off the light and turned toward the closed door on the other side of the stairs. She flinched before taking a full step away.

"What's in there?"

She tensed up. "It's nothing."

I reached for the knob.

"Wait!" She pulled my hand back. "It's… it's just a room Dad made for me. A practice room. I don't go in there anymore."

"Oh."

"So yeah. It's nothing. Maybe you can turn it into a playroom for the baby or something."

Her words hit me like a dagger to the chest, and I knew I couldn't let it go on any longer. "Maddie." I pulled in a jagged breath. "I-I lost the baby."

Maddie let out a shaky laugh. "What do you mean you lost it? It's not even born yet."

"I mean… I had a miscarriage."

Maddie dropped onto the bottom step, and the air whooshed out of her lungs. "How? When?"

"A few weeks ago."

She turned toward me in slow motion until our eyes met. "A few weeks ago? How is that possible? You grounded me. We were here together the whole time."

"Before that."

"How much before?"

"The week before you moved in."

"What?" Maddie jumped to her feet. "That was over a month ago. Why didn't you tell me? I'd just gotten used to the idea of... God, you *lied* to me. You let me think you were still pregnant."

"I'm sorry." I took her spot on the stairs and let my head fall into my hands. "I-I just didn't know how to say the words. It devastated me. I'm still devastated. Just everything happened so fast."

"So no baby. Dad's gone, and now there's no baby?" For the first time since we'd met, Maddie looked less like an angry teenager and more like a lost little girl.

I shook my head. I couldn't say the words. Not again.

Her eyes glistened with tears. "How is that even fair? How is *any* of this fair?"

Neither of us spoke for several minutes. Then I asked the question that had been nagging at me since she'd told me about the room behind the door. "Maddie, why'd you stop dancing?"

Her mouth fell open, and she just stared at me for a moment. Then the rage I'd become accustomed to bubbled up and brimmed over. "Because *you* came to Lake Edna and ruined *everything.* And now I have nothing, and it's all your fault."

"*You need a book on how to raise a teenager.*" I mimicked Natalie's voice as I drove to the bookstore. "A book will solve *all* your problems." *Right*, as if a book was what I needed. A shrink. A vacation. A damn kick in the ass for agreeing to be someone's guardian when I could barely take care of myself. That's what I needed. Not a stupid book.

I parked my car and stomped across the frozen parking lot before practically tearing the door from the hinges as I let myself in. Damn Natalie and her stupid ideas.

Without asking for directions, I followed the signs straight to the self-help section, where I found dozens of books on parenting teenagers. Everything from *How to Raise Your Teenager Right* to *Yes, Your Teen is Crazy.* "I could have told you that," I mumbled as I flipped through the pages. But as much as I knew I needed the help, I wanted nothing to do with the subject matter.

Instead, my eyes wandered to the shelf across from me. *Getting*

Naked Again, caught my eye, and I put down the parenting book and pulled the new one from the shelf. It was a book about finding romance again after death or divorce. I dropped it as if it were on fire then picked it back up again to return it to the shelf.

"Alex." His voice drew me away from the shelf, and my eyes followed.

My mouth dropped open. *Really?* As if the universe hadn't already set me up for failure at every turn. "Ben?"

"Wow, I was beginning to believe you'd fallen off the edge of the world. I haven't seen you in weeks." He looked good in loose-fitting jeans and a blue-and-green flannel shirt.

I struggled to find my voice. "It hasn't been that long."

"It has. Two weeks on Sunday."

"I didn't know we were counting the days." It made me angry to know he'd kept track. He wasn't supposed to be so available because I wasn't.

He crossed his arms and scowled. "I didn't know you were trying to avoid me. I thought we were *friends*." I hated the way the word sounded as it tumbled from his lips. And even worse as it formed on mine.

"We *are* friends, and I wasn't trying to avoid you." I flipped aimlessly through the pages of the book I still held.

"The hell you weren't." He pushed his hand through his hair. "Hiding in Natalie's storage closet? Really, Alex? Not very mature of you, is it?"

"What makes you think I was hiding in a storage closet?" How did he *know* I was hiding in a storage closet?

He raised an eyebrow and stared at me without saying a word.

"Fine." I slammed the book shut. "I was hiding in a storage closet. But I wasn't avoiding *you*. I was avoiding the situation."

"We have a situation?"

"Are you—" I took a breath. "Are you following me?"

"No." Ben let out a nervous laugh. "What makes you think I've been following you?"

"You seem to know a lot about my whereabouts. And for that matter, what are you doing in the bookstore in the middle of the afternoon?"

He shifted his weight from one foot to the other. "Looking for a book. But stop changing the subject."

"Oh, really? What book?" I snatched the paperback from him and read the title out loud. "*What Women Want and How to Give it to Them*?" My lips quirked up, and I tried not to laugh. "A manual on how to attract women? Really, Ben?" I vacillated between exhilaration and terror.

"Haha. Very funny. So what book are you getting?"

"It's not import—" He yanked the book from my hand before I could stop him. "Hey! That's not even my book, I just—"

His eyebrows shot up as he read the title. "*Getting Naked Again*? Sound advice."

I laughed. "Shut up."

"Oh, come on, Alex. You walked right into that one. And let's face it, we can't deny the tension between us." He reached for my hand, and I stepped back.

My heart slammed against my ribs as I remembered the kiss we shared in the bar. "I have no idea what you're talking about."

"You're the one who said you were hiding from the *situation*. What sort of situation would prompt you to hide from your friend?"

Friends. Right. I've never fantasized about Natalie *naked.* And those daydreams about Ben terrified me so much I'd taken to surrounding myself with memories of David. I slept in his clothes, wore his cologne, immersed myself in every photograph ever taken of us.

"Ben." I turned to the shelf, thumbing along the spines of self-help romance books until I felt his breath on my neck. "I don't know how to be just friends with you."

He leaned in closer and brushed my hair away from my shoulder as he whispered in my ear. "What are you saying?"

"I'm saying you occupy my thoughts more often than I'm comfortable with." I spun around to face him, our bodies almost touching. "More than a little. Are you happy now?"

Ben blinked a few times without saying a word. Then he stepped back and shoved his hands into his hair, messing it up more than it already was. "I think about you too. I've missed seeing you these past few weeks. I know we should take things slow, but frankly, I don't want to." He dipped his face down close enough to brush his lips across mine. But instead, he held perfectly still. "Come home with me. I'm off today. We can just talk. I promise I'll let you set the pace."

"I can't."

"Why?"

"I just—" I shook my head, and my mouth went dry as I struggled to come up with the words.

"Alex…" My body shuddered as his hands slowly made contact with my shoulders, pulling me closer. "Stop making excuses," he whispered against my temple. "Just spend time with me. Let me take care of you today."

My eyes fluttered shut as my heart hammered behind my ribs. Of its own accord, my body leaned into his, and my hands skated up his arms until they locked behind his neck. With a whimper, I gave in, melting into his embrace. My lips found his, and the world around us disappeared.

"Get a room," a woman whispered before scooting around the corner to the next aisle.

We pulled apart, my face flaming. "Oh my god. I can't believe we just got caught making out in a bookstore."

Ben cleared his throat. "Maybe we'd better do what the lady said."

"What, get a room?" I felt my eyes go wide.

Ben chuckled. "I just meant we should go someplace else. To talk. Or whatever."

"Or whatever?" I slapped his arm.

He smirked. "You did kiss me."

"Uh-huh." I turned my back to him, pretending to pay attention to the books in front of me.

"Well…" He leaned over my shoulder to whisper, running his nose along the shell of my ear. "I really liked kissing you."

"I liked it too. Too much." I moaned, spinning around to face him. "Okay, let's go. But we're just going to talk. That's it."

His face broke into a wide smile. "Talk. I can do that." Then he grabbed my hand, pulling me out of the store toward his shiny black Ford pickup.

One minute, I was buckling my seatbelt, feeling lighter than I had in months, and the next, I was sprawled out on Ben's bed, half-undressed with his delicious weight bearing down on me from above.

"You're so beautiful." Ben's hand slid over my shoulder, sweeping my hair aside as he kissed his way across my collarbone. "I've missed you."

"I-I missed..." I stumbled over the words, not sure what exactly I missed. The feeling of closeness with a man? The intimacy? Or Ben himself? "It's been too long."

"Shh... don't think. Just feel."

I froze in his arms, and a sudden pang of guilt stabbed me through the chest.

"Hey—it's okay, if you're not ready—"

"No. I want this. With you. Just... less talking, more kissing." I pulled his face down to capture his lips with mine.

Ben took the hint and went to work peeling away my remaining clothes. As he stared into my eyes, his hard body settled between my legs. He didn't say anything, but his eyes spoke volumes, and I wasn't sure I was ready to hear it.

With my head nestled against Ben's chest, I listened to his heartbeat as it slowed to a normal rhythm. "Best idea ever," I said, and his body shook with silent laughter. I sat up to scowl at him. "What's so funny?"

He pulled me back down, tucking me against him again. "Nothing. I'm just really happy to have you here... and out of Natalie's closet."

"Well, I can definitely say"—I breathed in his sweet mint scent—"you *do* smell a lot better than her old mop."

His chest vibrated as he laughed. "Better than *Eau de Coffee Shop Floor*, huh?"

"Much better... and much more satisfying. A few minutes here beats a few *hours* over there."

"Hey." He leaned over me with playful scowl. "It's been longer than just a few minutes. I'll have you know, we've been in this bed for almost two hours."

"And it's the best two hours I've spent in a long time." I grinned up at him. "And I wouldn't mind—" My cell phone went off, interrupting my next thought. "Oh, can you—" I pointed to my phone on the bedside table. He reached over and grabbed it, handing it to me. "Thank you," I mouthed as I took the call. "Hello?"

"May I speak with Mrs. Barrett?"

"Speaking."

"This is Mrs. Walker, Maddie's principal?"

I stiffened as my hand gripped the phone. It didn't matter where I hid. Reality had a way of finding me. "What has she done now?"

"Well, actually that's the problem. She hasn't *done* anything. She wasn't in school today, and while I realize the past few months have been difficult for her, she's still failing two classes, and I'm concerned there won't be time for her to catch up if she doesn't buckle down and get to business. Now, we do offer after-school tutoring and extra credit. I know her teachers are more than willing to work with her, but I'm afraid Maddie just doesn't realize or care how dire her situation is."

"She didn't go to school?" I sat up, throwing my legs over the side of the bed, so my back was to Ben. For two hours, I'd almost forgotten I wasn't Alex, the single girl, rolling around in bed with the sexy doctor. I was Alex the grieving widow with a teenager to raise, and I didn't have the luxury of taking time off. "I don't know what to say... that's a lot to take in at this moment. We had an argument this morning, but I was sure she'd gone to school."

"Am I catching you at a bad time?"

I bit my lip to keep from crying. I'd forgotten about Maddie... and David for the better part of the day, and that truth cut like a razor. "No... it's not a bad time." Ben sighed, and I reached to pull the sheet around me.

"Mrs. Barrett? Is everything all right? I'm sorry if I've made you cry... I know you've been going through a difficult time yourself."

What did she know about difficult times? "No... no, I'm fine. You just caught me by surprise. I wasn't expecting to hear from you today. Certainly not with this kind of news. I'll speak with Maddie as soon as I get home."

"Good. I'll look forward to hearing back from you then. Enjoy the rest of your day."

Ben whispered, "Are you okay?"

I cleared my throat, blinking back the sting of tears, and nodded. "Thank you." I disconnected the call and stared at the phone in my hand.

"Hey, you're not okay." He spun me around, pulling the phone from my hand and dropping it on the floor. "You look like you're about thirty seconds from a complete meltdown."

"Did you hear what she said? Maddie ditched school again, and she's failing her classes. I need to get home and deal with this. David would never forgive me for... any of this."

"Wouldn't he want you to live your life?"

"I have no idea what he'd want anymore. I don't know what I want anymore. I only know what's expected of me. And that has everything to do with taking care of his daughter and nothing to do with me." I stood up, tucking the sheet around me, and grabbed my clothes. "I need to go."

To his credit, Ben did nothing to stop me.

CHAPTER 19

MADDIE

SHE SHOULDN'T HAVE WAITED A month to tell me. She should have told me the minute it happened. I'd just gotten used to the idea of a baby, and now it was gone. I walked the two miles to my mom's house, replaying the argument I'd had with Alex. How could she have kept something like that from me? That baby would have been my little brother or sister. *I guess there's nothing tying us together anymore.*

My key got stuck in the door, and I had to wiggle it to get the lock to turn. Mom had promised to get me a new one, but she never had the chance. God, I missed her. I dumped my bag, coat, and shoes by the door then headed down the hall. My breath hung in the stale air like miniature clouds, and I shivered from the cold. I hadn't been there in weeks. Alex had switched the mail and turned the heat up just enough to keep the pipes from freezing. The cable, internet, and house phone had been shut off, but the power still worked. The fridge was empty, but I knew where I could find something to drink.

Standing at the top of the steps leading to the basement reminded me of the conversation I'd had with Alex just hours ago. *Conversation?* More like shout-a-thon. I couldn't believe her. She'd lied to me. Kept secrets from me. And then expected me to confide my darkest secrets to her? Right. Bitch had a screw loose.

I descended the creaking wooden steps to where my mom kept her stash of wine. At the bottom, I pulled the chain for the single bulb that hung from the ceiling and stared at the fifteen or twenty bottles on a rack across from me.

I looked at several of the labels and finally decided to take the one that read... Sarah and David Barrett, August 20, 1996. Their wedding day. I wondered why they'd never opened it. Maybe they were waiting for an anniversary that never came. And never would.

"I might as well celebrate for them," I said to the cold, dank room.

Tucking the bottle in the crook of my arm, I turned the basement light off and scurried up the steps to the warmer main level. I opened the wine then grabbed the single joint Brody had shoved in my coat pocket and headed down the hall to my mom's room. She'd kept a lighter in her top drawer. She always said she'd know where to find it if the power went out, but I knew she snuck a cigarette every once in a while. I placed the bottle on the nightstand and lay on her bed. It'd been weeks since she'd slept there, but I could still smell her floral perfume on the pillow.

"Mommy." I hugged the pillow tighter then let go and lit my joint just before taking a swig of the wine straight from the bottle. *Why bother with a glass?*

What the hell is that buzzing? I looked around for the source of the annoying noise and vibration that were disturbing my perfectly nice high. *There it is again. What is that?* I moved my hand under the pillow I was holding then pulled it back out. *Oh! Ha! My phone.*

There were two texts, one from Haleigh asking if I was okay, and one from Brody asking if I was having fun. In other words, was I enjoying his gift? But there was no text from Grey, which kind of stung a little. I told myself he'd had his phone confiscated in Mr. Well's class again, but I didn't believe it for a minute. Maybe he was waiting for me to make the first move.

With as woozy as my head was, I had to really concentrate to type all the letters correctly.

Me: I'm sorry.

Then I waited for what seemed like a million hours until Grey texted me back.

Grey: 4 what?

Me: Idk

Grey: Then why r u apologizing?

Me: Idk, I'm kind of wasted right now and I prob shouldn't have told you that.

Grey: Where r u? Did u skip?

Me: Yeah I'm at Mom's.

Grey: What do u mean u r wasted? Alex let u get wasted?

Me: Hella no. I said I was at my mom's house, with her hidden stash of grapes.

My eyes crossed as I read the next reply. *Stay put! I'm on my way.*

Me: Thought you were at school.

My stomach fluttered at the thought of Grey coming to get me. I needed to check myself in a mirror. Maybe brush my teeth… touch up my makeup. I pulled myself off the bed and staggered to the bathroom.

"Oh, my God," I giggled. Smudged mascara under my eyes made me look like a rabid raccoon. I wiped the streaks away until I looked halfway decent then brushed my teeth using a leftover tube of toothpaste and my finger.

Once I was confident my breath smelled okay, I stumbled my way back to Mom's room and cracked open the window so the house wouldn't reek of pot. Then I grabbed the half-empty bottle of wine and took it to the kitchen.

"What the hell, Maddie?" Grey's voice startled me, and I nearly dropped the bottle.

"What do you mean, *what the hell, Maddie*? What the hell, *Grey*?" I slipped on the polished floor and almost fell, but Grey grabbed me around the waist, pulling the bottle from my hand. My heart fluttered as his body pressed against mine, and for a moment, I remembered I was excited to see him.

"Aren't ballerinas supposed to be graceful?"

"Don't call me that. I don't dance anymore. How'd you even get in here?"

"You left the damn door open." His jaw flexed so hard I worried it might shatter. "You're lucky it was me and not some nutjob coming in to rape you or something."

I pushed away from him. "In Ed Lakna? Really? The only crime around here is Mrs. Walker's fashion sense. I half expect to see a pile of skinned Dalmatians in the school parking lot."

He held up the bottle. "Did you drink this by yourself?"

I burst into a fit of giggles. "Do you *see* anyone else here? Oh wait... I forgot, my buddy Mary Jane had a glass."

Grey's face scrunched up. "Who the hell is Mary Jane?"

"She's my fairy pot-mother."

"Jesus, Maddie, you were smoking weed too? You know what? I'm done. I can't believe I ditched swim practice for this. I thought you wanted to get better... to *be* better. I warned you about Brody. Hell, after what he did, you still went back to him? I thought... damn it... I even asked you out! I should have known when you avoided answering me and ran off. Fuck! Why do I always fall for the troubled ones? Why can't I just *once* fall for a sweet girl who likes me back? Just fucking once!"

"What? What do you mean I avoided answering you? I said all right. That's yes, in case you didn't know. And for your information, if I hadn't run off to English, she would have docked my grade again, and you of all people should know I can't afford to lose *any* points in that class. And as for Brody? I want *nothing* to do with him. He stuck that joint in my pocket while I was trying to figure out why you were being so pissy. And for the record, I never once asked you to ditch swim practice for me. God, why are boys so stupid?"

"Because they're always thinking with their—" Even with my head spinning and Grey's presence further clouding my thought processes, I recognized her California girl accent.

"Alex!" I gasped.

CHAPTER 20

ALEX

"W-WHAT ARE YOU DOING HERE?" Maddie stumbled away from the boy and gaped at me. This wasn't the same bubbly girl who'd helped me put boxes in the basement, just hours earlier. Unfortunately, I recognized the deathly pale train wreck in front of me. I'd seen *her* several times already. *Jesus, what would David say?*

"I should be asking you the same thing. What the hell are *you* doing here? Besides drinking and"—I sniffed the air. "Is that pot I smell... *again*?"

"Ma'am, I know—"

I cut the boy off before he could start in on his lies. I could see how he'd charmed Maddie, and God knew I'd seen *his* kind before. The kid belonged in a pair of Calvins on a giant LA billboard, not the after-school special my life had become. But since he'd invited himself into my nightmare, he might as well get the full experience. "I don't think you do know... anything for that matter. What are *you* doing here? You do realize Maddie is under age, don't you? I should have you arrested for corrupting a minor."

"Oh my God!" Maddie stumbled in front of the boy, tucking him behind her. "Grey didn't do anything wrong. And for your information, he's a minor too!"

"No, Maddie. It's okay." He stepped around her to face me again. "I know this looks bad, but it's not what you th—"

"Oh, I'm sure it's *exactly* what I think." I looked at the bottle in his hand then to my clearly inebriated stepdaughter as I caught another whiff of marijuana.

Maddie rolled her eyes at me. "You just managed to show up in the wrong place at the wrong time. Big surprise."

"I'm pretty sure I showed up at precisely the *right* time." I turned to address the boy again. "I think you need to go, and be thankful I'm not calling your parents."

"I understand, thank you, ma'am." He set the bottle on the counter then turned to Maddie. "I'll talk to you tomorrow."

"Don't count it," I mumbled as he hurried out the door and closed it behind him.

"God, Alex." Maddie slumped against the counter. "You didn't have to be such a bitch to him. I told you he didn't do anything. He just came to check on me."

"Yeah, right... to check on you. You mean to check you out? You're so gullible. Do you have any idea what a teenage boy could do while you're in a compromised state?"

"He wasn't going to *do* anything. *Grey* isn't like that. Why do you always think the worst of everyone?"

"Because, in my experience, people end up proving me right. Case in point... this makes the third time you've royally screwed up while on my watch. What exactly am I *supposed* to think when I get a phone call from the school telling me you've skipped school again, *and* you're failing two classes, *and* instead of trying to catch up, you're here getting drunk and high. You know what they say, three strikes, you're out."

"Oh, so now you're kicking me out? That's fine. I didn't want you in my life anyway." Her expression turned icy, and she crossed her arms, her mood flipping like a fish on a boat.

"That's not what I meant." Once again, Maddie had me frazzled beyond words. "I mean, you're grounded, *again* and... and I'm selling this house."

Maddie blanched, her expression going from shock to anger in a heartbeat. "You can't sell it. It's mine!"

My blood pressure skyrocketed, taking my heart rate with it. "No, technically, it's mine, and it's nothing but trouble. We both need to move on, and the only way I can see that happening for you is if I take this house out of the equation. No more escaping reality and coming here. No more secret bottles of wine and hidden joints. No more sleeping around."

"For the last time, I'm not sleeping with Grey. And you're *not* selling my mom's house."

"Just watch me." I grabbed the half-empty bottle of wine from the counter and poured it down the drain.

"This is *my* home." She stomped her foot like a five-year-old. "You can't just sell it. God, no wonder Dad was going back to Mom. You're such a bitch!"

My legs tried to buckle beneath me at her declaration, but I managed to stay upright. "Yeah, well, this bitch is in charge of your life. Get used to it."

Maddie turned and made as if she were walking out the door. "I'll just go stay with Haleigh… or Grey."

"Like hell you will." I yanked her back by her sweater. "You'll stay away from that boy. He's nothing but trouble."

She wrenched out of my grip. "How can you judge him like that? You don't even know him."

"I've known plenty like him. They're all the same."

"So basically, you're saying my dad was a player who slept around?"

Her words were like a slap to my face. "You're the one who keeps reminding me he was leaving me for your mom, so yeah… that means he was just like the rest. And since he's left me with you, I get to make the rules. And the first rule is to be in the house by curfew, or I'm calling the police. Now get your stuff, and get in the car."

"No way? She was drunk *and* high?" Natalie hit me with the question the minute the last customer walked out the door.

"Again."

"And no grandmother to blame this time?" She cleared the coffee cups from the counter and wiped it down.

"Nope."

She shook her head. "Wow, you hit the jackpot with this one, huh?"

"Don't remind me." I'd done nothing but replay every moment of our confrontation. Lack of sleep was beginning to become the norm for me.

She tossed the damp rag across the space, hitting the sink dead center. "Oooh, two points... so, are you still trying to find some long-lost family member to take her in? Some rich Daddy Warbucks who can't wait to embrace little orphan Maddie?"

"I wish." I blew on my hot coffee, thinking how I was *this close* to sending her to live with Grandma Rose. But my conscience wouldn't allow me to stoop *that* low.

"Come on. She can't be that bad. She's a kid. A teenager. It's not a terminal illness, I'm pretty sure they all grow out of it. I mean... I never did." She winked. "But I hear most kids do."

"Thanks for the reassurance." I ran a hand through my tangled hair. "I can feel the gray coming in as we speak."

Natalie burst out laughing. "Well, at least you can afford frequent trips to the salon. I foresee weekly visits once you finish that game you're working on."

I laughed. "Yeah, right. I've spent more time stuck in 'gamer's block' than I have working."

"Maybe you need to take a day off and relax. Oh, I know! Why don't we play hooky tomorrow and hit the spa. You and me. Grownup girl time."

"I've spent quite enough time playing hooky from life. And since you mentioned it, I think it's probably time for me to pull on my big girl panties and start *acting* like a grownup."

Natalie let out an exasperated sigh. "I get that you're trying to be responsible. And that's great, really. But you deserve a life too. Maybe it's time for you to come out of the closet—literally—and call Ben. I'm not suggesting you sleep with him, per se. But if you did—"

Her comment hit just a little too close to home. "I'm not discussing Ben." Especially after running out on him the day before.

"Oh come on. Who else am I supposed to live vicariously through? It's not like I can talk to my coffee boy about *his* nonexistent sex life."

My eyebrows shot up. How did we end up discussing the sex lives of teens? "How do you know anything about coffee boy's sex life?"

"Oh my god, you can practically *see* the sexual tension rippling off him. It's so bad it's got *me* taking cold showers. Besides, I overheard him talking to a girl on the phone, and I got the distinct impression they haven't made it to the boinking stage yet."

"You're so gross."

Natalie shrugged. "You wish you were as gross as me."

"I wish you'd just serve coffee without the creamy commentary."

"You two sound like you're having a good time. I can hear you giggling from the parking lot." Ben grinned as he came through the front door.

"Hi, Doc." Natalie waved.

"Good morning, Natalie... Alex." He nodded to me.

I managed a smile. "On your way to work?"

"Yep." Ben sat on the stool beside me, brushing against me to whisper, "Though I'd much rather spend another day in bed with you."

"Mmhm." My face flamed, and I had nothing but hot coffee to douse it.

"Okay, what are you two whispering about over here? And wait just a damn minute..." Natalie pointed at me. "Why aren't you hiding in the storage closet?"

My mouth fell open. "I, um... well, we..."

Ben chuckled at my embarrassment. "Alex has decided to come out of the closet... at least where I'm concerned."

"Well, I'll be damned." She stared at Ben. "How'd you pull *that* off?"

"It was my good looks and charm."

I choked on my coffee. "More like your superior stalking skills."

"Hey, I was looking for a book." Ben laughed.

"How could I forget?"

"So basically, you worked everything out?" Natalie asked.

"Something like that," I mumbled, shifting my weight so I leaned away from him.

Natalie's head bobbed a few times. "Good. I approve."

Ben stiffened beside me. "Well, as long as *you* approve."

"So what does the doc think of your teenager dilemma?"

"I think Maddie just lost both her parents." I could feel his eyes on me. "She needs time to grieve and come to terms with life without them."

Natalie nudged my hand with hers. "Listen to the doc. He's a smart guy."

I sat up straighter. "She's not the only one grieving."

"Aww, sweetie, that's not what I mean at all." Natalie came around the counter to wrap an arm around my shoulder. "We haven't forgotten what you've lost."

"Hey, I wasn't trying to make light of it." Ben leaned in but, thankfully, didn't touch me. "I'm just saying, she's a kid. She doesn't have a handle on her emotions in the best of situations. This is going to be doubly difficult for her."

"I know. Of course, I know this, rationally. But dealing with her on a daily basis is testing my ability for rational thought."

The bell on the door jingled as someone came in. Natalie hurried back around the counter to play hostess again, and Ben sat upright on his stool, maintaining a careful distance from me. I was torn as to whether I wanted him to move away or come closer. Maybe I wasn't so different from a teenage girl myself these days.

"Listen, I'm sorry I said anything." Ben leaned in again. "The absolute last thing I meant to do was to drag up painful memories."

"It's fine." I forced a smile, but his expression told me I'd failed to fool him. "No, really. I am. I'm fine."

"You're sure?"

I nodded.

"Can I see you later?"

"When?"

"I get off at nine."

"I don't know. It's a school night, and I just grounded Maddie again."

"Maybe I could swing by? I'd really like to spend some time with you."

"I don't think that's a good idea. Maddie—"

"Sure. Of course, I understand." His smile was strained. "I need to run, or I'll be late." He bent down as if to kiss me but changed his mind when I flinched. "I'll talk to you later?"

I nodded.

His eyebrows furrowed. "You're not going to start hiding in the closet again, are you?"

I hesitated for a minute. A minute too long. He stood to leave.

"Ben." I grabbed his hand, giving it a little squeeze. "I'll text you later. Have a good day."

This time, his smile was genuine. "My day's already looking up."

CHAPTER 21

MADDIE

Alex grabbed her keys from the kitchen counter and searched the space in front of her as if she'd lost something. "Where did I put the grocery list?"

I waved the folded paper like a flag. "You gave it to me ten seconds ago."

"Oh, right, too many things to remember these days." She shook her head and snatched the list from me, tucking it into the pocket of her fancy, gray wool skirt. Her designer outfit didn't belong in a Michigan winter. "Do you have your math homework?"

I slung my backpack over my shoulder with a drawn-out sigh as we headed for the garage. "Yes, I have my math homework."

"And what about your English paper?" She unlocked the car. Why she felt the need to lock it while it was in the garage, I'd never know.

"I can't believe you called all of my teachers."

"I should have called them a long time ago," she muttered and started the car as I put on my seatbelt. The temperature was still somewhere south of freezing, and I shivered as she backed out of the driveway.

"One of these days, I'll remember to start the car before we need to leave."

"Right, and then we'll both be dead from the fumes. You know, Haleigh could give me a ride." I almost said Grey could pick me up since he lived closer, but Alex refused to listen to me about him. Plus, he and I weren't exactly on great terms. Well, I assumed so anyway, since he'd basically ignored me, refusing to respond to a single one of my texts.

"Haleigh doesn't need to go out of her way when I already drive right past your school on my way to the coffee shop. And you didn't answer me about your English paper."

"Yes, I got it done a day early since it's not due until tomorrow. I also studied for my history test today and finished my science worksheet. We just started a new section in my computer class, so I don't have anything due yet, and if you really want to come watch me run around the track in P.E., you're welcome to. Is that everything, or do you want bathroom updates too—because I can call you when I pee." I waited for a reaction, any reaction, but got nothing.

"No, that's fine." She rubbed her eyes while we sat at a red light.

I stole a glance in her direction. "You're going to rub your mascara off if you keep doing that."

"What? Oh." She checked the mirror for a sec before the light turned green.

"You're awfully dressed up for a Tuesday. You got a hot date waiting for you at the coffee shop?" I hadn't seen or heard her with the mystery guy in weeks. I had to wonder if she'd already kicked him to the curb.

"No! I..." She shook her head then slowed to turn into the school parking lot. A long row of cars queued up by the entrance, stopping to let students out. "I have a meeting—on Skype."

I shrugged. "Whatever."

"Okay, I'll pick you up at two-thirty." She dug for something in her purse but seemed to give up after just a few seconds.

"I can get a ride home."

"No!" she snapped. "I'll pick you up and drive you to school every day until I can trust you."

"Fine." I got out and slammed the door behind me. She could be mad about that if she wanted. I didn't care.

I made my way through the halls and dumped my backpack off before heading to P.E. As much as I joked with Alex about watching me run a mile, I had to admit my time was slower, and I couldn't seem to catch my breath.

In second hour history, I managed to finish my test just in time for Mr. Wells to grade it. He handed it back to me with a smile before class was over. As soon as the bell rang, I hugged my exam to my chest and dragged myself to third hour. Grey hadn't exactly spoken to me since

Alex threw him out of my mom's house last week, but he'd have to say something about my better-than-passing grade. I waited for him outside the door, eager to see him.

"Here." I shoved the paper at him before he could walk past me into the classroom. God, he looked good in jeans and a black turtleneck. I didn't know many boys who could pull that off.

"What's this?" He twisted his pillowy lips into a scowl.

"Just look at it, please?" I actually whined like a middle schooler. God, I was pathetic.

He rolled his eyes then lowered them to my test. I knew as soon as he saw the grade, he was happy. He tried—hard—to hide his smile, but it tugged at his perfect lips anyway. "A hundred and four?"

I bounced on my toes, a smile threatening to rip my face in two. "Yeah. I got every answer right, *and* I did the extra-credit question."

"Congratulations." He handed the paper back to me and turned to go in.

"Wait." I reached out to grab his arm but stopped myself. "I wanted to tell you I finished my English paper a day early, too."

He stopped and stepped out of the way of the other students. Once they'd passed, he looked at me. "What do you want me to say, Maddie? I tried. You know I tried. But not only did you get wasted, you almost got *me* in trouble, and I didn't do anything besides try to help you."

"Grey, I'm sorry. How many times do I have to apologize before you believe me? It was stupid of me, and I'd like to make it up to you. I'm bringing my grades up. I've told Alex at least a hundred times you were only there to stop me from doing something stupid. And if Brody even *looks* at me, I walk the other way." I leaned against the brick wall, tired all of a sudden.

The one-minute bell rang, and he glanced toward our class. "I'm happy you're trying to turn things around for yourself. At least I hope it's for yourself, because if you're doing it for me..." He shrugged.

I wiped at a bead of sweat on my forehead. It was as if someone had jacked the school's furnace all the way up. "You don't like me anymore, do you?"

"I—hey, are you all right?" He put his hand under my chin and raised my face to his. "You're really pale."

"I'm fine. We have to get to class." I shook him off and pushed away from the wall, but the action made me dizzy, and I stumbled.

"You are not fine. What did you take?" His eyes turned hard as he stared into mine.

I gaped at him. I supposed I deserved that, but I'd really been trying to be better. "Nothing, jerk." The tardy bell rang, and we were officially late. "Great."

"Maddie." He grabbed my arm. "I think you should go to the nurse."

"You know what? As of right now, you're not allowed to care about me," I snapped and pulled away before he noticed the tears working their way to the surface.

"But I do," he murmured.

Mrs. Shoeman stuck her head out in the hall. "Grey, Maddie, are you going to join us for class today?"

"Maddie's not feeling well," he blurted before I could say anything.

"Hmm." Mrs. Shoeman looked at me. "Maddie, is that true?"

I shook off her concern and reached for the bottom hem of my sweater. "I'm just warm. I can take this off."

She looked at me more closely then turned to Grey. "Why don't you walk her to the nurse's office? But don't take all hour."

"Yes, ma'am." Grey nodded, putting his hand on my arm again and urging me down the hall.

Our classroom door closed behind us, and I scooted away from him. "Don't touch me."

"Sorry." He pulled his hand away but kept his eyes trained on me in a way that made me warm for a completely different reason.

I stopped walking. "You know, ten minutes ago, I wouldn't have minded. Hell, I probably would have *liked* you showing me that kind of attention. But as of right now, if you don't like me, then you are not allowed to worry about me, and you are not allowed to look at me like, like… that." I waved my hand at him. "So stop it. Just stop all of it. Right now."

The smile that had almost been there when I showed him my history exam came to his lips, full force. "You must really not be feeling well. I think you're delirious."

I let my shoulders slump and huffed out a breath. "What's that supposed to mean?"

He took my hand, and I tried to pull away again, but he held it tighter and tugged me toward him. "I do like you, Maddie, a lot. I won't stop worrying about you, and as far as looking at you... well, I have a hard *enough* time keeping my eyes off you, so I'm pretty sure that's not going to stop either. I'm just disappointed. I was hoping we would have gone out by now, or at the very least hung out together. But you decided getting wasted was more important, and now your stepmom thinks it's my fault."

"I... I stopped listening after you said you liked me."

He laughed then put both his hands on my cheeks. "Shit. You're burning up." He dropped his hands and wrapped his arm around my shoulders. "Come on. Mrs. Shoeman won't be happy if I don't get back soon."

Once we'd reached the clinic, Grey wrapped his arms around me, giving me a too-quick hug. "I'd better get back, but I promise to text you later, okay?" As soon as I nodded, he turned to Mrs. Jones, the school nurse. "She's all yours."

Apparently, I had a fever, and as much as I begged Mrs. Jones not to, she called Alex to come get me. Thirty minutes later, Alex stood in the clinic doorway looking more than a little disheveled with her coat half-zipped and her hair in a wild mess.

I blinked at her a few times. "What'd you do, run here?"

"Are you sure she's sick?" Alex crossed her arms and scowled at me as she spoke to the nurse.

"I'm sure." The nurse nodded, handing me my backpack. "She should go home and get some rest."

Alex sighed. "Okay, let's go."

We stopped at my locker so I could switch out my books and get my coat then trudged through the snowy parking lot to the car. "I told them I was fine."

"I'm sure you did." She rolled her eyes as she climbed into the driver's seat and cranked on the engine.

I scanned her messy appearance again. "Did you miss your meeting?"

She glanced at me. "What meeting?"

I leaned toward her, tilting my head to the side to stare at her confused expression. "The Skype meeting?"

"Oh! Uh, no, not really. I had to… cut it short though."

"What exactly do you do? I never see you go to an office, but you always seem to be working. And no one *I* know gets to work in their pajamas, so spill." I flopped back into my seat, sinking into the warm leather.

"Mostly, I write code."

"Code? Like secret messages and stuff?"

She laughed. "No, computer code. I des—"

"Stop right there." I held up a hand between us. "I've heard enough. Dad already tried to explain that crap to me once."

Thankfully, she didn't say another word, and we were quiet all the way home. When we got there, I grabbed a bottle of water from the fridge and went up to my room. After changing into my PJs, I sent a quick text to Haleigh, so she wouldn't be looking for me at lunch then crawled into bed. A minute after Haleigh texted me, I got a text from Grey.

Grey: Since u stopped listening, I do worry. Especially 2day.

My eyelids were so heavy, I had a hard time replying, but I eventually sent a message back to him.

Me: Thank you. I just need some rest. TTYS

Grey: Not soon enough.

I hugged my phone then plugged it in and put it on my nightstand before drifting off to sleep.

CHAPTER 22

ALEX

Armed with a cereal bar and a cup of her favorite tea in a travel mug, I knocked on Maddie's bedroom door for the third time that morning. "Once, Maddie, just once I'd like to get you to school on time. If you're not out here in one minute, I'm coming in with a cold bucket of water and a whistle." I almost laughed, remembering my mother threatening me with the same thing when I was a teenager.

It wasn't so much getting her to school on time I was worried about—though it would be a bonus—but after running out on Ben, yet again, the day before, I was kind of hoping to catch him before he had to go to work. I raised my hand to pound on the door one more time when a thought hit me like a wrecking ball. I lowered my arm, grasped the handle, and slowly cracked open her door. She was still in bed with the covers heaped over her, and it looked like she must have grabbed an extra blanket sometime in the night.

"Maddie," I whispered. "Are you still not feeling well?" I waited for her to respond, but when she didn't, I crept closer. "Maddie, did you hear me?"

Still no response.

My breath hitched, and with trembling hands, I reached down to pull back the covers from her face. Ice flowed through my veins as I stared down at her still form and images of David, lying cold in his coffin, flooded my brain. I brushed her cheek with my fingers, realizing she felt warmer than Natalie's hottest cup of coffee. And although she seemed to be shivering, a thin sheen of sweat coated her milky-white skin.

"Go 'way," she murmured. "Sick."

Just like in the movies, everything seemed to skid to a stop for just a moment, then I couldn't move fast enough. I darted from her room to mine and snatched my phone from the nightstand. "Shit! Of all days." I threw the dead phone on my bed and raced down the stairs to my office. After flipping through a few pages in the phonebook, I picked up the landline and dialed.

"Bean There. Donut—"

"Natalie, I need Ben's number," I blurted.

"Alex? What are you doing? Don't you have his—?"

"My phone died, and I need to talk to him right away."

"Okay. Okay. Calm down. What's gotten into you anyway?" I heard the jingle of the coffee shop door in the background. "Hi there. How are you today?" she said to someone.

"Natalie. The number?"

"This'd better not be some phone sex emergency."

"No! It's Maddie. She's sick, like really, really sick, and I have no idea what to do. I don't know who her doctor is or if she even needs a doctor or if I should just take her to the emergency room."

"Why didn't you say that in the first place?" Natalie sounded flustered.

She rattled off his number, and I hung up and dialed him. It rang several times then went to voicemail. "Damn it, answer your freaking phone!" I dialed him again, and he picked up on the third ring.

"Hello?" He sounded super sleepy.

"Ben, it's Alex. I'm sorry to wake you like this, but Maddie's sick. She has a high fever, and I don't know what to do."

"Um..." I could hear him roll over in his bed, and all I could think about was being there with him and—*stop, Alex, concentrate.* "Did you give her anything for the fever yet?"

"What?" My brain had trouble focusing.

"Tylenol, Motrin, something to get the fever down."

"Oh, no. I just found her soaked in sweat in her bed and called you." All of a sudden, I felt ridiculously stupid for not thinking to give her any medicine before running to Ben for help. I was clueless when it came to people being sick. I'd rarely, if ever, been sick myself. I never caught colds or the flu. My mother always teased that I had an immune system built like Fort Knox.

"Do you have anything in the house?" he asked.

"I think so, yeah."

"Give her two of whatever you have, and if it's not down in…" he paused, "in an hour, call me back, okay?"

I nodded then realized he couldn't see me. "Okay, thanks. And I'm sorry I woke you. I was… well, I was going to try to surprise you this morning and come over after I dropped Maddie at school, but that obviously didn't happen."

"I would have liked that." I could hear the smile in his voice. "You're always welcome. Why don't you call me back either way? Just so I know she's all right."

"Thanks… again."

"Any time."

After disconnecting the call, I went in search of something to reduce a fever and found Tylenol in the medicine cabinet above David's sink. I hadn't bothered to empty or even open the cabinet since he'd been gone, and just then I was glad I hadn't. I took the bottle and a glass of water into Maddie's room. She'd pulled the cover back over her face and continued to shiver.

"You need to take some medicine." I shook the bottle. She groaned and wrapped the blankets tighter around herself. "Maddie, please? It will make you feel better." I set the water glass on her nightstand and shook two tablets from the bottle into my hand. "Here…" She opened one eye to peer at me then wiggled her fingers out of her blanket cocoon and took the pills. I handed her the water, and she carefully sipped some without sitting up. "I'll leave the glass here in case you want some more, and I'll come back to check on you later."

She gave a little nod then tugged on her blankets again. "Alex," she said in a raspy voice.

"Yes?"

"Don't forget to call school." She closed her eyes and was back asleep in less than thirty seconds.

Her cell phone sat charging on her nightstand, and I double-checked to make sure it was turned to silent before heading back to plug mine in and going downstairs. I went to my office and called the school then sat at my desk, staring at the wedding pictures that served as my laptop's screen saver for longer than I should have.

"I know I should have checked on her last night," I said to David's smiling image. "Am I ever going to get the hang of this?" I imagined his voice in my head saying, *probably not,* but I shook it off. He would have had faith in me. More than I had in myself.

An hour later, she was still burning up, and her blankets were damp to the touch. I grabbed my phone from the charger and hit the autodial for Ben.

"How's the patient?" He sounded much more awake than he had earlier.

"She still has a fever." I rubbed my temples with my fingertips as I spoke. "Should I give her more Tylenol?"

"Do you have anything else?"

"No. I looked."

"You'd better wait a little longer. With all her drinking, I don't want to compromise her liver any more than necessary."

"You don't think she's ODing or has alcohol poisoning or something?" My voice jumped an octave.

"I haven't examined her, Alex. But probably not since it started yesterday, and it sounds more like the flu than anything else."

"Yeah, yeah. She promised she wasn't doing any of that stuff anymore. You're probably right."

"You don't sound convinced."

"It's just... I want to be sure, you know?"

He was quiet for a second then asked, "Do you want me to... come over?"

"I... um... would you mind? I hate to bother you, and I know you'll be in a hurry to get to work, but I just can't stand seeing her like this and not knowing what's wrong or what to do to make her better."

"It's not a problem. I'm on my way."

CHAPTER 23

MADDIE

THE WEIGHT OF SOMEONE SITTING on my bed and fingers gently brushing my hair from my face brought me slowly out of sleep. "Maddie? I need you to wake up for a minute. There's a doctor here to see you." Alex used a softer tone than I'd ever heard from her. With my eyes closed, I could almost pretend she was Mom.

This must be a dream. Mom's gone, and Alex isn't that nice, and... "Doctors don't make house calls." It hurt my throat to talk.

"Hi, Maddie. I'm Dr. Hudson," the man said, and he sounded too solid, too present to be a part of a dream.

I clenched my blankets around me, trying to stop my body from shaking, and forced my eyes open as far as I could. Alex sat with her hand on my shoulder, and a handsome man with sandy brown hair and an oval face stood next to my bed. "I know you," I mumbled.

"We met before at the hospital. I worked with your mom. Would you mind if I examined you? Alex is worried."

I shifted my eyes to her, but she was looking at the doctor, glaring at him actually. Did they know each other? Alex stood and moved around to the other side of the bed while I sat up. My whole body ached, and my head felt woozy.

"That's good enough. You can stay like that." Dr. Hudson set a black bag down on my nightstand and pulled out a stethoscope.

I didn't think doctors carried bags like that anymore, but maybe he made a lot of house calls. I also didn't remember him personally, just that I'd met him once. But I remembered Mom saying how nice he was, and how some lucky girl would grab him up one day.

He did all the regular doctor stuff: listened to my heart and lungs, looked in my throat and nose, and took my temperature. Alex stood right next to my bed the whole time, fidgeting.

Dr. Hudson put his stethoscope away and smiled at me. "Does your throat hurt?"

I nodded.

He looked at Alex. "I'm pretty sure she's got strep. I'll do a quick swab to make sure, but I'll go ahead and write a prescription for her."

"Oh, um, okay." Alex twisted her hands in front of her.

"Are you allergic to any medications?" he asked me before shoving a giant Q-tip down my throat.

I gagged as he swiped the end of the stick across my tonsils then managed to shake my head.

"All right. I'll run up to the hospital and get something for you. In the meantime, I brought some ibuprofen, and you might want to gargle with warm salt water."

"You don't have time to go and come back," Alex said. "You'll be late for work."

Dr. Hudson glanced at me. "Dr. Kowalski is covering my shift today."

"But—"

"I want to make sure Maddie is taken care of. Sarah would appreciate that." He sat on the edge of my bed and gave me a conspiratorial smile. "I'll be going right past 7-Eleven. Would you like me to bring you a Slurpee? It'll feel good on your throat."

I nodded again. Great bedside manner *and* Slurpee delivery service. Mom wasn't wrong about this guy. He patted my shoulder then stood and grabbed his bag from my nightstand.

"I'll show you out." Alex hurried to my door and waited for Dr. Hudson to catch up.

They left the room, and I snuggled back under my blankets, glancing at the clock. It was ten forty. Grey would be going to lunch any minute. I grabbed my phone and pulled it under the blankets with me.

Me: How was 3rd?

Grey: Boring without u there. How r u feeling?

Me: Better now. But I have strep.

Grey: ☹ Wish I could bring you something to make you feel better.

I didn't dare tell him I was already getting a Slurpee, but I would choose seeing him over that any day.

Me: Wish you could too. Txt you later.

Grey: K

I put my phone back moments before Alex walked into my room again. "Would you like to get up and take a shower? It might make you feel better, and I can put clean sheets on your bed."

"How do you know Dr. Hudson?" I sat up.

Alex looked at my dresser then at me. "I met Ben at the funeral."

"Ben?"

"Dr. Hudson, he… said to call him by his first name… since he knew your mom."

Either I was sicker than the doctor told me or there was something fishy going on, because Alex never acted that nervous. "Sure, whatever you say." I slid my legs over the edge of the bed, and my feet fell to the floor like bricks.

She took a step toward me. "Do you want me to—?"

"No!" I held my hand out. "I can do it myself."

"Why don't you take a bath in my big tub? Then you won't have to hold yourself up in the shower."

My mood perked at the thought. "You don't mind?"

"Of course not. Wait here, and I'll go get the water started."

"Thanks."

She scurried out of my room but was back a few minutes later. I'd managed to stand and get a clean set of pajamas to take with me. Alex hovered until I made it down the hall and into her ginormous bathroom with the Jacuzzi tub. I undressed and eased myself into the warm, bubbling water.

It wasn't that I liked being sick, but it was kind of nice having everyone paying so much attention to me. The only person I knew who was ever this attentive was my mom. The last time I'd gotten this sick was over a year ago, just before Thanksgiving. Dad had flown out to see Alex, and I'd ended up with the flu. Mom made me turkey-shaped orange Jell-O, and we'd watched *A Christmas Story.* I sank lower into the bubbles, thankful for the roar of the tub's jets drowning out my sobs.

When the water got cold, I flipped the switch, turning off the

Jacuzzi, and climbed out of the tub, wrapping myself in the oversized towel Alex had set out for me. For a moment, I just sat on the edge, watching the water swirl down the drain, wishing it could take my pain and guilt with it.

"I'm sorry, Mom and Dad. I'm really, really sorry. I'll do better. I'll *be* better. I promise." I rocked back and forth, begging—for what—I didn't know. My parents were gone. There was no bringing them back. And it was all my fault.

"Maddie? Are you all right? Do you need help?" Alex called from the other side of the door.

"I'm fine," I choked out. "Don't come in." I didn't need, or want, her pity. I wanted my mom. I wanted orange Jell-O. And I wanted Alex to stop pretending to care about me and to leave me alone.

CHAPTER 24

ALEX

"I THINK I GOT EVERYTHING ON your list." Ben set an armload of grocery bags on the kitchen island. "But I'm not sure why you didn't just let me get a couple cans of chicken soup."

"Maddie's allergic to chicken." I smiled, remembering David reciting the list of foods Maddie couldn't eat before I'd even met her. He had such high hopes for us hitting it off. If he could see us now… "Did you get orange Jell-O? She likes orange. Is this her medicine? I'd better take that up to her right away."

"Alex." Ben clasped my hands in his. "Yes, I got orange. You told me three times before I left. Why don't you let me take up her medicine with the Slurpee while you start the soup?" He held my hands for a second longer then let go and left me there alone in the kitchen.

David's kitchen.

Ben was here in *David's* house, taking care of *David's* daughter.

I shook away the nagging sensation and unpacked the bags. He'd gotten everything on my list, including the Jell-O and the vanilla yogurt granola bars Maddie and I both liked. After putting away what I didn't need, I washed the vegetables.

"What kind of soup are you making?" Ben startled me as he stepped back into the kitchen.

"Well, I've never been much of a cook. You can thank my mother for that." I dried off my hands and took a knife from the block on the counter. "But even I can follow simple directions. I found the recipe on the fridge in Sarah's handwriting. Apparently, it's Maddie's favorite. How is she?"

"She's fine." He leaned against the doorframe, and I could feel him watching me. "I got the impression she'd like to be left alone for a while."

"I really appreciate you coming over and—well, *everything*." I glanced at him over my shoulder. Even slightly rumpled and majorly sleep deprived, the guy oozed sexy. "But you don't have to stay if you don't want to."

"Why does that sound like you're kicking me out?" He pushed off the wall, sauntering over to stand behind me. Cool hands rubbed my neck and shoulders.

A little voice told me I should move out of his reach, but I couldn't. His hands were firm and comforting as I peeled and sliced carrots. "I'm not... it's just... I mean this is where—"

He dropped his hands and stepped back. "This is *his* house."

I set the knife down and turned to face him, but as much as I wanted to say something, I couldn't find the words. My insides were jumbled and twisted, and I was certain my expression mirrored that.

"It's fine." He looked down then back up again with a sad smile. "I won't touch you. I want to, but I won't. I took the day off though, so can I at least stay and help you cook?"

I nodded and handed him an extra knife. "I don't know if I can do this," I whispered after a while of peeling and cutting in silence. A wave of sadness came over me, and I had to push back the threat of tears.

"*This* what? Cut potatoes, take care of Maddie, or be with me?" His voice sounded hollow, and I hated that I'd made it that way. "Never mind. Don't answer that. Why don't you go take a hot bath. You've had a rough morning. I'll finish the soup."

"Ben—" I set down the knife, feeling the weight of the world pressing down on me.

"One day at a time, Alex. Let's get through today... and tomorrow"—he shrugged—"we'll figure that out when the time comes, okay?"

"Okay, you're right." I blew out a breath and turned to walk out of the kitchen then stopped. "The recipe calls for thick chunks, but I think we should keep them small. They won't hurt her throat as much."

Ben smiled at me before taking three long strides and wrapping me in his arms. "I know I said I wouldn't touch you, but I can't help myself.

And in case you don't know this, you're an amazing woman. I think you're doing a great job with Maddie. You can tell me to go any time you want, but I hope you'll let me stay."

I hugged him around his waist and buried my face in his shoulder. He smelled good, fresh-vegetables-and-spices good. "Thank you, for everything." I kissed him. It wasn't meant to be much of a kiss, but I couldn't seem to pull my lips away.

"Go. I'll still be here when you're done."

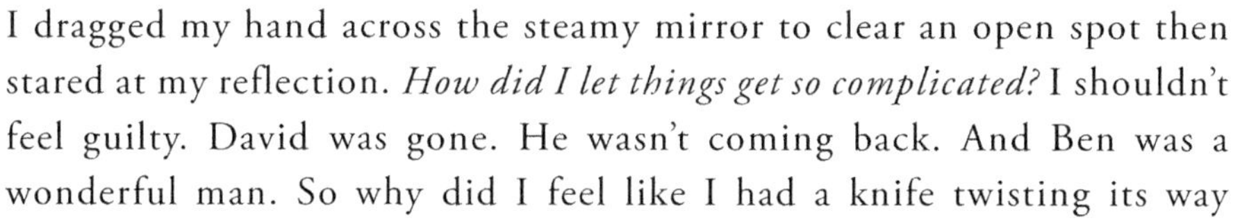

I dragged my hand across the steamy mirror to clear an open spot then stared at my reflection. *How did I let things get so complicated?* I shouldn't feel guilty. David was gone. He wasn't coming back. And Ben was a wonderful man. So why did I feel like I had a knife twisting its way through my gut as I watched him standing in the middle of my kitchen as if he belonged there?

"Knock, knock?" Ben's voice and the sound of his knuckles rapping against the doorframe shook me out of my thoughts.

I swiped away a few tears before poking my head out of the bathroom to find him standing across the room in the open doorway.

"Hey." I forced a smile.

"Feeling better?" he asked, and I nodded. "Good. I just checked on Maddie, and she's sound asleep. I think the soup is finished. I left it simmering on the stove."

"Oh, okay... good. Thank you." I took a step out of the bathroom, hitching my towel up a little and tugging it tighter around me.

"I... um... I guess I'm gonna go. Give you some space." He looked down at the carpet, seemingly tracing the pattern with his eyes before tipping his face back up and locking them with mine. "I'll call you tomorrow, okay?"

He turned to leave, but I wasn't ready to let him go. "Ben... wait."

He shifted his weight. "This is obviously too difficult for you... having me here. I don't want to cause you any more stress than I already have."

He was right. I wanted him to leave, but I *needed* him to stay. "Please, don't go."

He took measured steps, crossing the room until he stood directly in front of me. "What am I going to do with you?" He cupped my cheek in his palm.

I leaned into his touch, tucking myself under his chin. "Can you just lie down with me for a few minutes?"

"I can do that." He kept me wrapped in his arms and guided me toward the bed, but he stopped at the edge of the mattress to lock his eyes with mine. "Are you sure?"

With a shaky smile, I untangled myself from his grasp and climbed into the bed, pulling him along until we were lying side by side on top of the covers. "No, but I don't want you to go." I shivered.

"You're cold," he murmured, rubbing his hands down my arms. "Here." He tugged off his navy thermal shirt then pulled it over my head until he'd enveloped me in his leftover warmth. "Better?"

I nodded, nestling into his chest.

"We're going to be okay, you know. I'm not going anywhere."

I propped myself up on one elbow to look down at him. "Why do you put up with me?"

"Because I can't imagine anyone more worth it." He smiled, running his nose along my cheek until his lips brushed against mine. Once, twice, then I kissed him back, allowing my tongue to tangle with his.

Before I knew what I was doing, I'd tossed the towel aside and tugged his shirt back over my head until I was naked beneath him, and his jean-clad hips had settled between my open legs.

He captured my bottom lip in his, sucking and nibbling as he freed himself from the confines of the denim. "Are you sure?"

I wasn't, but I nodded anyway. Ben had this amazing ability to make me forget myself and everything around me. Then as he settled between my legs again and I felt him *there*, I realized what we were actually doing—where we were—and then Maddie coughed down the hall, and the panic set in. "Get off me. *Get. Off.*" I couldn't get out from under him fast enough, shoving his chest until he jumped back, a mask of confusion twisting his handsome face.

He tangled his hands in his hair as he stared down at me as if he didn't recognize me all of a sudden.

"Stop looking at me like that!" I tugged the damp towel around me as I pulled myself to sitting.

"Did I hurt you?" he whispered.

"No, you didn't hurt me." I covered my face. "I just—I thought I could, but I can't."

Ben dropped to his knees in front of me, pulling my hands from my face to brush the tears from my cheeks with his thumbs. "Hey, it's okay. I get it. What can I do?"

"I think you should go." I looked him straight in the eyes and watched as I shattered his heart. "It's not you. It's me. It's just too much too soon."

His mouth fell open for an instant, then he scrambled to pull his jeans back on. "I'm sorry, Alex. I-I should have known better. I just… I love you, and I—"

"Please don't. I can't deal with that right now." I turned away from him. The tears came so quickly I couldn't blink them back fast enough. "I'm sorry. Just go and I'll—I'll call you later, okay?"

"Yeah. Okay, sure." He nodded absently, and I could tell I'd destroyed him. "I'll just go then."

I didn't wait for him to clear the room before falling face first into my pillow and letting the sobs rip free. I'd made such a mess of my life.

CHAPTER 25

MADDIE

ALEX CAME INTO THE KITCHEN wearing some of my dad's old sweats—just like she'd been doing the past few days—and started making a pot of coffee.

"It's Monday. Aren't you going to the coffee shop after you drop me off?" I asked as I poured skim milk on my Honeycombs.

My throat didn't hurt anymore, and I was anxious to get back to school. Okay, not to school per se, but I wanted to get out of the house... and to see Grey. Alex and I had spent most of the last four days lying on the couch watching *Fast and Furious* movies and *Project Runway* reruns. We both thought Mrs. Walker could take a fashion lesson from the designers. Late Friday night though, I'd caught Alex watching the video of her and Dad's wedding. I don't know if she saw me, but I could tell she was crying.

She rubbed her eyes then reached for a mug. "Do you think Haleigh could give you a ride today? I'm not feeling well."

"Yeah, sure. You probably got sick from me. You should call Dr. Hud—"

"He's busy," she snapped as she poured her coffee then replaced the decanter and left the room.

I finished my breakfast and put my dishes in the dishwasher before calling Haleigh. Half an hour later, we were on our way to school.

"You missed the assembly." She twirled one of her signature curls around her finger while we waited for the traffic light. "It was lame though."

"Yeah, Grey told me. He said the best part was Mrs. Shoeman almost lighting Mr. Lesage on fire during the safety demonstration."

"That was so funny. So you've been talking to Grey?" She gripped the wheel at ten and two like always, wearing a smirk that created a set of dimples I'd never noticed before.

"A little." I shrugged. I didn't want to go into it right then, but Grey had called me after school on Wednesday, Thursday, and Friday, then three times over the weekend. That didn't include the hundred or so texts we'd sent each other. It gave me a warm fuzzy just thinking about him.

"That's nice. Did he tell you about Kelsey and Brody getting into a huge fight on Friday? I didn't see it, but I guess Kelsey was screaming, and Mrs. Walker had to call her parents."

"He mentioned it." He hadn't mentioned how upset Kelsey had been, but maybe he didn't know. I hoped he didn't care… *too* much.

Haleigh parked her car, and we both climbed out. "I'm so sick of this!" She swatted a few fluffy white flakes as our feet crunched down the layer of snow already coating the parking lot. It was mid-March, and we still had several inches on the ground. The forecast called for another storm, and this time it was probably right.

"I guess that thing Mom used to say isn't true this year, is it? Something, 'out like a lamb'?"

"In like a lion. Out like a lamb." Grey walked up beside me, taking my hand. "Hey."

"Hey" was all I could manage to get out as his fingers curled around mine. Any chill was completely gone, and I had the sudden urge to roll around in a nearby snow bank.

"Yeah, that's—oh, hi, Grey." Haleigh blushed. "Um, I'll see you later." She scurried ahead of us.

"Why do girls always run away from me?" he asked with a straight face.

I summoned the courage to tug his sleeve a little. "I'm not running."

He smiled. "No, you're not, are you?"

We stopped just inside the building and moved out of the way of the doors. It just about killed me to do it, but I let go of him to take off my gloves and shove them in my pockets.

He did the same with his then grabbed my hand again. "May I walk you to your first hour?"

I nodded, trying not to stare at him, but the slight pinkness of his cheeks and brightness of his eyes made that pretty much impossible. "I have to stop at my locker first."

"Lead the way." He moved his free arm in a sweeping motion. "So are you really feeling better, or are you just tired of being stuck in your house with Alex?"

"Both." I laughed. "But I think Alex got what I had." I shoved my backpack in my locker, and we continued toward the gym, holding hands again, the feel of it becoming more natural with every step.

"Yeah, that happens. Marissa's always worried Chase will catch whatever bug is going around. Speaking of Chase…" We stopped outside the girl's locker room, and Grey brushed my hair back from my face. For a second, I thought he was about to kiss me, but he didn't. "Um, if this snow keeps up, my dad will be really busy plowing, and Marissa handles a lot of the calls coming in so—" He let go of my hand and shook his head. "Never mind. Alex probably won't let you."

All my warm fuzzies turned to prickly frost at the thought of Alex keeping me from seeing Grey. "What were you going to say?"

He rubbed the back of his neck. "I was wondering if you could come over after school for a little while and help with Chase. I don't really *need* the help, but it'd be nice to have the company… *your* company."

Yes. Yes. Triple yes! "I'll ask her. She might not care since she's sick." I doubted that, but it was worth a try. "I'll text her later, okay?"

His lips twitched into a small smile. "Okay. See you in third hour." He took off down the hall.

I might have been feeling well enough to come back to school, but in P.E., I wasn't up to par with the rest of the class yet. As if a room filled with sweaty boys and nasty old sock stench wasn't bad enough, we were doing circuit training, and I could only make it through about half the stations before getting winded. Coach Pollard was nice enough to let me take a few breaks then let me go early to get a shower.

I took my phone from my gym locker and sent a text to Alex.

Me: How r u feeling?

I figured I'd start with something nice, hoping it would distract her from my real request.

Alex: Not great. Why aren't you in class?

Me: On my way to shower after PE. I was asked to babysit after school. You cool with that? I'll be home in time for dinner.

It took her a few minutes to reply, but the wait was worth it.

Alex: Fine. You'll probably have to fend for yourself for dinner though.

Me: Thanks!

I grabbed my stuff and hurried to the shower. History dragged since, by the time second hour started, everyone knew school would be closing early for the day. I didn't mind waiting through third hour though.

"Did you ask Alex?" Grey asked as soon as I sat down at our table in earth science.

My stomach did a weird flutter thing at how hopeful he looked. "Yep, we're good to go."

"Wait, she said yes?" He sounded surprised.

I giggled. "Do you want to see her text?"

"No, it's just... not what I was expecting. But I'm glad, really glad." He put his hand over mine on the table.

I squeezed his fingers. "Me too. Maybe all that nice stuff I've been saying about you finally worked." I wasn't lying, technically. I did text her, and she did say it was fine. It wasn't my fault if she didn't bother to ask for more details.

CHAPTER 26

ALEX

"WHAT THE HELL?" I SAT up, letting the blankets pool around my waist.

At first, I thought the chime had been part of a nightmare, but then the doorbell sounded several times in rapid succession before the banging started again. With a groan, I climbed out of bed and looked at the clock. It was almost noon. I'd slept the morning away.

The chime went off again, followed by more banging. "Hang on!" I shouted as I dragged myself down the stairs to open the front door.

"About damn time! Where the *hell* have you been?" Natalie brushed by me.

I stared at her for a second before slamming the door. "Hi, Natalie. Come on in."

"Don't *Hi, Natalie* me." She crossed her arms over her jacket. "You haven't been in the coffee shop in a week. Why are you avoiding me? And don't you dare use the sick kid excuse. I already know she went to school today, so that won't hold water."

I used both hands to push my ratty hair out of my face. "I wasn't avoiding *you*."

"I guess that would explain why Ben keeps coming in and asking if you're hiding in the closet." Natalie popped up an eyebrow and waited for me to respond.

I nodded. The mere sound of his name made my stomach twist into knots. The thought of him was never far from the forefront of my mind, but I repeatedly pushed it back, unwilling to deal with the aftermath of what I'd almost done with him in my husband's bed.

"I should have known something was up by the look on his face. I figured he'd lost a few patients, or maybe his dog died." She gave me a look that said she knew exactly what had happened—or at least close enough to guess.

"He doesn't have a dog." I turned and made my way into the kitchen with Natalie close on my heels.

"You know, it's one thing to avoid the doc, but me? You always come see me when you're upset. I was the first person you called when you found out about David. Not your mom… me. And don't even try to say it's just my coffee."

"Speaking of coffee… if you're going to be here, can you at least make yourself useful?" I pointed at the coffee maker.

She rolled her eyes before grabbing the filters from the cabinet. "You seemed almost happy the last time I saw you. I thought things were good. So, when did everything go to shit?" She paused to look me over. "And speaking of shit… no offense, but you look like total crap. When did you go back to living in David's old clothes? You really need to burn these." She pulled on the sleeve of my sweatshirt, and I tugged my arm back.

"I'm not burning them. What are you doing here anyway? Shouldn't you be at the shop?"

"I closed early." She hit the button on the machine, making it come to life with the magical sounds and smells of fresh coffee. "I should be pissed at you, you know. Ben is my friend too."

"We had sex…" I paused at her *duh* face. "But we almost did it *here*. In my bed. In *David's* bed." I choked back a sob. Knowing what I'd done and saying it out loud were two different things.

"Oh, sweetie." Natalie pulled me into a hug. "You didn't do anything wrong. Your husband isn't on a business trip. He's dead." Her tone was gentle despite the weight of the words she'd used.

I pressed my cheek against her shoulder. "Ben told me he loved me."

"Wait? He did? Where? When?" She leaned back to look me in the eyes.

"Just before I kicked him out of my house."

"Oh, sweetie, you didn't! Is it really that surprising… or *awful* for him to love you?"

"Yes. No. I don't know." I shrugged out of her embrace to pace the room. He hadn't known me long enough to love me. Love took time. And I hadn't even had time to mourn the love of my life. How could I even begin to consider the love of another? "I have no idea what I'm doing. He can't fall in love with me."

Natalie patted my shoulder. "You're a little late for that, don't you think?"

"It doesn't matter. *I* can't fall in love with him." I shook my head. "I just can't."

Natalie barked out a laugh without a trace of humor. "I hate to be the one to say this, kiddo, but it's beginning to look like he opened his heart to you, and you ripped it out, treating him like a damn yoyo. Does the guy even know what he did wrong?"

"I don't know. I just asked him to leave. I haven't really talked to him since."

"Don't you think you at least owe him that?"

"Yes. Of course, I do." I slammed my ceramic mug against the granite counter, creating a web of cracks along the side. "But I have no idea what to tell him."

"Tell him what you told me. And do me a favor. Don't wait too long. Either be with him, or cut him loose. What you're doing isn't fair, Alex. He's a good guy. He deserves better."

What if I didn't have it in me to give him what he deserved? What if I was still too broken? I took a gulp of too-hot coffee to avoid answering her.

Natalie zipped up her coat and smoothed her honey hair behind her ears. "Listen, I need to go."

"Yeah, you should get back to the coffee shop. It's the lunch rush."

"No, I told you I closed early. The whole town is closing up. Haven't you noticed there's a damn blizzard out there?"

My eyes shifted to the window and the blanket of white outside. "I guess I was too distracted to notice. I should probably call Maddie to make sure she has a ride home from school."

The shock in her expression was unmistakable. "Sweetie, the school's been closed for almost two hours."

"Oh." I blinked a few times, watching the snowfall outside the kitchen window. "She said something about going home with someone after school."

"She'd better get a ride before she's stuck there all night. And I'd better get *my* ass home before you're stuck with me all night."

I flashed a weak grin, abandoning my cup to walk her to the door. "Yeah, get outta here. I don't think I can deal with fending off your advances for a whole day."

"You know you love me and my wandering hands." Natalie bumped my shoulder with hers then opened the door. The air swirled with snow as she stepped outside. "Don't forget to call him, okay?"

"I won't." I gave her my word then closed the door and leaned against it, taking a few deep breaths to clear my head. Natalie was right. I needed to call Ben, but that would have to wait. First, I had to find out where Maddie was. I reached into my pocket to pull out my phone and hit the speed dial.

"Hey, Alex." Her voice was more cheerful than I'd ever heard it. At least one of us was happy.

"Where are you? Why didn't you come home after they let out school?"

"You said I could babysit?" She spoke slowly, as if addressing a small child.

I shook my head to clear it. I had no idea what was wrong with me. "Oh, that's right. Well, tell them I'll be right over to get you."

"Uh..." She cleared her throat, and I could hear her shifting the phone. "You don't have to get me. I have a ride home."

I held my breath for a long moment before letting it out. "Where are you exactly?"

"I told you. Babysitting at a friend's house. He'll bring me home later."

"He? He who?" My earlier lifelessness evaporated as irritation rushed in to replace it. "I want a name, Madison."

The phone line crackled while I waited for her reply.

"Grey." Maddie sighed, and I could practically hear her eyes rolling in their sockets. "I'm with Grey."

Of all the sneaky teenage behavior! "So you lied? What happened to babysitting?"

"I *am* babysitting. At his house. He has a little brother."

"Semantics, Maddie. You knew you weren't supposed be with him." I held my temper at bay, but it hung by a thread. "The address?"

I heard her whispering before she came back on the line. "One-Three-Two Elm, but I'm perfectly safe. His dad said—"

"Stay right where you are. I'm coming to get you."

"Alex, wait—"

I disconnected the call and ran to get my coat.

"*Goddamn it!*" I slammed my fists against the steering wheel.

My all-terrain Porsche Cayenne was stuck in a ditch on the outskirts of town, and Triple-A said it would be over two hours before someone could rescue me. And just my luck, my phone's low-battery light flashed up at me.

I hit the autodial for Natalie and fidgeted with my coat zipper while I waited for her to pick up.

"Miss me already?" Natalie chuckled.

"I need help."

"Didn't I say that this morning? Lucky for you, I don't think you're beyond helping, but it's—"

A gust of wind whipped around the car, and even though I was safe and warm inside, a deep shiver cut through me. "No joking, Natalie. I'm stuck in a ditch."

"What!" She screeched into the phone. "Where? What are you doing out in this weather?"

"Maddie went to that boy's house. I was trying to pick her up before she got stranded."

"Condom boy? Or liquor boy?"

"Liquor boy." I fumed, thinking about Maddie's shitty taste in boys.

"Geez, you can't catch a break, can you?"

"No. I can't. And my phone's dying, but if I keep the motor running to charge it, I'm likely to run out of gas."

"I told you not to let your tank get so low. You're lucky you haven't run out of gas several times since I've known you. Jesus, that's so dangerous." Neither one of us said it, but it was clear from Natalie's tone that she knew as well as I did it would get cold—and fast—without the engine running.

"Hey, no 'I told you so's. I need help, not a scolding."

"Okay, okay. I know someone with a truck. I'll send him to get you out of the ditch."

"Thank you! I'll owe you, big time."

"Nah, trust me. You won't owe me a thing."

CHAPTER 27

MADDIE

GREY THREW HIS XBOX CONTROLLER on the floor and grumbled under his breath.

"It's just a game, Grey. Start it over, and we'll figure it out."

He sighed. "Did you hear from Alex yet? It's been awhile since she said she was coming to get you."

"No, I tried calling her when you checked on Chase, but it went straight to voicemail. You're not really worried about her, are you?" My heart rate picked up a little at the anxiety in his voice. I didn't want to think about what could happen to Alex on a night like that.

"No, it's not that." He lowered his head to his knees.

"Um, okay. What is it then?"

"You."

"Me?"

Before I had a chance to react, Grey had rolled to his knees in front of me and put his hands on my thighs. My heart slammed so hard against my ribcage I was sure it would leave bruises. But I couldn't think about that. Instead, I focused all my attention on how good Grey smelled and how safe I felt with him around, and how much I wanted to…

He brought his lips to mine, gently at first then more firmly as I leaned forward to wrap my arms around his neck. But even with our chests pressed together, he still wasn't close enough. I eased my legs apart and scooted to the edge of the couch while he knelt on the floor. His arms circled my waist, and I held him so tight I thought I might be choking him, but he didn't complain. Instead, his mouth opened just enough for my tongue to slip inside, and he let out a surprised breath. He kissed me a moment longer before pulling back and resting his forehead against mine.

"Do you know how long I've wanted to do that?" he said between raspy breaths.

"No." I smiled. "Tell me."

"Too long." Then he kissed me again, this time leaning me back onto the couch.

I tugged at his shirt, my fingers just barely grazing his skin before he jumped away from me. I pushed myself upright and ran my hand through my wild tangle of hair. Then I stared at him, wondering what I'd done wrong.

As if he could read my mind he said, "Oh, crap. Maddie, it's not you." He knelt down in front of me again and took my hands. "I'm just, well, I'm... ticklish."

"Oh... kay..."

"I mean I'm super, crazy ticklish."

I studied his expression, and then an idea struck me.

"Uh-oh," he said, just before I attacked him.

I tackled him to the floor and started tickling him, everywhere—his stomach, his ribs, his legs. He laughed so hard he couldn't fight back, so I kept going until I was laughing just as hard. Before I realized it, his arms were around me, and we were kissing again. I'm not sure how long we stayed like that when we heard the garage door open.

We scrambled onto the couch, and he turned the TV to some random channel while I straightened my hair again and tried to keep myself from blushing. Staying calm proved to be nearly impossible with Grey staring at *me* and not the TV. He leaned over and kissed me once more, just seconds before his dad appeared in the doorway.

"Did you two eat yet?" Mr. Daniels asked.

"We made a frozen pizza," Grey said. "Chase went down about an hour ago. How are the roads?"

"It's stopped snowing, so they're clearing up. Why don't you take my truck to get Maddie home?" He tossed Grey the keys.

Grey caught them with one hand then stood up. "Um, okay."

He had to have been thinking the same thing I was... *Alex.* I could only hope she'd bailed on the mission when she realized how bad the roads were. I sent her a quick text, praying she wouldn't show up at Grey's house spitting fire and brimstone when I wasn't there.

"Did my boys behave themselves today?" Mr. Daniels looked at me.

I glanced at Grey fiddling with the keys. "They were both perfect gentlemen."

"As they should be." He smiled. "Have a good night, Maddie. And Grey, be safe on those roads."

"I will," Grey said just before his dad left the room. "Perfect gentlemen?" His lips curved up at the corners.

I shrugged to hide the shiver running through me. Did he have any clue he owned me when he stared at me that way? "Your parents were nice enough to let me stay without adult supervision. I didn't want to disappoint him. Besides, you were."

"Yes." He pulled his lip between his teeth. "But rolling around on the floor tickling me wasn't exactly very ladylike."

I jumped up from the couch and grinned at him. "Don't tell me you'd prefer me in a corset and chastity belt."

"Maybe the corset." He tugged me toward him and kissed me again.

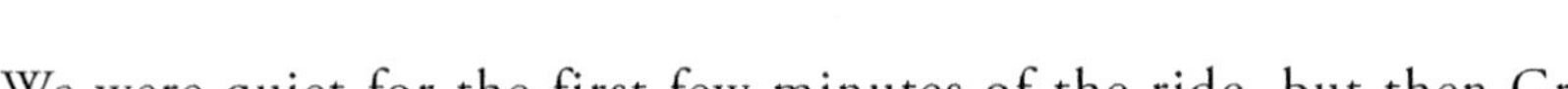

We were quiet for the first few minutes of the ride, but then Grey slid his hand into mine. "Thanks for coming over today."

"I had a good time. Even if we couldn't get past that one part of the game—Mystic whatever."

"*Mystic Realms Three*?" He smiled and squeezed my fingers. "Yeah, well, that'll have to be the highlight of some other evening."

"Oh, and what exactly was the highlight of this one?"

He laughed. "I think you can guess."

"Sure, but I want to hear you say it." I didn't know why, but I *needed* to hear it.

He rolled his eyes.

"Please."

He glanced at me then smirked. "Watching you change Chase's diaper."

"What?" I let go of his hand and glared at him.

He laughed again then grabbed my hand and brought it to his lips. "Don't start pushing me away now. Not now that I finally have you." He kissed my fingers again then rested our joined hands in my lap.

I worked very hard to stay calm when he said he 'had me' because I wasn't exactly sure what that meant.

"Maddie?"

"Yes?"

"I feel really weird asking this, but since I never actually defined it with Kelsey, and that didn't work out so great for me, I guess I just need to be clear about, I mean about what we're... you know."

I loved it when he was flustered. His normally confident expression completely disappeared, and he had an innocence to him. "If you're asking me to be your girlfriend, then the answer is yes. If you're talking about something else, I have no idea."

"No, no. The girlfriend thing. That's it. So yes, yes you're my girlfriend." His face lit up the whole truck.

We turned down my road, and Grey let go of my hand to park his dad's truck. There were a few lights on in the house, and the garage door was open, but Alex's car wasn't in it. *Shit.* I told myself she'd gone to see her friend, but my stomach twisted at the idea of her showing up at Grey's house, pissed that I'd sent her on a wild goose chase.

I pushed all those worries to the back of my mind as Grey turned in his seat to face me and leaned closer, licking his perfect lips. "Can we revisit the highlight of my night before you go?"

I put my hand out to stop him. "I am not changing a diaper right now."

"You know that wasn't it."

"Do I? You never actually said."

"Fine. The *best* part of my night was finally kissing you. Now will you please—?"

I smashed my lips to his. Unfortunately, that was as close as we could get with the console between us. So I pulled away after not even *close* to enough time kissing him.

"I'll see you later." I jumped out before either one of us could stop me.

CHAPTER 28

ALEX

ANOTHER SHIVER RAN THROUGH ME. It had been almost an hour since Natalie had promised to send help, and so far, the cavalry had failed to show up. My phone had long since died, and even with my conservation attempts, my gas tank was beyond the red zone. And it had gotten darker, and colder, as if that was even possible.

I was just about to get out of the car and walk home when a wash of headlights blinded me. Part of me was excited by the roar of an approaching truck, but another part conjured up the image of some axe-wielding stranger out to dismember stranded women on the side of the road. I wasn't sure whether I should jump out and embrace my savior or lock the doors and climb under the seats.

A gloved hand rapped against the driver's side window, and I jumped.

"Alex?" Ben brushed the snow away to stare at me through the foggy glass. "Are you okay? How long have you been out here?" He pulled on the handle, but the doors were still locked.

"I've lost track." Another shiver wracked my body. "I think my brain cells are half frozen."

He tugged on the handle again with no luck. "Is the door locked or is it stuck?"

"Oh!" I blinked at him a few times while the realization hit me. Natalie had sent Ben to rescue me. "Yeah, it's locked." I hit the button, and he yanked open the door.

I leaned against his body as he helped me out of the driver's seat.

"Jesus, you're a damn Popsicle." Ben's large hands rubbed up and down my arms. "You know you can freeze to death in your car. Why didn't you have the heat on?"

"I ran out of gas." My teeth chattered. "I conserved what I h-had... just turning it on every f-fifteen minutes or so. B-but that only lasted so long."

He shook his head, but thankfully, he didn't comment on my lack of survival skills. "Come on, grab what you need. I have the heat on in my truck."

"Th-thank you." I forced a smile, but in my frozen state, I imagined it looked more like a grimace.

He led me around to the passenger side and helped me into his truck, then vanished into the blowing snow until he reappeared on the driver's side. "You know"—he climbed in and shut the door—"when Natalie said I needed to rescue you, I was pretty sure she was pulling some sort of matchmaker crap again. I had no idea you were actually freezing to death out here, or I would have hurried. What the hell were you doing, anyway?"

"On my way to pick up Maddie." I rubbed my hands furiously in front of the vents. "I'm really sorry to drag you out in this. Natalie didn't tell me she was calling *you*."

"I would have come if you'd called me yourself, you know."

I felt his eyes burning a hole in the top of my head, so I kept mine riveted on my bluish fingers. "I know."

"Alex." The pain in his voice was evident.

I lifted my face to his and swallowed a sob. It hurt to look at him. Memories of his body moving above mine flooded my thoughts faster than I could push them back. I craved his touch and hated myself for it.

"You haven't returned my calls. You haven't been at the coffee shop, not even hiding in the damn closet. You wouldn't even come to the door when I knocked. Did you think I didn't know you were home? Do you think I don't know what you're doing, now?"

I pulled my eyes from his to focus on the swirls of snow in front of us. "Ben, I can't... I just can't do this."

"You can't do *what?*" He growled like a wounded animal. "Remember to put gas in your car before going out in a blizzard? That's obvious. What else can't you do?"

I struggled to put my thoughts together in a way he would understand. "I can't start a relationship with you."

"We're already *in* a relationship. I'm in love with you, Alex."

"No." I shook my head. "You can't be in love with me. I can't let you."

He laughed, deep and throaty. "You can't *let* me? You don't exactly get to choose. I'm sorry to say, sweetheart, it's too late. I'm there. Head over heels, stupid in love. Emphasis on the stupid, it would seem. And whether you want to admit it or not, you're in love with me, too."

"No." I was unable to form complete sentences. How did he not understand? I was David's wife. I wasn't *allowed* to love anyone else.

"Yes. You are." He reached out and took my hand, squeezing my still-frozen fingers in his. "I see it when you look at me. I feel it when you kiss me. You're just as much in love with me as I am with you."

"Stop." I pulled my hand away. "Stop saying that. Take it back. Take it back, right now. I am *not* in love with you. And you *can't* be in love with me. This was just supposed to be sex. That's it. S.E.X."

Ben put his fingers under my chin and lifted my face until our eyes locked. "No, Alex. It was never just sex. Not for me. I didn't mean for it to happen, but it did. And I won't take it back. I'm in love with you."

I shook my face out of his grasp. "But I can't love *you*. I'm supposed to love David."

"Damn it, Alex." He slammed his fist against the steering wheel. "David's gone. I'm sorry, but he's not coming back."

Hot tears streaked over my cheeks. "Don't… don't say that. I know he's gone, but it doesn't change how I feel." The minute the words were out of my mouth, I shattered. Sob after sob wrenched out of me as I sat, staring ahead into the driving snow.

"It's okay. I've got you. I'm here." Ben pulled me into his arms, hugging me against his solid frame. "I knew this was too fast. I knew I should have stayed away until you were ready. I didn't give you enough time to grieve." He rocked me back and forth, muttering to himself.

"Why… why are you here? Why do you keep coming *back*?"

He chuckled. "Because I keep thinking you'll wake up one morning and realize we belong together. God knows the timing sucks. But it's not like we can choose when to fall in love. Sometimes, life just shoves someone in your path."

I pressed my face against his chest. "You should just give up on me."

"Sorry, can't do that."

I looked up at him—at the strong lines of his jaw and his mesmerizing eyes—and I wanted to kiss him, to thank him, for not letting me self-destruct on a dark piece of road in a blizzard. "Kiss me."

Ben blinked a few times, then his lips spread in a wide smile before descending upon mine.

As if on autopilot, my body reacted of its own accord, melting into the warmth of his. My fingers tangled into his snow-dampened hair to keep him from pulling away. Not that he would have. It was evident in the way his mouth attacked, capturing mine again and again until we were both quite warm and completely out of breath.

"I think I'm warm enough now."

He laughed. "I've missed this." Ben's fingers trailed up the length of my coat to the zipper and slid it down slowly, never pulling his eyes from mine. "We don't want you to overheat in this heavy coat."

"No, that would be bad."

"Very bad."

After removing my parka, Ben slipped out of his as well, and before I realized what was happening, I'd straddled him in the center seat. His hands rested under my thighs, holding me hostage as he ravaged my mouth.

"You probably won't believe me when I say this, but I've never done this in a car before."

I smiled against his lips. "This?"

"Make love."

I froze on top of him.

"What's wrong?" He pulled his face back to look into my eyes.

"I'm sorry." I climbed off his lap, settling into the passenger seat, and pulled the seatbelt across my chest, locking it into place. "Can you just take me home, please?"

Ben scrubbed a hand across his face. "What the hell just happened?"

"I was supposed to pick up Maddie forever ago. She'll be worried."

"Alex—"

"I can't do this. I'm sorry, Ben. I just can't."

He closed his eyes, laying his head against the back of his seat. He was quiet for several minutes before gripping the steering wheel so hard his knuckles went white. Then he flipped a switch, and the windshield wipers jumped to life, clearing the snow with an angry squeal. "Fine. Whatever. I'll take you home."

CHAPTER 29

MADDIE

ALEX'S SHRIEKING DOWNSTAIRS BROKE THROUGH the amazing dream I was having. "What the hell?" I rolled over and hugged my pillow to my chest before pulling it over my head, muffling my scream. "Why is she up so early when she knows they'd cancelled school today?"

Another angry screech carried up the stairs, and I sat up in bed, throwing my covers to the side so I could get up.

"Damn it, Alex!" I shouted as I pulled on my mom's old fuzzy robe and slippers, making me look like Cookie Monster's spawn. Under ordinary circumstances, I wouldn't have been caught dead in that get-up, but it was freezing in my room, and the blue fleece still smelled of Mom's perfume.

I stomped down the stairs with as much fury as I could muster in the thick cushioned Muppet slippers. The big white googly eyes clicked together as I went.

"No!" Alex yelled, throwing her game controller into the couch cushion just as I rounded the corner into the family room.

I pressed my balled-up hands into my hips and glared at her. "What the ever-loving-hell are you doing up at this hour... playing video games?"

"Gah!" Alex spun around, her hand pressed to her chest and her eyes matching the ones on my feet. "Maddie? You scared the crap out of me."

"Well, I'd say we're even, but that *still* doesn't make up for you ruining the best dream I've ever had. Are you crazy? I didn't have to get up until at least lunch."

She shrugged and pulled her controller out from between two leather seat cushions. "Sorry, I was a little preoccupied."

With a series of electronic whirs and hums, the game roared to life again, and Alex turned her attention back to the TV.

"Hey, I know this game. You're supposed to grab the ledge on the left."

Alex's jaw flexed as she gritted her teeth. "I know what I'm *supposed* to do. I can't get the stupid thing, and I don't want to go around the entire maze to get the other side when I *should* be able to go through right here."

"Well, Grey said there's a glitch in the game. The ledge looks like it's there, but it's just the image. The actual *whatever* isn't there. You know… the thing in the program that lets you grab it? He said the programmer screwed up."

Alex turned around with a look that should have turned me to stone where I stood. "Oh, is that what *Grey* says? I'm pretty sure *Grey's* never designed a complex video game before. Does he have any idea how difficult writing that many lines of code is?"

"Geez. How much coffee have you had? It's just a *stupid* game with a *stupid* glitch. Take the maze, and go around. You're just wasting your time trying to grab a ledge that isn't really there."

She muttered something under her breath and tossed the controller on the floor before storming off into her office, slamming the door behind her.

"You're just pissed off because your *freaking* Porsche is still stuck in a snow bank," I yelled at the top of my lungs. "It's not my fault you decided to drive in a blizzard. I had a perfectly good ride home."

The door opened with a whoosh, and Alex stood there, panting as if she was building up to breathe fire or something. "My *freaking* Porsche wouldn't *be* stuck in the snow if you hadn't been with that *boy* after I'd forbidden you to see him!"

"You have no reason to forbid me to see Grey."

Alex put a hand up between us. "Don't even say it. I don't wanna hear his name mentioned again, or I'll… I'll ground you for the *rest of your life*."

"Well, I guess that's gonna suck for you, isn't it? You'll be stuck with me twenty-four seven. That doesn't leave much time for *your* boyfriend, does it?"

"It's a good thing I don't *have* a boyfriend, isn't it?"

I glared at her and let my lips curl up in a wicked smile. "Oh, did he kick your ass to the curb, too? Your odds aren't so good with men, are they? Dad was just about to drop you, and now Dr. *Hotson* gives you your walking papers. And funny... wasn't he my mom's boyfriend first, too? Sucks to be you, always picking up my mom's leftovers." I'd known the instant I saw them pull into the driveway in Dr. Hudson's truck. That same truck had picked Mom up on more than one occasion.

But when Alex had slid out of the front seat, landing ass first in the snow, and Ben ran around to haul her to her feet, I knew I was in for a show. *Alex should really learn to curb her temper while she's standing in the middle of the driveway.* The sexual tension poured off them like hot maple syrup. It didn't take long for me to put the pieces together. Finding out he'd dated my mom too was just the icing on the cake.

Alex turned three shades of red, and I was about to step back before her head exploded when she stomped her foot like a five-year-old. "No, for your information, I broke up with him because I'll be way too busy packing up your mother's *leftovers* and putting her house on the market."

"What do you mean, *putting it on the market?*" My mouth fell open, and I just stared at her for a minute. "Are you saying you're going to sell my house?"

Her face didn't show a drop of emotion. "That's exactly what I'm saying. Don't sound so surprised. This isn't the first time I—"

"But you can't sell my house!"

"Oh, but I can. Because it's not *your* house—it's mine." With another gust of air, Alex slammed the door again, leaving me stunned.

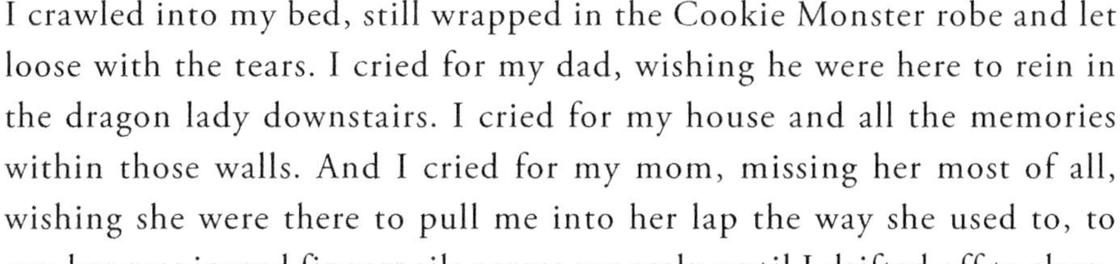

I crawled into my bed, still wrapped in the Cookie Monster robe and let loose with the tears. I cried for my dad, wishing he were here to rein in the dragon lady downstairs. I cried for my house and all the memories within those walls. And I cried for my mom, missing her most of all, wishing she were there to pull me into her lap the way she used to, to run her manicured fingernails across my scalp until I drifted off to sleep.

And grabbed my phone and sent Grey a text.

Me: Alex is selling my mom's house!

I snuggled into my pillow and waited, but I'd barely nestled in when the chime sounded, letting me know I had a new message.

Grey: Sorry. Wish I could make it better.

Me: Wish you could come over.

Grey: Want me to climb up your trellis and hide out in your room?

Me: LOL. Yes.

I'd barely hit send on my message when the phone rang in my hand. Before I could form the word hello, his voice came through the line like warm cocoa on a cold day.

"If you had a trellis, I would," he murmured.

I rolled to my back, twirling a piece of hair in my fingers. "What about an old ladder?"

"A trellis is more romantic. Think... Romeo and Juliet."

I laughed. "Cliché much? Besides... didn't they kill themselves at the end?"

"Minor detail. I'm thinking more along the lines of the balcony scene. You know... moonlight, secret rendezvous... *kissing*." He lowered his voice on the last word, and it made my tummy flutter. "But you'll definitely need a trellis."

I giggled. He obviously took his Brit Lit seriously. Only an idiot would discourage this romantic side of him. "Guess you'll have to build me one in the spring. I think we have a few scraps of wood in the garage."

"I'll *definitely* build you one... if you promise to let me steal a kiss."

"One... a dozen... whatever."

Grey didn't respond, but I knew he was still there. I could hear him breathing.

"Is something wrong?"

"I'm really sorry your stepmom is selling your house. That's pretty shitty. I know how hard it is to leave the memories behind. I was lucky though. Dad sat me down, and we talked about it before he got remarried. We made the decision together, but it was still hard."

"She said it's not even my house. It's hers. It's as if she doesn't even care how I feel about it. I hate her!" I ground up the words and spit them out. "I wish my dad had never met her."

"It won't always be like this, you know."

"Yeah... sure. Time heals all wounds, right?" I barked out a hollow laugh.

"Well, it's a cliché for a reason. But I can certainly think of a few things that would make time go by a little faster."

"Yeah, like what?"

"You were saying something about an old ladder. Do you think Alex would notice if I propped it against the house and climbed in your window tonight?"

"Seriously?" I sat up in the bed, pulling the blue fleece around me with a smile. "I think I could distract her long enough for you to get in. But I can't guarantee I'll let you back out once I have you."

"I think I could live with that."

"Wait, Maddie. I'm not going to do this with you right now." He pulled away and hopped off the bed.

I sat up and stared at him for a second before dropping my eyes to my lap. "You don't want me?"

"Whoa, whoa, whoa." He sat next to me and put his hands on my cheeks, forcing me to look at him. "You're beautiful and intelligent and funny and amazing, and I could go on and on, but the one thing you're not is ready."

"How the hell would you know?" I tore myself away from him and went to the other side of the room near my dresser.

He lay back on my bed then rolled to his side, propping his head up with his hand. "You really have no idea how hard it is for me to say no to you. I'm so crazy hot for you right now I'm pretty sure I could bring the lake to a boil. But I don't want the reason you're doing this to be because you're getting back at Alex."

"Why not? My dad's not even in the ground yet, and she found herself a fuck-buddy. She probably thought she could get rich off that doctor, too."

He groaned and fell back again. "Do you even hear yourself? I want this to be about you and me. Not you, me, and Alex. I wish you'd just stop hating her so much."

"Fine. We'll just never have sex then."

"That is not what I said!" He sat up and swung his legs off the bed.

"Well, I'm never going to stop hating her. So if that's the condition, then you might as well go." I pointed to the window.

He shook his head then stood and went to the same window he'd climbed in an hour ago. "You're sure you want me to go?"

I didn't respond because the truth was I never wanted him to go. But having him take Alex's side cut me worse than I could've ever cut myself. The worst part was feeling like, maybe in a way, he was right.

Being around Grey made me whole in a way I hadn't felt in a while. I wanted to hold on to that as long as I possibly could. He turned his back to me then lifted the sash, but my body betrayed me and grabbed him around the middle. I pressed my nose to a spot between his shoulder blades and breathed in his scent.

"Don't go," I whispered.

He turned and wrapped his arms around my shoulders. I didn't want to cry, but lately, it was one of the few things I did well. He held me until I calmed down then kissed my tear-streaked cheeks and finally my lips.

"Can you try, for me, for us? Please?"

I held him tight and buried my face in his chest. "Okay. I'll try. If you help me."

"Of course, I'll help you. I'd do just about anything for you." He bent down and pressed his lips to mine.

CHAPTER 30

ALEX

I stared down at the white plastic stick in my hand and swallowed back the growing lump in my throat. It couldn't be. We were careful. Weren't we? My legs gave out, and I dropped down to sit on the edge of the tub, still clutching my fate between my fingers.

"What am I going to do?" I whispered the words just as a sharp knock startled me out of my trance.

"Hurry up! I'm gonna be late for school." Maddie called from the other room.

My heart jumped at the sound of her voice. Ever since our argument, I'd tried to backtrack. Tried to explain my position. I'd even broken down and created a spreadsheet to explain the costs involved with maintaining a separate residence we weren't actually living in, the innumerable problems associated with her running there as a way to escape reality, and the constant worry hanging over me with regard to drug parties and other assorted illegal activities.

Maddie refused to hear any of it. She couldn't get past the way I'd sprung my decision on her. And truly, I hadn't meant to lash out at her the way I had. For some reason, I couldn't stop myself from dropping to the level of a sixteen-year-old girl when I got angry. She didn't help the situation at all, but I could hardly blame the actual sixteen-year-old for acting her age.

I tucked the pregnancy test into a drawer before opening the door. "Can you get a ride? I, uh, I'm sick."

Maddie looked me up and down, taking in my worn sweats and ratty hair. Her barely veiled hatred of me burned me where I stood. "Wow, yeah… you look like crap."

I squeezed the brass knob until my knuckles went white and blurted out the only thing I knew would reach her. "Can Grey come get you?"

"Is this some sort of April Fool's Day joke?" Maddie leaned against the doorframe and stared at me. "Or is it a test you hope I fail?"

I froze at the word *test.* "No!" I squeaked then cleared my throat. "I just really don't feel well. I'm not up for playing games, and I'm well aware you still talk to him despite what I've said. He may as well do me a favor. I know you're going to call him first anyway."

A wide smile brightened Maddie's face for the first time in days. I wanted to be annoyed but found myself filled with a bone-deep sense of relief. "Cool."

"I'm glad my… *circumstance* works to your advantage."

"Most definitely!"

"I was being sarcastic."

"Oh, I know." She beamed at me then bounced back out the door and down the stairs, dialing as she went.

I had no idea how long I stood frozen in the bathroom, but the slam of the front door brought me back to the situation at hand. My feet came unglued from the cold tile, and I hurried to the bedroom to get my phone from the new charger Maddie'd insisted I buy after the snowstorm incident. Apparently, I couldn't be trusted to remember to charge my phone, so the rapid charger and the emergency backup taking up space at the bottom of my purse would save *her* grief in the future.

My fingers trembled as I dialed Natalie's number.

"Hey, you're late." She'd unintentionally hit the nail on the head, and I gasped. "What? I even made your favorite muffins this morning."

"There were two lines, Natalie. Two!"

"What are you talking about? What two lines? Where? Are you at Walmart? What did I tell you about—?"

"The thing! I peed on the thing, and it came up with two pink lines. But that can't be right. I can't be—"

"Whoa… hold on there. Back up. Are you saying you took a—" Natalie lowered her voice. "—pregnancy test? And it was positive?"

"That's what I said! Weren't you paying attention?" I paced over the carpet until my entire body had stored enough static electricity to charge an army of cell phones.

"How many did you take?"

"What do you mean, how many did I take? Isn't one enough?"

"Oh, sweetie... one is *never* enough. Go drink a few gallons of water, and I'll be right over." She didn't bother to say goodbye. The line simply went dead.

Two hours and six tests later, Natalie and I sat on my rumpled sheets staring at the pile of plastic sticks. I can only imagine my expression matched hers exactly. I was in shock.

"I thought you were on birth control."

I glared at her. "It's not foolproof."

"Condoms?"

"Can you lecture me some other time? Seriously, Natalie. What am I going to do?"

She didn't answer me right away, but when she did, she was adamant. "You have to tell Ben."

I dropped my voice to a whisper. "I haven't even spoken to him since the snowstorm."

"I never said it would be easy." Natalie patted my leg.

"Three weeks, Natalie. I haven't seen him for three weeks." I slid off the bed to pace the room, my hands clenching and unclenching the soft fabric of my sweatshirt.

"Well, I haven't seen him either, since you've effectively run him out of my life too."

I stopped pacing to gape at her. "I never told him he couldn't come into the coffee shop."

"Right, because he wants to bump into the girl who broke his heart. That's hardly the best way to start each day. Caffeine and heartache to go."

"I didn't mean to break his heart." I let my face fall into my hands. "I didn't ask him to fall in love with me."

"Love doesn't work that way, and you know it. And you *also* know

Ben isn't the kind of guy to take something like this lightly. You need to tell him you're carrying his baby."

"Ugh, I know." I flopped backward onto the bed and stared at the ceiling. "I'm just not ready to say it out loud, okay? I mean, what if I lose this one too?" I turned my head to look at Natalie as hot tears welled up in my eyes.

She lay beside me and took my hands in hers. "You don't know that you'll lose this one. Maybe you should go see a doctor before thinking all gloom and doom. And while you're at it, you need to call Ben. He still loves you. Maybe it's time you let him."

It sounded simple, but what she was asking could easily be the second hardest thing I'd ever do.

The sound of a door slamming followed by heavy footsteps broke through the fog in my brain.

"Hey, are you still sick?" Maddie leaned over the back of the sofa, her thick hair falling like a curtain around me as her face hovered above mine. The angry expression I'd come to expect from her had lifted, and she actually looked happy. Or maybe she just found joy in my possible illness.

"Umm... yeah." It took me a minute to get my bearings straight. I shooed her away and sat up, wiping away the line of drool creeping down my chin and removed the video game controller from my lap. "Wow, I guess I fell asleep."

"Ya think?" Maddie perched on the arm of the couch with something that looked suspiciously like a smile teasing the corners of her lips.

"Don't be a smart-ass—and don't sit there, you'll break it."

"What? You mean sit here?" She bounced a few times before I leveled a skin-melting glare at her. "Fine. You're so touchy. Are you PMSing?" Maddie slid off the arm and into the cushions beside me.

I did a quick mental calculation before reality came crashing down. "No!"

"Geez, sorry. Could have fooled me. Maybe you just need a few doses of chocolate. We could go get some fudge. I wouldn't mind a decadent chocolate concoction myself."

My stomach rolled. "I'll pass."

"Come on! Let's go to Mercier's and get some chocolate cherry—oh, or the chocolate peanut butter—come on, come on, come on." She yanked on my sleeve to punctuate each word. I didn't think I'd ever seen her so lighthearted.

Unfortunately, with every tug, my stomach threatened to open its gate and send back everything I'd ever eaten, along with several things I'd only thought about. Basking in her mood would have to wait. "Maddie, please! Not tonight. Just go dig through the freezer. I think there's a pint of Chunky Monkey in there."

"Oh sure. From months ago. It's probably freezer burned and gross. But whatever—deny me my last request for fudge. See if I care."

"God, it's not like you're on death row. There'll be other chances to eat fudge."

"Sure, you say that, but how do you know? Maybe I'll never eat fudge again, and it'll be... All. Your. Fault." She'd said those words before, but this time they didn't carry any of the same malice. I almost wanted to hug her. *Almost.*

"Give it up." I grabbed my head in my hands. "You're not getting fudge unless you make it yourself."

"Fine." Maddie exhaled, and I could have sworn she muttered "Miss PMS" under her breath, but I wasn't sure.

"So... who drove you home?"

"Do you really need to ask?"

I groaned but said nothing.

"Don't make that sound. You don't even know him. He has a good job, he helps take care of his little brother, and he's nice to me." Maddie wound the hem of her shirt into a knot. "I like him, and nothing you say can change that."

David should have been having this conversation with his daughter, not me. "You're too young."

Maddie picked up her head to scowl at me, all traces of good humor gone. "I'll be seventeen in a few weeks. And before you ask, I haven't gotten drunk or high since we've been together."

"What do you mean by *together*?"

"I'm not sleeping with him, if that's what you're asking. He hasn't even tried. He's a good guy. You should give him a chance."

"It wasn't that long ago you thought Brody was a good guy, too." I twisted sideways to face her on the sofa. "I haven't forgotten what boys his age are like."

"Whatever. Grey is nothing like Brody." Maddie scoffed. "And for the record, I never thought Brody was a good guy. And just so you know, it's been… like a hundred years since you were a teenager. You have no idea what boys are like now."

"Right. That's exactly what I said to my mom when I was sixteen."

Maddie crossed her arms and sank deeper into the cushions. Her teeth came together with a clack. "You're not my mom."

"That's not what I meant." I sighed. "Look, I'm not trying to be your mom. I'm just trying to be the best stepmother I can. I'm pretty much learning as I go here."

"Well, you have no reason to treat Grey like he's a criminal. He's not one of the *Sons of Anarchy*. He's my boyfriend."

"Boyfriend, huh?" I blew out a breath. "I guess I could try."

Maddie smiled.

I forced back my own grin. "I'm not making any promises. I said I'd *try*. Maybe he could come over, and I could meet him under less crazy circumstances?"

"I'll ask him." Her smile got wider. "So does that mean it would be okay for Grey to take me to the Imagine Dragons concert in Grand Rapids in June?"

"Don't push it." I wagged a finger a few inches from her nose. "But I'll think about it."

Maddie swallowed a squeal before reining herself in. "Fair enough."

I dragged myself out of the cushions and staggered to stand. "I'm going to lie down."

"You just woke up."

"And I've been awake too long already. Lock up before you go to bed. And don't forget to make sure the garage door is shut."

I trudged up the stairs and fell into my bed, well aware that I wouldn't be drifting to sleep any time soon.

CHAPTER 31

MADDIE

I FLUMPED DOWN IN THE PASSENGER seat of Grey's black Focus. For the past three weeks, Alex had been letting me ride to school with him. She hadn't entirely given up on her crusade against him, but she'd stopped trying to forbid us from seeing each other. Despite what she'd said about meeting Grey under better circumstances, there just never seemed to be a good time. And she still wanted proof his parents would be home before letting me go over there.

Her complete lack of attention also seemed to directly coincide with her working and being tired all the time, but she hadn't even come out of her room this morning to wish me—

"Happy birthday!" Grey leaned over to kiss me.

I forced a smile. "Thanks."

"Don't tell me you're one of those people who hates her birthday." He threw his car into gear, flashing a quick smiling before gunning the engine. "You're only seventeen. You can't be feeling old yet."

"No, this is just the first one without my parents." Unlike every year for as far back as I could remember, I'd woken up to a silent house. No whipped cream slathered blueberry pancakes in bed. No over-the-top presents rivaling Christmas morning. And I already knew there'd be no dinner at Beverly's, and no decadent German chocolate cake topped with Clara from *The Nutcracker*—an ornament Mom had picked up for me when I was five and just starting dance—the paint had faded, and it had a big chip on the bottom, but Mom never forgot it.

"Oh, right, I'm sorry." He clasped my hand over the center console.

"It's okay. It's not even that. I mean it is, but it's... Alex."

The light turned red, and he took that opportunity to catch my eyes. "I thought you two were getting along better. Didn't you say she took you out for a midnight ice cream run a couple nights ago?"

"We're only getting along because she practically ignores me. And yes, we went out for ice cream—and fudge a few days before that—but only because she didn't wanna go alone. She's been a junk food junkie for the past few weeks, and I'm just there to tag along. Green light."

"Oh." He didn't tear his attention away from me until the car behind us honked. "I'm sorry. But it's gotta be better without her harassing you all the time, isn't it?"

"I guess. I just thought... I don't know, I thought maybe she'd at least try to make my birthday special. But she didn't even get out of bed this morning."

We pulled into the school lot with plenty of time to spare, and Grey parked the car and cut the engine. "Well, I plan on making it special. Since today's only a half day, and I have a surprise for you later, can you try not to be grumpy?"

My heart beat faster at the promise of a surprise from Grey. "Do I get a hint?"

"No." He laughed then pressed his lips to mine in a quick kiss before climbing out of his car. "Not even a little one."

The dreary April showers had finally cleared out, leaving a bright sunny sky in their place as Grey and I walked across the parking lot, hand in hand, avoiding the last remaining puddles.

"Happy birthday, sweetie!" Haleigh skipped up behind me, wrapping her arms around my middle in a breath-stealing hug, then shoved a brightly colored card at me before grabbing Todd's hand. Sometime in the last few weeks, they'd officially become a thing.

"Thanks. Do you want me to open this now?"

"Oh, no." Her cheeks turned pink. "Later is fine. Are you doing anything special today?"

"We are." Grey draped his arm over my shoulder and pulled me against him.

"Aww." Haleigh's eyes glistened as she watched us. "So, what did Alex get you?"

I had to swallow the lump in my throat. "She, um..."

"She's giving Maddie her gift later," Grey said, saving me from explaining the whole thing again.

"Well, that's cool." Haleigh nodded, but I could tell she felt the tension in the air.

"Grey's giving me my gift later too, but he won't give me any hints." I ducked under Grey's arm, but he snagged my jacket and yanked me back with a laugh.

"You're going to love it! It's—" Haleigh clapped her hand over her mouth.

"Hey!" I shot a glare at Grey. "You told her, but you won't even give me a hint?"

"Sorry, Grey," Haleigh squeaked out.

"It's okay." He smiled at me, not at all bothered by my sorry attempt at looking sour. "I had to make sure you would like it."

"Fine." I relaxed into him with a huff. "I guess I'll just have to wait."

"It'll be worth it." He pressed a kiss to my temple then spun around to back down the hallway to his first hour, watching me the entire way.

"You ready for your surprise?" Grey slid an arm around my shoulder as we exited third hour.

"Are you kidding? I've been ready all morning."

He laughed. "Well, you're going to have to wait a little while longer."

"Hey, no fair." I hip-checked him, and he caught me around the waist, hauling me into the air to carry me to the car.

The weather was unseasonably warm, almost summery, so I threw my jacket in the back seat. That's when I noticed the big black box with the silver bow.

"Is that my present? Was that here this morning?"

"Yes. And yes. But you were too crabby to notice." He laughed. "Now get in. I want to take you somewhere."

We drove through town and up the coast of the bay. We'd gone several miles north before I recognized where we were. "There's a roadside park up here my dad used to take me to."

"I know." He grinned. "That's where we're going." He pulled into the gravel lot and parked near the path that led to a small picnic area with a bay view.

He climbed out of the car, grabbing my gift from the back seat, then hurried around to get my door for me. The wind coming off the water had a bite to it—Dad always waited until later in the season to make the trip—but it didn't matter. The look on Grey's face made every icy gust worth it. He grasped my hand and dragged me down the deserted path to sit on one of the picnic tables. Then he placed the rectangular box in my lap.

"Happy birthday."

I squealed as I pulled the ribbon away from the box and lifted the lid. Inside, I found a leather-bound sketchbook. "What's this?"

His smile nearly split his face in two. "Open it."

I carefully flipped open the cover and gasped at the first drawing. "Grey..." The girl in the picture looked a lot like me, only she wore a sort of combination of battle armor and a long gown with a small gold crown on her head. Under the drawing he'd scrawled, *Princess Madison, beloved heir to the throne*. "It's beautiful." I glanced up at him, his face blurred by my tears. "I don't feel very royal though."

He rubbed my back then put his arm around my shoulders. "Keep looking," he whispered.

I turned to the next page, surprised to see an image of Alex. Considering he'd only seen her a few times, he'd done a pretty amazing job capturing her likeness. He'd sketched her wearing an intricate black robe that reminded me of a Disney villainess, but the thing that drew my attention were her eyes. He'd managed to capture them almost exactly, right down to the deep sadness within. I ran my finger over the caption as I read it aloud. "*Queen Alexandra, keeper of lost souls.*"

The next page had Grey himself in knight's armor, wielding a sword. Haleigh and Todd both had pages too. He'd always been so private about his art, only letting me see a few here and there, but for my birthday, he'd created an entire book full of his drawings.

Just for me.

I flipped through the rest of the book, following the story of the princess who'd lost her family and had no choice but to battle her way through Queen Alexandra's realm and free the souls of her parents to claim her birthright. Toward the end, he'd sketched Princess Madison with her arms over a crouched Queen Alexandra.

"She defeats her." I ran my fingers over the drawing, feeling the indentations where his pencil had pressed into the paper.

"No, Maddie." He gently pulled my hand from the page and held it in his. "She frees her from her own misery."

"You think she's miserable. Is it because of me?"

He shook his head. "I think she misses your dad as much as you do, and it might be easy for her to take things out on you because you remind her of him."

"She's been so unfair to you, and you're defending her?" I pulled my hand away.

"She's just trying to protect what little of your dad she has left. And this can't be easy for her either. She's not really old enough to have a teenager, is she? And besides, I'll win her over eventually."

I leaned my head against his shoulder and flipped through the last few pages of the book. They were of the princess and her knight, and they were very… *intimate.*

"I wouldn't show those around to anyone." His face turned bright red.

I tilted my head up and pressed my lips to his. "I won't. I guess you weren't kidding when you said you liked corsets. But maybe we could act it out some time."

He took the book from me and set it aside then shifted our positions so I was straddling his lap with my arms around his neck. "*That* is very tempting," he whispered in my ear before kissing his way across my jaw to my mouth. We kissed for a long time, long enough that the sky clouded over again, putting a fresh chill in the air. "We still have a little time before Alex expects you home. Do you want to come with me to get my paycheck?"

"Yeah." I shivered and only partly because of the cold. "Maybe a hot chocolate while we're there."

It didn't take long to get to the coffee shop, but as far as I was concerned, we could've driven around all day as long as we were together.

Grey parked in the alley behind the building, giving me one last toe-curling kiss before climbing out and opening my door for me. "Come on. Let's get your cocoa. Do you like marshmallows or whipped cream?"

"Definitely whipped cream."

"Whipped cream it is. I'll even add special birthday sprinkles." He grabbed my hand and led me to the backroom, where he plucked an envelope out of his cubby and tucked it into his pocket.

I flashed him a wide smile as he dragged me through a storage area and another door until we were standing behind the counter, face to face with Alex.

She looked up from her coffee and gasped. "Maddie? What are you doing back there? And you." She blinked up at Grey. "What are you doing here?"

"So, I see you've met coffee boy." Alex's friend, Natalie, smirked.

CHAPTER 32

ALEX

I GAPED AT NATALIE. "YOU MEAN liquor boy, right?" My attention shifted to my stepdaughter and her boyfriend. I felt almost foolish using the silly nickname we'd given Grey before I'd known his name—even more so as he stood in front of Maddie as if protecting her from me.

"*This* is liquor boy?" Natalie motioned toward Grey and when I nodded, she burst into hysterical laughter. "Oh, that's—" She doubled over, heaving in breath after breath.

"Why is that funny?" I looked to Maddie for an answer.

She shrugged, leaning into Grey.

Natalie wiped tears from her cheeks. "I'm sorry, but that's hilarious. This is *Grey*, my *coffee* boy."

"*The* coffee boy? The same golden child who doesn't smoke, drink, or do drugs?" I asked, flabbergasted. Not that I still held the same unfair opinion of Grey since Maddie and I had talked, but I wasn't sure how to reconcile the two different versions of him in my head. Part of me held onto the belief that he'd somehow influenced Maddie's reckless decisions.

"It would seem so. Apparently, *liquor* boy and *coffee* boy are one in the same."

I stared at the dazed and confused expressions worn by Maddie and Grey. "But—"

"Oh, this gets even better. That means you"—Natalie choked back a giggle as she turned to Grey—"are the kid who figured out the glitch in her video game."

Maddie pointed at me. "*Her* video game?"

"Yep. Seems like your boyfriend has a bad case of hero worship for your stepmom—or at least the games she designs."

"*You're* Alex Spencer?" Grey's eyes bugged out of his head.

I nodded, unable to find the words to respond. I'd gotten used to the reaction from teenage boys over the years, but that didn't make me any less uncomfortable under his scrutiny.

"Oh my God!" Grey pulled Maddie around the counter and perched on the stool next to me. "You're like a-a legend! You've designed three of the decade's most amazing video games. I got this job just so I could afford the new system to play *Mystic Realms Three*. Stores can't even keep them in stock." He sputtered on as if he were a teenage girl, and I was the newest boy band crush.

"And you really don't drink?"

Maddie leaned around him to glare at me. "I've been telling you that for weeks."

"And you don't smoke *or* do drugs?"

"Sweetie..." Natalie patted my hand. "Can I get you a glass of water? You look like you might pass out."

Grey shook his head. "No, I'm fine. I just can't believe I'm actually sitting here with Alex Spencer. In the flesh. Well, you know what I mean. And holy shit! I figured out the glitch in your last game!"

Natalie barked out a laugh. "You sure did, coffee boy. Bragging rights for life, I'd say."

"Hey, Alex?" Grey fished into his pocket and pulled out an envelope. "Can I get your autograph?"

"Are you kidding me?" Maddie huffed and parked herself on a stool several seats away. "Can't a girl get a hot chocolate in this place?"

"Shit." Grey stuffed the envelope back into his pocket and rushed to Maddie's side, pulling her into a loose hug. "Babe, I'm sorry. I can get an autograph anytime. Natalie, can we get a hot chocolate for the birthday girl?"

"Oh, my God." *Her birthday? How did I miss that? I'd combed through every entry in David's calendar and never stopped to note Maddie's birthday?* The look on Natalie's face gave me my answer. I'd been too preoccupied with my own issues to pay attention to anything else. I cleared my throat. "Happy Birthday, Maddie."

"Thanks." She glanced at me then turned back to Grey. "You know what? I've changed my mind about the hot chocolate. Can we just go?"

Grey snuck a peek at me with an apology in his eyes. "Um... yeah, of course. Come on." He grasped Maddie's hand and helped her from the stool. "We can stop by Mercier's on the way home."

"I'll see you at the house later." I flashed what I hoped was a friendly smile.

She gave me a fake one in return. "Yeah, sure. Later."

It's official. I'm going to be a terrible mother.

For the third week in a row, I found myself hugging the toilet good morning. Somehow, I'd managed to keep my condition a secret from Maddie, but it would only be a matter of time.

In fact, time was running out, in more ways than one. First of all, I faced a constant barrage of nagging from Natalie to tell Ben about the baby. She just didn't understand. I wasn't ready. Then there was pressure from the higher-ups to come up with a fresh idea for a game. But that was at least the good kind of pressure—the kind I was used to. In the midst of everything, I'd stumbled on gold.

"Wow. Did Grey draw all these?" I flipped through the first few drawings of Maddie in warrior gear, surrounded by an entire cast of supporting players, myself included. "He's really talented."

Maddie rushed toward me and snatched the book out of my hands. "That's not yours. I never gave you permission to—did you look at all of them?" Her mouth dropped open, and she hugged the book to her chest.

I threw my hands up in surrender. "Sorry! I didn't know. It was just lying on the coffee table. I only saw the first few pages." I narrowed my eyes at her. "Why? What did I miss?"

"Nothing. It's none of your business. I shouldn't have left it out. Grey gave it to me for my birthday. You know, the day you forgot about?"

I let out a sigh. "How many times do I have to apologize? I even got you a gift."

"Right. Of course. The fancy dress I can't even wear until spring. You probably pulled it out of your own closet."

"I did not! And it's not fancy. It's a sundress, and I got it special for you." Tears pricked my eyes, and I blinked them back before she caught me crying. My current emotional state was on par with a hormonal teenager. And the last thing we needed was two of us around the house.

"So special you ran out and got it at the last minute. Thanks a lot."

"I'm sorry I forgot your birthday." I choked back a sob, trying to hold the waterworks at bay. "I'm a horrible person. I should have put the date on my calendar."

"Ah, *finally*, we agree on something." Maddie grabbed her jacket from a hook and flashed me a quick smile, her momentary pique forgotten. "Grey's waiting for me. You wouldn't want me to be late for school, would you? Tell Natalie I said hi."

Between the two of us, I was going to get whiplash from the rapidly changing emotions in the room. "Okay. Will do. Have a nice day."

"It's been three weeks. You're just about out of excuses, missy." Natalie shook a finger in my face as she poured another decaf coffee for me with her other hand.

"I know." I adjusted myself on the red vinyl stool. "I just need time to figure out what I'm going to say."

"What's there to figure out? 'Hey, remember those times we—'"

"Um, no. I'm not going to play the 'remember when' game. Besides"—I plastered a fake smile on my face—"lots of people wait until they're out of their first trimester to share the *happy* news."

"Just don't wait until the baby's crowning, okay? Seriously, you need to tell him, sooner than later."

"I will. I should be able to hear the heartbeat at my appointment next week. Once everything feels real, I'll tell him."

Natalie banged her hip against the counter with a groan. "He should be there for that."

"Jesus, don't start in on me about that too. Could you maybe leave a little bit of my ass intact? I might need it to give birth."

"I'm just saying." She shrugged.

"Drop it, Nat. I'm under enough damn pressure as is." I let my head fall into my hands. "I'm trying to work on a new game design, I'm living with a rabid teenager, hell-bent on my destruction, and I have to get Sarah's house ready to put on the market."

"Does Maddie know you're selling her mom's house?"

"Yes. She knows. She just doesn't know when."

"So, lemme get this straight. You haven't told Ben about the baby, *and* you haven't told Maddie about the house?"

I blew out a ragged breath.

"I'll give you a break on one but not both. Promise me you won't leave Maddie in the dark."

CHAPTER 33

MADDIE

Mother's Day hung over me like Poe's swinging blade, each tick of the clock bringing me closer to my doom. I had no idea what disaster I had to look forward to, but for some reason, my world felt off.

"Thank you for coming with me." Grey reached over the center console to take my hand. "I know that couldn't have been easy for you."

"No, it's fine. I'm fine."

Grey wound us around the cemetery drive, and I stared out the window at the long shadows crawling forward from the perfect rows of headstones lined up like sentries. After an early lunch with his family and visiting his mother's grave, memories of my own mother invaded my thoughts. I wasn't even sure whether Mom would be buried beside Dad or not. How did that even work after divorce? Would Alex be the one to decide, or would I get a say?

Grey pulled my hand to his lips and kissed my knuckles. "Where to? Should we swing by the coffee shop for some of Natalie's world-famous blueberry scones? Or Mercier's for chocolate cherry fudge?"

I gave him a weak smile then went back to watching the scenery go by. "I'd like to go home."

"Home? I mean, I know Mother's Day must be really hard for you, but I figured if we spent it together, you wouldn't feel so alone."

The hurt in his voice caused me to turn and face him again. "Not my dad's house. *My* house. I want to see if my mom's tulips are blooming." I squeezed his hand as the memory caught me off guard. "She used to fill a vase every Mother's Day and take it to the senior center. I think I'd like to do that."

Grey smiled at me. "I think that's a great idea."

I leaned my head toward him on the seat as he maneuvered us through town. A line had formed outside of Beverly's Café for the annual Mother's Day dinner, and the mouthwatering aroma of their chocolate-laden, peanut butter, caramel-filled cake reached me all the way in the car as we passed by. Mom and I always shared a slice even though we'd end up fighting over the last few bites.

We'd just turned down Maple Drive when Grey's voice shattered my memory of Mother's Days past. "This can't be good."

I gaped at the smoky-gray Porsche Cayenne parked in my mother's spot in front of the garage. The tailgate hung open, exposing a stack of broken-down moving boxes, and a *For Sale* sign leaned against the rear bumper.

"What the hell?" I had my seatbelt unbuckled and my door open before Grey had come to a complete stop. A bone-deep chill rattled through me. "What does she think she's doing?"

"Maddie?" Grey threw the car into park and reached for his own buckle as I jumped out.

"No, Grey." I whirled around to stop him from following me. "I need to do this myself. If she thinks she's going to sell my mother's house out from under me, she has another thing coming."

"What if things get out of hand, and you need a ride home? What about the tulips?"

I glanced over my shoulder at the front door, imagining Alex pawing things she had no business touching. "I'll call you if I need you."

His face fell, but he nodded. "Yeah, okay."

I spun around on my heels and marched up the front steps as he gunned his engine and pulled out. I threw open the front door, making it swing wide and bounce off the wall with a bang.

Alex flinched from her seat on the floor, dropping a roll of clear packing tape. "Maddie!" She put her hand over her chest. "You scared me. What are you doing here? I thought you and Grey were spending the day together."

"What am *I* doing here? What are *you* doing here? This is my mother's house. My mother's stuff. You have *no right* to pack her things like she doesn't matter." My pulse pounded in my ears as I stood, panting in the doorway. I took another step inside and grabbed the door to slam it shut.

Alex cleared her throat and pulled herself from the floor to take a step toward me. "We talked about this. I even showed you the numbers on the spreadsheet. It's the best thing for both of us. We can't move forward if we don't put the past behind us."

"No. You talked. And I couldn't give two shits about your dumb-ass spreadsheets." I closed the distance between us and poked a finger into her chest. "You never asked me what I wanted. You never gave me a choice. And if you had, I would have told you it's not the best thing for *me*. I don't want to put my parents behind me like they never even existed."

Alex shook her head, her ponytail bouncing behind her. "You're a kid, Maddie." She tried to use her new "mom" voice, but it didn't work on me. I knew she didn't care. How could she when her parents were still alive and well and living on a beach somewhere in California? "You don't have the capacity to make these types of decisions. The house *needs* to be sold. Her things *need* to be packed. You weren't going to do it. So I had to."

I clenched and unclenched my fists with every word she uttered. "You should have *asked* me. You should have given me that option."

Alex sighed and scrubbed a hand over her face. "We *did* talk about this, but I'll agree I wasn't exactly in the most receptive mood for your argument the first time. You said some pretty horrible things to me, too, if you recall. But I thought for sure you understood my position the last time we talked."

The memory of our first discussion about Mom's house flashed back in all its intensity. She'd deserved every nasty word I'd hurled at her. And so maybe I didn't pay that much attention the second time she'd tried to talk to me, but she still should have given me the choice. "You're *not* selling my house!"

"Maddie, time is running out. I'm not going to debate this anymore. We can't afford to keep an empty house. It's not practical. And you're seventeen. You couldn't possibly understand what it's like to live in the shadow of someone you can never compete with." Alex grabbed an empty box and began tossing in my mom's collection of Jane Austen novels.

As her hand wrapped around the worn copy of *Pride and Prejudice*, I lost it. "Don't. Touch. That. You're damn right you can't compete with her. You're not good enough to touch her things. You're nothing. You didn't deserve my dad, and you don't deserve to be standing here in the same house where they loved each other!"

The book slipped from her fingers, landing on the floor on its spine with the pages spread open on either side. Her face flushed crimson, and her hands shook. "Why do you hate me so much? Because I fell in love with your dad? Because I'm not your mom? I can't change any of that. And you have no idea how hard it is to take care of someone who despises you. So fine. You want to do it? You do it. But this house *will* be sold. And I don't care if it's filled to the brim with your mother's precious stuff when it happens." She tripped over the box, knocking it over and spilling the books across the carpet as she stormed out. I was still gaping at the open doorway when she returned with an armload of broken-down boxes. "You might need these." She dropped them on the floor and slammed the door behind her as she left.

As the adrenaline ebbed out of me, I dropped down beside the open book and let my tears fall. How did Alex expect me to pack up the tulips and the nights when my parents tucked me in and the time in the backyard I told my dad I wanted to be a ballerina? Was I just supposed to leave those things behind?

I wished I hadn't sent Grey away and fished my phone from my pocket to text him.

Me: She's really doing it. She's selling my mom's house.

I clutched the phone to my chest while I waited, but the reply came almost immediately.

Grey: So sorry baby. It'll be ok. U'll get thru it.

Was Grey right? Would it be okay? Would I ever really get through it? I didn't think so. My heart shattered, all the tiny pieces stabbed me from the inside, and I couldn't breathe.

Me: Wonder if anyone would buy the house w a dead body in it.

Grey: What dead body?

Me: Mine.

Grey: Not funny, Madison. Don't even joke about shit like that.

I tossed my phone into the couch cushions and curled into a ball on the carpet. My phone beeped with a new message, but I no longer had the energy to respond. Instead, I leafed through the pages of Mom's favorite book, stopping at the scene near the end where Elizabeth refuses to agree to the demands of Mr. Darcy's aunt. I knew right then I didn't have the strength to be like Elizabeth Bennet. Standing up to Alex, being better for Grey, fighting to keep the memory of my mother alive... it was just too hard.

I pulled myself from the floor and made my way to my mom's room, stopping for a moment in the bathroom to grab a bottle of cough syrup. The shoebox on Mom's top shelf in her closet was where she'd hid her prescription medication: the stuff she didn't want me to know about, the antidepressants, the sleeping pills, and the strong pain meds she didn't really need for pain.

I reached for the box, but instead of finding a stash of meds, I found my pointe shoes. My throat squeezed shut as I held the worn satin and leather in my hands. Everything I'd done was for nothing. I'd given up dance to bring my parents back together, and they'd died. Those stupid shoes were like a flashing neon sign reminding me of everything I'd lost.

"I hate you!" Tears burned my eyes as I hurled them, one at a time, across the room, the ribbons cutting through the air like flags on a windy day. I could still hear the slap they made against the wall as I walked over and picked them up again. I felt nothing. No exhilaration. No adrenaline. Nothing. Once upon a time, dance had defined me; now I didn't even know who I was.

I toed off my sneakers and sat down to slip them on in their place, tying the ribbons around my ankles on autopilot, waiting for the slightest spark of something. *Anything*. But it never came. I rose up on my toes for a painful instant before tearing through everything in my mother's closet, searching for the pills I knew she kept hidden from me.

I found what I was looking for in the bottom of Mom's favorite bag—a handmade straw weave tote in teal. Dad had got it for her the last summer they were together. We'd gone to Mackinac Island, and she'd stashed sandwiches for the ferry ride in her bag. How ironic that she'd stash the drugs she'd started collecting when Dad moved out in the same bag.

I dumped a handful of pills from each bottle into my palm, mesmerized by the way the different colors pooled in my hand. I stood there contemplating my options until the sweat in my palm made the pills sticky. Then with one last deep breath, I shoveled them into my mouth and reached for the codeine cough syrup chaser.

"Maddie, NO!" Grey's hand shot out, slapping the cough syrup from my grasp. Thick red liquid splattered the wall, and the balance of the contents soaked into the cream-colored carpet like blood. He snatched up a crystal dish from the dresser, dumping out my mother's favorite collection of earrings. With his free hand gripping the back of my neck, he held the bowl to my lips. "Spit them out."

The chalky residue coated my tongue, making me gag as I pushed the gooey mess out of my mouth.

Grey shoved the dish back onto the dresser and grabbed my face with both hands. "Open up." He shouted at me, his breath coming out in jagged blasts as he peered down my gaping throat. "Did you swallow any?"

I tried to shake my head, but his grip was too tight.

He tipped my face back until his wild eyes locked on mine. His fear radiated off him. "Madison, did you swallow any of those fucking pills?"

"NO!"

His hands shook as he held me. "Don't you lie to me. I swear to God, I'll drag you into the bathroom and stick my finger down your throat until you puke."

"I didn't." I choked back a sob. "I didn't swallow them."

Grey let out a shuddering breath as he released me then pulled me into a crushing hug. "What the hell did you think you were doing? Damn it, I'm too young to have a stroke." His heart thundered in his chest as he held me, his body trembling in time with mine.

"I can't do it anymore. I tried, Grey. I really tried, but I'm not strong enough to hold myself together. Not even for you."

"Jesus, Maddie, you need to do it for *you.* Not *me.*" He stepped back, holding my shoulders and staring me right in the eyes. "I love you. Do you hear me? I. Love. You. But you shouldn't be doing *anything* if it's just for me. You're important enough all by yourself. I've been where you are, and I'm going to stay with you every step of the way. I know you can do this."

"Grey." I sobbed out his name as tears streamed down my cheeks.

He leaned down, pressing his lips to mine for a quick kiss. "I love you. I cannot lose you. But you need to get rid of that gross taste in your mouth."

An unexpected laugh bubbled out of me. "Yeah, probably."

He darted out of the room and came back with a cup of water. I gulped it down, cooling my burning throat.

"Better?"

I nodded.

He pulled me against his chest again. "When I came in here and saw you standing there with the cough syrup to your lips, I was so scared."

"I'm so sorry. I just—what if I'd—what if you hadn't…?"

"But I did. This time. But Maddie, I might not always be there. Not because I don't want to be, but because next time you might not text me first." He stiffened in my arms. "You need to talk to someone—like a therapist or something—someone who can help you deal with this stuff. I'm seventeen. I don't know what the hell I'm doing."

"There won't be a next time." I tried to wriggle free, but he held me tighter.

"Still. You should—"

"Stop." The last thing I wanted was to revisit my darkest moment. "I don't want to think about that right now. Can you please just kiss me?"

He nodded as he wiped my tears with the rough pads of his thumbs then cupped my face and pressed his lips to mine… soft and tentative as if he thought I might break. But as I gathered his shirt in my fists, dragging him closer, the kiss spun out of control.

My stomach tumbled like a dryer on high, the heat making its way down my neck to my toes. In that instant, I felt more alive than I had in months. I wasn't Sarah and David Barrett's orphaned daughter—the girl so desperate to cling to her dead parents she'd do almost anything to destroy herself. And I wasn't the misunderstood stepchild, punishing Alex for being… well for being *alive.* I was just Madison Barrett—girl in love.

A sense of urgency came over me, and I tugged at the hem of Grey's cotton tee, inching it up to expose his hard abs, then let my fingers run over his lean muscles. "I want you."

He pulled back, the look of desperation in his eyes warring with his obvious concern for my well being. "I told you I wouldn't do this if it was about—"

"It's not," I whispered. "I swear. It's about *you*. I've wanted to do this since the first time you kissed me." I pushed his shirt up his chest, and he grabbed it, lifting it the rest of the way over his head, and dropped it on the floor.

Grey stood in front of me shirtless. Nothing but his ragged breathing broke the silence between us. Neither of us said a word for what seemed like forever. We just stared at each other like everything around us had been put on pause. Then he whispered my name and crashed his lips to mine.

His hands trembled as he unbuttoned my blouse, letting the silky fabric slide over my shoulders and pool on the floor at my feet.

I reached up to unfasten my bra, but he grabbed my hand, towing me through the bedroom. "You don't want to do this in here." It wasn't a question. "Come on." He led me across the hall to my room and hauled me up to toss me on the bed. Like I was flying down a sand dune on Lake Michigan and into the cool water on a hot summer day, my stomach continued to dip and swirl. Exhilaration clouded my thoughts, edging back my pain as I clung to Grey like a life raft.

We fumbled with the rest of our clothes, our limbs tangled and our mouths connected the entire time. My lips still carried the hint of a chalky residue under salty tears, but Grey tasted of cherry ChapStick and peppermint gum, and that overpowered everything else.

With my heart threatening to beat its way out of my chest, I ran my hands everywhere I could reach. I savored the feel of him under my palms at the same time his fingers explored me, making me insane with need, desperate to feel all of him. "Grey, I, um, I'm not on the pill."

He pushed up on his elbows and flushed. "I keep a condom in my wallet. I mean, it's not like I thought I'd be using it today. I just carried it around, you know, in case. But it's not like I *always* carried one with me. It's just... since that night in your room, I figured it might be a good—"

I covered his mouth with my hand. "It's okay. I'm glad one of us planned ahead. Now shut up and kiss me."

He smiled against my palm then dragged my arms over my head.

CHAPTER 34

ALEX

NATALIE EXHALED INTO THE PHONE. "You know, I hate to say I told you so, but I—"

"Yeah, yeah. I know. You told me so. But you don't understand. It wouldn't have mattered if I'd told her. I mean, I did try to tell her... more than once. She just wouldn't listen. And trust me. She would've freaked out either way." I flipped on my blinker and got into the left lane.

"Do you blame her? She showed up on Mother's Day to find you packing up her mom's stuff. Could you have possibly been any more insensitive?"

Natalie's disappointment rang through the line, and I wanted to tell her it wasn't my fault, but somewhere in the back of my hormone-addled brain, I knew better. I shouldn't have reacted the way I did. I never seemed to say or do the right thing where Maddie was concerned. I should have—who knew? Whatever it was, I didn't do it. Another wave of tears fought free. "Whose side are you on?"

"There are no sides. But I think you could have done things differently. And what about Ben? Your appointment is tomorrow. Have you told him yet?"

Ben. Just thinking about him caused a bone-deep ache and a fluttering low in my stomach. It seemed as if even my unborn child had taken sides against me. But that was ridiculous. I wasn't far enough along for that.

"Well? I'm taking your silence to be a no."

"You don't understand."

"That seems to be your mantra lately. Well, I've got news for you. No one understands. And do you know why? Because you're *wrong.* You can't keep these things from people." Natalie's frustration was evident even through the phone.

"But—"

"I'll give you a few buts. Maddie may be a holy terror sometimes, *but* she still deserves to know what happens with her mother's house. And I know you miss David. I know you're buried in guilt about your feelings for Ben, *but* he still deserves to know he's about to be a father. And I'm sorry, sweetie, *but* it's time to pull on your big girl panties and start acting like someone's mother because whether you like it or not, you are. You're the only mother Maddie has now, and you have an innocent baby growing inside you who needs you to stop hiding under your blanket of grief."

I didn't want to believe she was right. I didn't want to think I'd been hiding all this time. The truth sat like a lead weight on my chest. I reached the end of Main Street and pulled over to the shoulder, too blurry with tears to drive.

Her voice turned soft as she seemed to run out of anger. "Are you still there?"

Everything that had happened over the past several months ran through my head. The ground had finally thawed, and soon I'd be burying my husband. A man who'd only been in my life for a short time, but who'd managed to so completely consume me that I couldn't seem to find my way out from under the weight of his loss. Was it love? Or was it the knowledge that he didn't love me as much as I loved him?

"It's just too much, Natalie. I'm only one person. How much can one person bear?"

"Hey, I know you can do this. Life is hard. But you can't stick your head in the sand and wait for it to go away. You have to deal with it. You have to start talking to Maddie about things that affect her, and you have to tell Ben about the baby. I'll give you one week to come clean. If you haven't told him by then, I'll do it myself. And hey, this is for your own good, you know?"

I sniffed and wiped the tears from my face with the back of my hand. "Fine. I'll tell him."

"Good. Now come on over, and have a cup of decaf and a blueberry scone."

"No. I have things I need to do. I'll—maybe I'll come over after my appointment tomorrow. If I feel up to it."

"Okay, sweetie. Take care of yourself. Call me if you need anything."

"Thanks, Nat."

Natalie's words stung. And the argument with Maddie had left me exhausted. But despite the weariness, I found myself on a course toward Ben's house with my stepdaughter still very much on my mind. I knew I needed to repair the rift we'd created, but I had to talk to Ben first. Maybe things would be better if I let go of the black cloud hanging over me and just told him the truth. Admitted my feelings and my fears. Told him about the baby.

Once I'd resigned myself to coming clean, I felt the weight lift. He'd loved me not so long ago. I could only hope he still did.

I pulled into Ben's driveway and jumped out of my car with the engine running. Ben's house was dark as purple streaks etched the sky, and the sun slipped down over the horizon. After ringing the bell and banging on the door to no avail, I sat on the stoop to wait. But the mid-May weather still carried a bite to it, and I wasn't dressed for the cold.

After climbing back into my car, I dialed his number, but it went straight to voice mail. I left a message for him to call me as I looped through town toward the hospital. Once I'd gotten it in my head to tell him, I became obsessed with carrying it out, even if that meant making my declaration in the middle of the emergency room.

Traffic on Main Street moved at a snail's pace, unusual for a Sunday evening. But a steady stream of cars exited the parking lot at Beverly's Café, crowding the road. As I waited at the light, I glanced at the smiling faces going in and out of the restaurant.

A familiar shock of golden-brown hair caught my eye, and I stared at his profile. Then I noticed the beautiful blonde at his side. He threw his head back, laughing at something she said, and wrapped an arm around her shoulders, kissing her temple as he guided her through the door.

Fuck my life. What were the odds I'd pass by the restaurant at the exact moment he was going in? Damn small towns.

I watched them until they disappeared within the building and a loud honk startled me. Ben had moved on without me. Natalie was right. I'd taken too long to make a decision, and he'd given up on me.

What am I going to do?

I continued down Main Street and took the first left, circling back toward the coffee shop. I could see Natalie through the window, laughing with the customers at the counter, and drove on, not wanting to be around smiling, happy people.

Alone. By choice, by design, by accident. But undoubtedly alone. Heavy droplets of rain pelted the top of my car as I headed up the coast. I didn't have a plan. I just drove. I stopped off for gas and a gas station burrito and sent Maddie a text to let her know I'd be getting home late. Not that she cared about me or my whereabouts. Not that anyone would.

Just after midnight, I pulled into my driveway next to Grey's car. The old me would have gone into hysterics, even though I'd half expected him to be there when I arrived. The new me understood—and was maybe a little jealous.

A light glowed above the stove, casting shadows over Grey's face as he sat, sketching at the counter. He looked up as the back door closed behind me with a click. "Oh, hey." He gathered his pencils and paper into a neat pile and sat up straighter on the stool.

"Where's Maddie?"

"She's, uh, sleeping. In her room. I stayed down here, 'cause I figured, well, you know. That you wouldn't want me up there." He fidgeted with a fat bubblegum-pink eraser.

"Oh. Okay. So…" I tossed my keys onto the counter and attempted a friendly smile. "Why are you still here?"

He reached into his jacket pocket and pulled out several orange pill bottles. "I-I caught Maddie trying to take these. At her mom's house. She actually had a mouthful of them when I walked in and was about to wash them down with cold medicine."

My stomach twisted as Grey told me what had happened, and my dinner threatened to make a reappearance. She'd tried to kill herself.

David would've never forgiven me had his daughter taken her own life on my watch. No matter how I looked at it, I'd screwed up.

"Is she... is she okay?" I collapsed onto a stool, dropping my purse at my feet.

"No. I mean, physically, she's fine. But—and I mean no disrespect when I say this, but—watching you pack up her mom's stuff really upset her. And then she found these." He reached into his other pocket and pulled out a pair of tattered ballet shoes.

I took them from him. "I don't understand. They're just shoes." Maddie hadn't danced since I'd known her. And who would want a pair of ratty old slippers anyway? I rubbed my thumb over the worn satin. "David always said she was an amazing dancer."

"She was. Do you know why she quit?"

I shifted my gaze to Grey. "No, he never told me."

"Ask her someday." His expression told me he knew the answer, but he wasn't about to share it with me. "And maybe have that conversation about her mom's house before you actually sell it."

"Oh my God. Natalie was right." I blinked back hot tears. "I'm a terrible person."

He reached out his hand but pulled it back at the last second. "You're not a terrible person. But maybe see if you can fix things?"

I nodded, wiping tears as they fell. "Of course."

"Well, I guess I'll go home." Grey hopped off the stool and shoved his art supplies into a backpack. "I just thought I should stay and tell you before I left."

"Thank you, Grey. Really." I reached out and squeezed his hand. I didn't know what to think about a teenager schooling me on the intricacies of life, but he had. He'd managed to sum up everything I'd failed at in a few words.

He nodded and turned to leave.

"Wait. It's late. Why don't you stay on the couch?"

"Are you sure?" He scratched the back of his neck.

"I'm positive. Stay here. I'll get you a blanket." I dragged myself off my stool and headed up the stairs to find a clean blanket and pillow and peeked into Maddie's room as I went by. She lay curled in a ball, cocooned in a ratty old quilt, something I'd seen at her mother's house just today.

How could I have been so wrong about so many things? And how would I ever repair the damage I'd done? Whether David had been faithful or not, his daughter deserved better than I'd given her. I vowed to rectify that immediately.

CHAPTER 35

MADDIE

THE BRUSH OF WARM FINGERS and a light kiss on my cheek woke me. I opened my eyes to see Grey's contented smile. He moved to sit next to me on my bed and hold my hand.

"What time is it? Am I late for school?" I asked him, trying to sit up and see my clock.

He held me in place though. "You're not late. I'm early. Actually, I never left."

"You... you spent the night?"

"Alex didn't get home until after midnight. She let me stay on the couch."

I blinked my eyes a few times before taking a good look at him. He wore the same clothes as the day before, and his hair was only a little disheveled. I put my free arm over my face. "How come you look so good first thing in the morning? I probably look like crap."

He laughed then eased my arm away from my face. "You're beautiful in every sense of the word."

My breath caught, and I tugged on his shirt to coax him down to kiss me. After a moment, he pulled back, a worried look in his eyes. "You told her, didn't you? That's why she let you stay."

"I had to, Maddie." He brushed a strand of hair from my forehead. "I don't think you have any idea how much you scared me. You need help—"

"I'm okay. I mean, I know I screwed up, but I won't ever do that again." This time I did sit up and wrapped my arms around his neck. "I'm sorry."

He hugged me tight and rubbed his hand up and down my back. "You know I'm going to watch you like a hawk now, right? And be completely overbearing and freak out if you so much as take a Tylenol."

"Yeah. I know."

"Maddie..." He sat back and studied my face. "This is serious. You have to promise me—swear on your parents' souls you will never try *anything* like that again."

"I promise. I swear." Seeing the fear in his eyes when he'd found me had sobered me up. I'd never realized what my selfish decision would mean to anyone else. I wished I could make him understand how much I meant what I said, but I guessed it would just take time.

He stared into my eyes for a moment then leaned forward and pressed his lips to mine. I wove my fingers into his hair and delighted in the fact that he'd been allowed in my bedroom without Alex giving me the third degree.

"Breakfast is ready!" Alex called from downstairs.

So much for that thought.

Grey pulled back then cleared his throat. "We should probably get down there. I don't want to take advantage of Alex's hospitality."

I sighed. "Yeah. Is she cooking something?"

"Can't you smell it?" He smiled. "She's making bacon-stuffed buttermilk pancakes. And she put about a gallon of syrup on the table."

I took in a deep breath and got a nose full of the salty-sweetness wafting up from the kitchen. "Did you guilt her into making those? The last time she made them was the day after she forgot my birthday. How is it she can be so shitty sometimes, like packing up *my* mother's house without even talking to me about it? But when it comes to food, she remembers every little thing I like and don't like or can't have."

He laughed. "Remember how we talked about giving her a chance? She cares about you, Maddie, more than she even realizes. And she knows she made a colossal mistake. But she also needs you, just like I do."

I raised an eyebrow at him.

"Well, maybe not *exactly* like I do." He gave me a quick kiss. "But you know what I mean."

"All right. All right. I promise I won't, *you know*, ever again. And I promise to try harder with Alex. As long as she tries, too."

"That's my girl." He stood up and reached his hand toward me. "Now come on, and eat some breakfast before it gets cold."

I let him help me out of bed and gave him another hug. "I'll be down in a sec, okay?"

"Okay. But don't take too long." He squeezed me and kissed the top of my head before leaving my room.

I ran to the bathroom then threw my tangled hair into a ponytail and splashed some water on my face. No matter how beautiful Grey found me, I wouldn't sit through breakfast with him while I looked like a total wreck. A moment later, I bounded down the steps to find Grey sitting at the kitchen table with a ginormous stack of syrup-laden pancakes in front of him and Alex pouring herself a cup of coffee.

"I thought you were trying to cut back," I said to her as I slid into the seat next to Grey. He grinned at me then put his hand on my knee under the table.

Alex turned and gave me a small smile. "It's decaf. How are you feeling this morning?"

"I'm..." I looked to Grey for reassurance, and he nodded. "I'm better."

"Good." She eased into the seat across from me, and we both loaded our plates.

After a while of silent eating, Grey sat back and checked the time on his cell phone. "I should go so I can get a shower before school. This was really delicious, Mrs. Barrett. Thank you." Hearing him call her by my mom's name unsettled me, but I fought back the hurt feelings.

"You're welcome, Grey. You'll probably be full until dinner."

"Alex, can you give me a ride today so Grey has a little more time?"

The two of them shared a look, and I set my fork down, ready for whatever they *thought* I should be doing.

"Actually, I was hoping you'd come with me to an appointment this morning." Alex took her napkin and dabbed her mouth.

"This isn't some kind of intervention, is it?" I turned to Grey. "I promised you I wouldn't... do that again, and I *meant* it. I really do promise. I don't want to go see some shrink."

"It's not an appointment for you, Maddie. Though, I do think we need to talk about some *things*," Alex said. "And we'll revisit the discussion about therapy. But not today. Today, I have an appointment I'd like you to be there for."

"Oh-kay. If you're sure you're not dragging me to some secret shrink appointment."

Alex shook her head and smiled at me. Awkward, but at least she tried.

"Cool. Can I drive?" I tossed out the question, knowing damn well she'd say no.

She glanced over at Grey then shrugged. "Sure. I'm kind of tired anyway, and you can get some practice in."

"Seriously?" I held my breath, glancing between the two of them again, and they both nodded. I let out a shriek and clapped my hands like a little girl.

Grey laughed before scooting back his chair to stand. "I should really get going."

He put his hand on my shoulder and leaned down to whisper in my ear. "I love you. I'll see you soon." Then he kissed my cheek.

I wanted to tell him I loved him too, but I couldn't with Alex sitting right across from me with her mouth hanging open like one of those singing fish. *That's right, Alex. He loves me.* Instead, I squeezed his fingers, hoping he knew what I meant. "Okay, bye."

After he'd left, I finished eating and helped Alex clean up the kitchen. We didn't say much to each other, but she kept staring at me as if I might vanish into thin air and disappear without a trace.

"Maddie?"

"Yeah." I handed her the last dirty plate to put in the dishwasher.

She clinked some dishes around to make room for it then reached for the package of detergent tabs under the sink. "I'm sorry about yesterday." She put a tab in the slot and shut the door. "I shouldn't have started packing your mom's things, and I hope you can forgive me."

I leaned against the island and crossed my arms, blinking back tears. "I just wish you'd talked to me first. I mean *really* talked, not just told me it was going to happen."

"I know, and I'm very sorry. I've been so consumed with what's going on in my own life that I forgot to think about you being a part of it. And I *want* you to be a part of it. I want us to make decisions together for our... family." She looked down then back up, the word *family* more tentative than any of the others.

"I get that we can't keep the house, but I'm... I don't know, not ready to let it go yet."

She twisted her lip as if she were contemplating something. "I'm not comfortable with it just sitting empty, so how would you feel about renting it? I can ask Natalie if she knows any people looking for a house. That way, we'd still own it. We'll give it a year and see how you feel, say... after graduation? How does that sound?"

I hated to admit it, but that actually seemed like a good plan. It'd give me a chance to go through my mom's things and get used to the idea of it not being my home anymore. "Yeah, I think I could go along with that."

"Okay." Her face lit up. "There's one more thing. I'd like you to go back to dance. Your dad wouldn't shut up about how good—"

My stomach clenched. "I don't dance anymore."

Alex's smile wavered. "Well, we can talk about it later, but for now, we need to get cleaned up. My appointment's in an hour."

I nodded then headed up to my room to get dressed. Whatever this appointment was for, she seemed anxious to get there on time.

CHAPTER 36

ALEX

"I seriously can't believe you're letting me drive your Porsche. I mean, you love this thing." Maddie bounced in the driver's seat, jingling the keys in her hand.

"It's just a car, right?" I forced myself to smile, thinking of all the potential disasters that could happen with a teenager at the wheel. I wondered if my heart could handle it. "Okay, you'll want to adjust your seat and the mirrors to make sure you can see out."

Maddie reached between the seat and the door to adjust the height then moved the rearview mirror into position. "Got it. Can we go now?" She squirmed in her seat, the excitement rolling off her in waves. It might have been the first time I'd ever actually seen a real smile on her face.

Her delight was contagious, making me laugh. "Yes, but be sure to check for cars before backing out."

She rolled her eyes. "You don't have to tell me everything. I *do* know how to drive."

"Right." I pressed my lips together and sat on my hands, the words "nervous mother" floating around in my head. "The cockpit's yours, captain. Don't dent it."

Maddie threw her head back and laughed. Then she eased the car out of the driveway and made a smooth turn onto Grant Street. "See? Piece of cake." Her brows furrowed as she concentrated on the road, her expression an exact duplicate of David's face when deep in thought. I realized I'd never noticed how much she looked like him. I'd always pegged her for a mini-Sarah, but she really had a good blend of them both. Watching her navigate the streets behind the wheel of my prized vehicle, I saw nothing but her father in her.

"You're kind of creeping me out with all the staring." Maddie turned on the blinker and got into the left lane. "And it might be a good idea to tell me where I'm going before I decide to take this baby all the way up the coast on a joyride." Even her saucy smirk was the spitting image of David's.

I shook my head to clear it then checked the road ahead. "Very funny. You can get into the right lane. We're heading toward the hospital." I couldn't decide whether to tell her exactly where we were going or spring it on her once we'd arrived.

"Are you sick?"

My stomach fluttered. "Not exactly."

Maddie eyed me as she took the first right onto Main Street. "I take it we're going to see your doctor friend?"

A burst of laughter bubbled out of me. "No. Not going to see Ben." I wished. He still hadn't returned any of my calls.

I checked my cell phone. No messages. And maybe that was for the best. After seeing him with the mystery blonde, I wasn't sure I wanted him to call me back. If only I hadn't waited so long. *Why did Natalie have to be right?*

Maddie kept her eyes glued to the road ahead of us. "Well, I sort of liked him."

"Liked who?"

"Dr. Hudson. He was nice to me. And I know Mom liked him. I think Dad would have liked him too."

I coughed, choking on my own saliva. "What do you mean your dad would have liked him?" The image of David and Ben sitting on either side of me on the sofa flashed behind my eyes.

Maddie stopped at the red light and turned to face me. "I think he would have wanted you to be happy. Now that he's gone, I mean. Not that he didn't want you to be happy when he was here. But he wouldn't want you to be so sad and lonely."

The same girl who'd moved heaven and earth to make sure I knew her parents were reconciling before they'd died was concerned about my happiness? The irony wasn't lost on me. I opened my mouth then shut it again. My instincts screamed at me to leave it alone, but in the end, I couldn't do that. "I know your dad was planning on leaving me for your mom. You don't have to pretend. You're not the only one who's made that perfectly clear." My thoughts flitted back to my conversations with Mr. Howard and Mike Allen. Even Ben had been aware of what everyone but me seemed to know.

"Um…" The light changed, and Maddie jerked the car forward without saying another word. Her expression wavered between guilt and uncertainty, making me uncomfortable.

"It's okay, Maddie. Really. I've accepted it and moved on." Heartbroken and forever changed, but still. The fault rested solely with David. He'd been the one to lie. The one who'd betrayed me. I might never really know what had actually happened, and I was finally okay with that.

"No." Maddie shook her head. "It's not okay." She gunned the engine, and the needle jumped on the speedometer.

"Watch your speed."

She nodded, and the car slowed. "It's just—and I feel really horrible about what I've done." Maddie's leg bounced, and I rested my hand on her knee. Her anxiety made my own heart pound.

"That day… Mom and Dad were going to see my school counselor."

My head spun as she stumbled around the words, and I tried to comprehend her meaning. "When? What do you mean they went to see your counselor? I don't understand."

"I mean, the day they died. They weren't on a date. I know I said they were, but they really had an appointment with Mr. Lindstrom. I'd gotten into big trouble right before Christmas. I got high at school. Not just me—there were a few of us—but I was the only one who got caught." She blew out a breath. "I *wanted* to get caught. Mrs. Walker wanted to expel me, but instead, she agreed to several counseling sessions with my parents."

"But…" I pressed my cool hands against my hot cheeks. I remembered David's so-called meetings when I was out of town. And his calendar. The dates with Sarah. My pulse raced out of control. *Why didn't he just tell me the truth?* "You said they were—"

"I know what I said." Maddie's voice cracked. "I lied. I was mad and hurt, and I knew Mom wanted to get back together with Dad. She never got over him, and then you came along."

"And then *I* came along?" My mouth went dry as the implications of what she'd said sank in.

Maddie swiped the back of her hand across her cheek. "Mom was so depressed. She'd lost weight. She didn't care about anything. Even my dancing made her sad because she had to pretend everything was normal, and it wasn't. So I quit. I realized the only thing that would make her smile again would be if *you* weren't in the picture anymore. So I did what I did—and then they were gone." She went quiet for a moment before her soft whisper broke the silence. "I-I just wanted my family back. Now they're both dead, and it's all my fault."

My heart thundered in my ears like the crescendo of some tragic opera. I heard her speaking, but the words didn't make sense. "So they weren't—and he never—he really did love me?" I choked out a sob.

Maddie brushed a few more tears from her cheeks. "He did. He loved you. I'm really sorry if I—"

"Do you have any idea what you've done?" Every angry word she'd uttered since the day I'd met her flooded back with a vengeance. Every sideways glance, every temper tantrum, every malicious grin burned into the back of my eyelids. I blinked and saw them staring back at me. Reconciling that person with the girl I'd grown to care for seemed impossible. "You took him from me. He was already gone, but you took what few memories I had of him and tainted them with your lies. I've been so angry with him when he didn't do anything wrong." Tears fell freely from my eyes as I stared past her, out the driver's side window. A young couple pushing a stroller along the sidewalk caught my attention. He had his arm over her shoulder, and she was laughing at whatever he'd said. I would never have that.

Maddie eased the Cayenne to a stop at a red light three blocks before the hospital. I couldn't wait to be out of the car. Away from her lies. Away from the memories dredged up simply by her proximity.

"I'm sorry. I know it was a horrible thing to do, and I shouldn't have done it. I've done so many things I'm not proud of, Alex. And I-I can only say I'm sorry."

I felt myself dangling on the edge of a precipice and fought to keep from jumping into the abyss. "Sometimes sorry just isn't good enough." Not after all the damage done. The light turned green, and the car behind us honked. "Just go, Maddie."

She lifted her head, and the car lurched forward into the intersection. I glanced to my right in time to see a flash of silver, bearing down on us from the cross street. "Oh my God!"

Sirens wailed in the distance and voices called my name. *Maddie?* I said… or I thought. I wasn't sure. I was so cold. And my head screamed at me. *Where am I?*

The whooshing of a heartbeat—not a heartbeat—a monitor, sounded to my right. I blinked my eyes open enough to see a blurry face hovering over me and flashes of light in the space around it before everything went black.

CHAPTER 37

MADDIE

"I'M FINE! I DON'T NEED to be in here. I didn't even get hurt." A man in a white coat flashed a light in my eyes. He was the third person to do that in a matter of a few minutes. I'd already told them my name, address, and when I'd had my last period. Did they need to know my favorite movie or what kind of ice cream I liked? "Where's my stepmom? Where's Alex?"

"I need you to take off your sweater so I can check out that shoulder."

I pulled the bloody sweater over my head and dropped it beside me. "There. Now you can check whatever you want, as soon as you tell me where they took my stepmom."

His cold, latex-covered hands glided over the tender skin at my collarbone. "She's being prepped for surgery."

"Surgery? Oh my God. How bad is she hurt?" I tried to climb off the gurney, and Dr. White-coat pushed me back down. "You don't understand. This is all my fault. I didn't even see the other car. I need to call someone. Natalie would want to know. And Grey. Oh my God, Grey's going to freak out. And… And… Is Dr. Hudson here? I need to talk to Dr. Hudson."

"I believe he's gone." The doctor lifted my arm and slowly bent it at the elbow. "His shift ended a while ago. But if you promise to stay put, I'll go see if anyone's seen him."

"Fine. But please hurry." I lay down on the uncomfortable hospital bed and counted the bloodstains on the ceiling, or maybe they were something else. But either way, I found little comfort in my surroundings.

My nose burned with the scent of rubbing alcohol and something else that reminded me of the nurse's office at school.

Like finding familiar shapes in summer clouds, I tried to pick out images in the stains above me. I'd just discovered a dog when I heard the squish of rubber soles behind me.

"Maddie?"

I sat up too quickly and had to lie down again. "Dr. Hudson?"

"Hey, we're old friends now. You can call me Ben." He smiled. "I was just about to go home. What happened? Jesus, you look like you've been in an accident." Ben ran his eyes over my bruised arms before pulling out his stethoscope. I waved it off before he could press the cold metal to my chest. "Does Alex know you're here?"

"Didn't that other doctor tell you?"

Ben froze mid-motion. His hands gripped his stethoscope as he held it over his head. "Tell me what?"

"I was driving her car. I didn't see it. Alex screamed, but—" I choked back a sob.

"What happened?" He whispered the words as he finally draped the instrument over his neck. "Where is she?"

"It hit us on her side. There was blood and glass everywhere. I didn't know what to do. I couldn't get her out of the car."

"Maddie." He grabbed my shoulders and gave me a little shake, his face a grim mask. "Where. Is. She?"

"I think they're still running tests. It's really bad. The other doctor said she needed surgery."

Ben jerked away from me and turned to sweep back the curtain. "I need to find her."

"Wait!" I shot up off the gurney and grabbed his sleeve to keep from falling over. "Please don't leave me here alone."

"Honey, I need to check on Alex, but I promise I'll come back."

"I heard Alex Barrett was brought in a little while ago." A familiar voice shouted in the hall. "Where is she? I need to see her."

I followed on Ben's heels as he bolted toward the nurse's station.

Natalie stood toe to toe with a tall man in a pair of faded blue-green scrubs. "Surgery?" She shrieked. "Is she going to be okay? What about the baby?"

The tall doctor flinched. "She's pregnant?"

Ben froze, and I crashed into him. *I knew it. I knew she was hiding something.*

"She's pregnant?" Ben choked out.

Natalie spun around to face him. Her mouth hung open, and her hands flew up to cover it. "Oh my God, Ben. I'm so sorry. You weren't supposed to find out this way."

"She's pregnant?" Ben shook his head as he said the words again.

Natalie's eyes filled with tears when she saw me. "Oh, Maddie. Are you okay? Does Grey know you're here?"

Grey. "I haven't had a chance to call him. How did you get here so fast?" I hugged myself as a blast of cold air came through the open ambulance bay doors. I didn't know what chilled me more: the wind, or the possibility of Alex dying.

"Oh. One of my customers mentioned seeing a Suburban T-bone a Porsche Cayenne around the corner from the hospital. When I couldn't get Alex on the phone, I came right over."

"She's pregnant." Ben's expression turned hard as he faced the other doctor, who'd been standing there watching the scene in front of him like a tennis match. "Dr. Craig?"

"Right." Dr. Craig nodded once then snapped at a nurse at the computer. "We need to get an OB consult right away. And order an ultrasound. Stat. I want monitors on both Mrs. Barrett and the baby."

"Who's the surgeon on call?" Ben asked.

"Green."

"Good. I'll go talk to her myself." Ben turned to Natalie as Dr. Craig spun on his heels and took off down the hall. "Why didn't she tell me?"

Natalie sighed and glanced at me.

What was I supposed to say? I had no idea she was keeping something so huge from Ben.

"She was afraid of how you'd react," she said.

"How I'd *react*?" Ben pushed his hand into his hair and stared down the empty corridor. "Jesus. She knew I was in love with her."

"But she also knew she'd pushed you away a million times." Natalie took Ben's other hand, and suddenly, mine felt empty. Where was Grey?

Had he heard about the accident yet? "She didn't want you to come back just because of the baby."

My heart broke at the devastation in his eyes. Alex had kept the secret from both of us, and I didn't know how I felt about that any more than he did. Maybe if we'd been closer. Maybe if I hadn't lied for all those months. But I'd never know that, would I?

Ben blew out a breath, and I felt every shudder that went through him. "Well, I hope like hell I get a chance to make her feel guilty for leaving me in the dark."

"You will." Natalie pulled Ben into a hug, and I wanted to jump in and make it a group effort. Instead, I watched them from a distance. "In fact, I'll even help you bitch at her for keeping it a secret."

His eyes got glassy, and he ran a hand over his face. "I need to talk to the surgeon. I'll be back. Take care of Maddie."

Take care of Maddie. With everything going on around him, he hadn't forgotten about me, and I wanted to hug him for real that time. But before I could wrap my arms around him, Ben hurried down the corridor, leaving me with Natalie.

"Now, how about we get you back into your room and call Grey?" Natalie squeezed my hand. "You're not exactly dressed for the hallway."

I glanced down at my see-through tank top. "Thank you."

Grey rushed into the waiting room, the Michigan State sweatshirt I'd only recently given back to him tucked under his arm. Without a word, he pulled me into the crushing hug I'd been desperate for, but when I winced, he let go. "Oh geez. I'm sorry, baby. I didn't even think about how much pain you might be in." Grey took a step back to gape at the black and blue patterns on my exposed skin. "Here." He pulled his sweatshirt over my head then brought me into another, more gentle hug.

"I'm so glad you're here." I nuzzled my head under his chin and melted into his embrace.

"I'm sorry I didn't get here sooner. Mr. Stone confiscated my phone in first, and I didn't get it back until lunch."

"Doesn't matter. You're here now."

"How's Alex?"

I shook my head. "Haven't heard yet. Ben said he'd come out and tell us as soon as he knows something. I guess she's still in surgery."

"How about you? I can see the bruises, but what about the rest of you? Are you okay?"

"She needs to be resting." Natalie put her magazine down and stood. "That was the agreement, right, Maddie? Grey can stay as long as you agree to sit still."

I felt the heat climb up my neck. "Right." I eased into the closest chair, and Grey sat beside me, clutching my hand in both of his. "I'm fine. They discharged me, but apparently, I can't *do* anything for a few days. What's the actual point?"

Natalie smirked, but I could see the tension rippling on her forehead. "You can rest there next to Grey and wait like the rest of us."

"Come on, babe. Natalie knows best. That's why she's the boss." Grey threw his arm over my shoulder and nestled me against him in the uncomfortable hospital chairs.

"Alex is pregnant." His shirt muffled my voice as I pressed my cheek against his chest. The idea hadn't fully sunk in yet, but I couldn't help replaying the words in my head until it did. After everything else we'd been through, would our relationship survive her losing another baby? And what if she didn't make it?

He shifted me in his arms. "Yeah, I figured something was going on, but I didn't know for sure."

"What am I going to do without her?" I huddled closer to him, hoping his warmth would calm my racing heart. "I didn't want to care about her, you know. I wanted to hate her and blame her for everything wrong in my life. But the truth is, she's not a bad person. She's been in as much pain as me. I've done some horrible things to her, Grey. How will I ever make it right if she dies?"

"She won't die," he whispered, kissing the top of my head.

"I hope you're right. Because she's the only family I have left."

CHAPTER 38

ALEX

"WHY HASN'T SHE WOKEN UP?" Maddie's voice cracked.

"I don't know. Her body's healing, but I guess she's just not ready yet." *Ben.* Why did he sound so sad?

I climbed further out of unconsciousness but couldn't quite break through the fog. I must have been dreaming. I didn't know of a reality where Maddie and Ben would be arguing over why I wasn't awake. And why couldn't I open my eyes?

The voices quieted, and I noticed a rhythmic beeping in the background.

"Is Grey picking you up after school?"

School? Why isn't she in school? Where are we? Not home. My bed is much more comfortable than this.

"He wanted to, but I told him I'm staying until she's awake."

"Sweetie, there's no way of knowing when that'll happen. And we already talked about you going home tonight. You need your rest too. And you pinky swore."

How long have I been sleeping? I tried to speak but couldn't find my voice.

"It's been over a week. And it's my fault she's in here."

Not her fault. I pushed against the blackness to say something—to argue with her—but the darkness pushed back. *Tell her, Ben. Tell her it's not her fault.*

"Hey, it's not your fault. It was an accident."

"But if I'd been paying attention. If I hadn't upset her. If I'd just told the truth from the beginning."

"'What if?' is a dangerous question."

"I just need to her to know how sorry I am."

"I'm sure she knows."

The bed shifted beside me, and a warm weight rested on my arm. Slim fingers slid between mine. I felt them, and yet no matter how hard I tried, I couldn't squeeze back.

"Ben?"

"Yeah?"

"Is she going to be okay?"

"Yeah, kiddo. She'll be fine. Everything will be fine." I recognized the uncertainty in his voice.

"And the baby?"

The baby? He knows?

"Really good." Ben's mood picked up. He sounded almost happy. "He's perfectly safe in his little bubble."

"He?" Maddie giggled. "What if it's a she?"

"He, she, doesn't matter. As long as it's healthy."

"Yeah. I'd like a chance to meet the kid, no matter what."

"Hey, I need to do rounds, but I can swing by the cafeteria on my way back if you're hungry."

"No, I'm fine."

"Maddie..." Ben used his stern voice. "When's the last time you ate?"

"Natalie brought me blueberry muffins for breakfast."

Natalie was here? Coffee?

"That was hours ago. I'll bring you something."

"Just not—"

"Chicken, I know."

A light gust of wind ruffled my hair as if a door had opened then fell shut again. The disquieting beeping filled the silence, and for the first time, I noticed the biting scent of disinfectant burning my nose. It reminded me of Ben.

Maddie's small hand clutched mine. "I'm so sorry, Alex. I wish I could take it all back. Dad would be so ashamed of me." She sniffled, and hot tears dripped onto my skin. "I hope you can forgive me for all the trouble I've caused."

I struggled to grip her fingers and cursed my broken body for not responding. *We were both to blame. I didn't give you a chance. I wish I could take it all back, too.*

"Alex?" The weight lifted from my arm, and Maddie squeezed my hand. "Can you hear me? If you can, squeeze my hand again."

I did it! My eyes wouldn't open, but I felt my fingers twitch then the pins and needles as the feeling came back in both hands.

Maddie squealed. "Oh my God! You're awake? I have to get Ben. Don't go anywhere. I'll be right back."

I'll be here. At least until I can get the rest of me to cooperate.

I lost track counting the beeps while I waited for someone—anyone—to come back. I curled my fingers around the cotton blanket, making fists in the fabric. My eyelids fluttered as I strained to open them. Then the first pinpricks of light broke through, and the blurred shapes of the room came into view.

Maddie chattered as she burst back into the room. "I'm telling you, she squeezed my hand. I didn't imagine it."

"Alex?" Ben stepped up to the bed, and I forced myself to focus on his hazy form.

My throat burned as I tried to answer him.

"Don't try to talk. We need to remove the tube first." He held my hand and turned toward the commotion at the door. "I need help in here."

"Can't you just take it out?" Maddie asked.

"No, I'm not actually allowed to act in a medical capacity because of our... er, *relationship*." Ben stepped out of the room for a minute, and when he came back, another person came with him.

Maddie hovered over me, her smile spread so wide I thought her face might split in two.

Ben shifted until the new person stood beside him. "She's awake. Has anyone paged Dr. Philips?"

"She's on her way. She wants me to go ahead and extubate."

"Good. Maddie, can you step out for a few minutes? We need room to work."

"Uh, yeah. Sure." Maddie scooted out, and the door shut behind her.

"Mrs. Barrett?" The woman leaned into my view, but I couldn't make out her features. "I'm Julie Wagner, the respiratory tech on call today. Dr. Philips will be in to see you shortly, but first, we need to take care of that tube. I need you to blow out for me. Can you do that?"

I gave as much of a nod as I could.

"Okay, good. We'll go on three, okay? One, two, three."

I coughed and sputtered as she wrenched the tube from my throat.

"Okay, great. Now take a deep breath." She pressed a stethoscope to my chest. "Good, good. The doctor will be right in to see you." She patted my hand and left.

The minute Ms. Wagner left, Maddie stormed back into the room. "I told them you were awake. How are you feeling? Could you hear me talking to you? Natalie said sometimes people in a coma can hear when you talk to them. I'm so freaking sorry for—*everything.*" Maddie took a breath. "I need to call Grey. And Natalie. And oh my God, your parents will totally freak out. Ben made them go back to the house to sleep. They've been here since that first day. Your mom keeps trying to feed me. She's a shitty cook, no offense. No wonder you're so thin. Are you going to be okay now?"

Ben chuckled. "Slow down, kiddo. Alex needs her rest. Go make your calls. I'll come get you in a few, and we'll get something to eat."

"Right. Sure." Maddie beamed and bent down to seize me in a bone-crushing hug. "I'm so glad you're okay."

A flood of emotions washed over me. Tears filled my eyes, and I squeezed her back as hard as I could.

Maddie kissed my cheek and flitted out of the room as quickly as she'd come.

"Hey." Ben sat on the edge of the bed and took my hand in his. "I was afraid you might not come back to me."

I cleared my throat. "Water?"

He reached behind him then put a cup to my lips. "Just a sip."

The cool water soothed the burn in my throat enough for me to speak. "Thank you."

"You're welcome." His lips curved into a sad smile.

"I'm sorry."

"Hey, none of that." He took my hand in his. "You need rest."

"No. I need to say this." I tried to sit up.

Ben gave me the doctor face. "Alex, you've been in a coma for eight days."

I shook my head. "Please."

He sighed and nodded.

"I shouldn't have run." The words scratched my throat, and I felt the burn of tears.

He rubbed circles on the back of my hand. "I shouldn't have pushed so hard."

"And I should have told you about the baby."

"You should have."

"I'm so sorry." The first tears fell. Was I too late? Was he only here because of the baby? "I've made so many mistakes. I was operating under the wrong assumptions on many levels."

He pulled up a corner of the blanket to wipe the wetness from my cheeks. "You really need to rest."

"But you need to know why I didn't tell you."

He nodded again, settling back onto the bed.

"I said awful things that last day I saw you. And Natalie told me I was stupid for letting you go. But David cheated—even if he didn't really, but I didn't know that then—and I wasn't ready to put my heart out there just yet. And then I changed my mind, and I tried to find you and tell you I love you, but I was too late. And now..." I looked at the display on the monitor.

His face lit up with the first genuine smile I'd seen from him in months. "The baby's fine."

"I was going to tell you. But then I saw you with *her* and decided maybe it would be better if I didn't."

"Her?"

"Hey there. It's good to see you awake." A perky redhead poked her head into the room.

"Dr. Philips." Ben stood and stepped away from the bed.

"How's my patient feeling today? Like you got run over by a truck, I'd assume."

I shrugged and immediately regretted it. I did, in fact, feel like I'd been run over by a truck. "Yeah, I guess I do."

"I'll come back." Ben kissed the top of my head then stepped out of the room.

Dr. Philips watched him walk away. "You landed a good one there. Hearts have broken all over the hospital now that he's off the market."

"I don't know what you mean."

"Oh, my goodness, you must really be out of it. Why don't you try to get some sleep?"

"No! I need to talk to Ben."

"There's plenty of time for that… later."

The bed dipped down, and I let my eyes flutter open. Ben's lean shape formed a silhouette against the midday sun streaming in through the window.

"Hey."

"I'm sorry I woke you."

"I'm not. How's Maddie? Did she eat?"

"Yeah. We grabbed a quick bite, then Grey picked her up and convinced her to go to her therapy appointment. You might need to take up baking when you're out of here, though. She's been staying at the house with your parents the last few days, and Natalie's been supplying them with a steady stream of baked goods. I'm pretty sure she's developed an addiction to blueberry muffins."

"That's too bad. My only attempts at muffin baking have been epic failures. I think Natalie gave me a flawed recipe just to ensure she doesn't have competition."

"Maybe it's genetic. I hear your mom burns Pop-Tarts."

I laughed.

"It's good to see you smile again." Ben's expression darkened, and he shifted his attention to our joined hands. "I've missed you so much. I was afraid we'd never get the chance to fix things."

I squeezed his fingers. "Me too."

"Speaking of fixing things… who's this mystery *her* you seem to think you saw me with?"

"Oh…" I dropped my eyes to the blankets.

"Let me guess, you saw me with a blonde at Beverly's."

My eyes snapped up to his, and I nodded.

"Mother's Day, right?" I nodded again, and he bobbed his head a few times. "My sister and I took our mom out for dinner."

"Of course." I slumped further into the pillows.

"Do you remember me telling you I loved you? Well, that hasn't changed. Believe me, I tried. But I still do, more than I know what to do with."

"And the baby?"

"What about the baby? Alex, I loved you before. And I still love you after. Nothing has changed. Except now I'll have someone else to fall in love with in a few months."

I shifted my weight, trying to get comfortable. "So you're not mad?"

"Mad?" He leaned down and pressed his lips to mine. "I've never been happier."

CHAPTER 39

MADDIE

THE FINAL BELL ON THE last day of school rang, and I bolted from class to meet Grey at my locker. It had been a long four weeks since the accident.

He smiled, wrapping his arm around my shoulders as we headed for the parking lot. "What's that look for?"

"Nothing, well something, but it's a surprise. I want to tell you and Alex at the same time."

"Hmm…" He squeezed me, and I winced. "Oh, sorry." He dropped his arm and took my hand. "Your shoulder still bothering you?"

"Just a little."

He walked me to the passenger side of his car then stopped short. I waited for him to open the door, but he just stood there grinning.

With his hands planted on the roof of the car to either side of me, he leaned in so his hip grazed mine. "I'd better be gentle then."

All the commotion and noise of students and cars drifted away. In that moment, Grey and I were alone. He touched his lips to mine in a barely-there kiss before pulling back to gaze into my eyes.

"You don't have to be *quite* so gentle. I mean, my lips feel fine. They can take the pressure."

He laughed. "They can, can they?" Before I could respond, he kissed me again, deeper this time.

I inched my hands up his chest and around his neck to keep him from pulling away. I wanted him to know I wasn't fragile, that I might be slightly bruised, but I wasn't broken.

"You've made your point, Princess Madison," he said against my lips. "You are soft and strong... and I won't be so gentle with you in the future."

"The near future?"

He nuzzled my ear. "I think I could be persuaded. But I thought you said we were supposed to meet Alex at the coffee shop?"

"I did say that, didn't I?" I pursed my lips as I contemplated my options.

"Come on." He laughed and kissed the tip of my nose. "We'll revisit this later."

We walked into the coffee shop, hand in hand. Alex sat at the counter, with a row of mugs in front of her.

"What are you doing?" I stepped behind her and peered over her shoulder. She smelled like citrus and cucumbers.

"Experimenting." Natalie held out a blueberry muffin, and I snatched it with a grin. "I think we're getting close."

Alex took a sip from her cup and groaned, putting her hand on her belly. "Not close enough."

"Are you okay?" A pang of worry stabbed me. "Is it the baby?"

"Yes. The baby does *not* like cucumber, no matter how many fruity things you mix it with." She shot Natalie a death glare.

Relief flowed through me. "Why are you drinking cucumbers?"

"She's forcing me to drink these—" Alex waved her hand over the row of steaming cups. "—concoctions of hers."

Natalie scoffed with a sour frown. "They're not *concoctions.* They're blends. With tea. As it turns out, coffee—even decaf—is bad for the baby."

"That may be true, but lack of coffee is bad for the mother."

"Deal with it." Natalie poured another drink and slid it in front of Alex. "Try this one. It's chai and vanilla bean."

Alex blew on the cup before bringing it to her lips for a tentative sip. She nodded a few times. "Not bad."

Natalie beamed. "Jackpot!"

"So... Maddie, what's the big secret?" Grey leaned against the counter and rested his head on his hand.

Alex spun around on her stool. "Secret?"

"I'm not sure if I should tell you the good news or the bad news first." I bit back the urge to grin like a crazy person.

"Let's get the bad news out of the way." Alex took another sip of her tea.

I squeezed Grey's fingers. "Well, you know how hard I worked to bring my grades up in History and English?"

"Yeah," Alex and Grey chimed in together.

"I was hoping to pass History with at least a C." I stared at their expectant faces. "I didn't get a C."

Alex laid a hand on my shoulder and squeezed. "This was a rough year. You'll do better next year."

"Sorry, babe. Summer school won't be so bad." Grey pulled me into a hug.

"I'm not going to summer school." Grey opened his mouth to say something, but I cut him off. "Because I got a B! And I got an A in English!"

"Oh my God!" Natalie jumped up and down on the other side of the counter. "That's amazing. It was those last-minute tutoring sessions I gave you, wasn't it? I could never get enough of Jane Austen."

Alex laughed. "You could never get enough of Mr. Darcy!"

"Isn't he everyone's favorite?"

I grinned. He was definitely my mom's favorite. And for the first time since she died, it didn't hurt to remember.

"I'm proud of you, sweetie." Alex pulled me into a hug. "We've come a long way in a short time, haven't we?"

I squeezed her back. "We sure have."

"Speaking of time..." Grey glanced at his phone. "I should get going. I'm on diaper duty if I want to go to the party tonight."

I giggled. "Make sure you wash your hands before you pick me up."

"Before you go, I have some pretty good news of my own." Alex looked like she was about to explode with excitement. "I just got an email from my production department. I took the liberty of sending some photos of your drawings along with a rough idea for a storyline, and they loved it!"

Grey's mouth dropped open. "Are you serious?"

"It's not a done deal yet, but the production team wants to see more. That is, if you're willing to do the artwork."

"Holy shit!" He shoved his fingers into his hair. "Of course, I'm willing. I can't believe it! I'm going to be designing a video game!"

Alex laughed. "Well, I'd actually be doing the designing. You'd be doing the artwork. But if they give us the go-ahead, you'll get credit right alongside me. And if you enjoy the process, you could be looking at a future apprenticeship with the company."

"Are you kidding me?" Grey scooped me up and spun me around the room. "I have got to be the luckiest guy in the world!" He set me on my feet and tipped my chin until our eyes locked. "Definitely the luckiest guy."

I put the truck in park in my mother's driveway. "Don't tell Ben, but I hate his truck."

Alex leaned in to whisper. "Only if you promise not to tell him I hate it too."

I couldn't wait for Alex's replacement car to come in. Ben had convinced her to go with the Lexus SUV instead of another Porsche. "Less flashy… safer for the baby," he'd said. At least she'd picked the red. Not that I'd get to drive it much. Alex even said she'd match whatever I saved over the summer to buy my own car.

"Are you ready to do this?" Alex opened the door but didn't get out.

I stared at the newly polished exterior and blinked back the tears. "It's now or never."

"Are you sure? We could still rent it out for a year or two. There's no rush."

"No." I glanced at the new roses blooming under the front window. We'd uprooted the tulips and planted them at Dad's. "It's time to move on. It's just a house. The memories will always be with me."

"Okay." Alex smiled as she climbed down from the passenger seat and walked around to the tailgate. She pulled out the blue-and-red sign and held it out to me. "You wanna do the honors?"

"Yeah. Let's get this over with. I have a hot date with a video game artist."

CHAPTER 40

ALEX

WHAT'S THAT SAYING ABOUT RAINY days being perfect funeral weather? Well, it wasn't raining. In fact, I woke up to a beautiful sunny day—not a single cloud in the sky. A pair of hummingbirds danced past the kitchen window, sipping from the bright fuchsia June blooms as if today were just any other day. It seemed both wrong and entirely fitting at the same time.

The house was too quiet. Ben had to run to the hospital to check on a patient, and Maddie must have gone off with Grey, because she wasn't in her room when I came downstairs, leaving me alone with my thoughts. For the first time in months, that wasn't a bad thing.

A noise in the basement drew me out of the moment, and I followed the shaft of light spilling through the crack where the door stood ajar. I padded down the stairs in my slippers, finding Maddie sitting on the wood floor of her miniature dance studio, tying the ribbons on her old ballet shoes.

Butterflies swirled in my stomach, and I stepped to the side so I could watch her without being seen. Sarah McLachlan's "I Will Remember You" streamed from the speakers as Maddie stood and stretched one leg across the bar.

She switched legs then turned, doing a graceful spin in place.

I watched in awe as each fluid turn morphed into something more beautiful than the move before. She glided across the room like a swan in water, never once faltering. And as she rose to the points of her toes, I held my breath. Tears filled my eyes. David had been right. Maddie was an amazing dancer.

As if suspended on a string, she spun around—one then two then three revolutions—abruptly stopping in front the mirror with a wide smile.

She did another spin, her hair whipping around her like a cape before she came to a sharp stop again.

I watched her until the song changed then turned for the stairs, afraid I'd break the fragile spell.

After taking a long hot shower, I stared at my reflection in the mirror, barely recognizing my body. At the sixteen-week mark, my abdomen had begun to swell, not to mention the rest of me. "This baby is making me fat," I muttered.

"Hey! None of that." Maddie barreled into my room and scowled at me. "Don't let her give you a complex." She crouched down and spoke directly to my stomach. "Your mom just isn't used to wearing maternity clothes yet. Wait 'til Auntie Natalie and I drag her out shopping this weekend. Then she won't complain anymore."

"Not *shopping.*" I groaned, but secretly I was excited to embrace this phase of my life.

"Ha! You'll love it. Now, hurry up. The guys'll be here in just a few minutes. Grey texted me. Ben just picked him up, and they're on their way." Maddie took one last lingering look at herself in my full-length mirror and adjusted the straps on her dress. The one I'd gotten her for her birthday.

"See… I knew you'd like that dress."

She flashed a grin. "Whatever. It's fine. No offense, but you're not exactly the authority when it comes to fashion."

I knew that was likely as good a compliment as I'd get from her, but I'd take it. And we both had our less-than-diplomatic moments. Thank God we'd learned to take turns. And hey, Rome wasn't built in a day, and she *was* still a teenager after all. I blinked back the threat of tears and went into my closet to find something big enough to fit over my growing shape.

Maddie poked her head into my closet. "Alex?"

"Yeah?"

"I think I'm ready for you to make that therapy appointment for me."

"Okay." I didn't know what else to say.

Maddie's smile fell slightly as she studied my expression. "Maybe we could have a few appointments together?"

I couldn't hold back my smile. "I'll check with Ben. I'm sure he knows someone. He might even be able to pull a few strings to get us an earlier appointment."

"Sounds good." She pulled my teal sundress from the rack.

"What about this? The skirt is flowy enough to hide the baby bump, and the top is nice and snug across your boobs."

"Do you think flashing the girls is the way to go at the cemetery?"

"Works for me." She shrugged. "Besides, it's not like you can *hide* them anymore. I'm sure everyone will be just *dying* to see them."

"Ugh, you did *not* just say that." I contemplated her suggestion for a minute and continued to rifle through my dwindling choices.

"Seriously, Alex. The sundress is pretty. Dad would have liked it." A smile lit her face. "And I doubt you'll hear Ben complaining."

"Fine." I blew my hair out of my face and sighed. "Are you sure you're okay with Ben being there? I know what people will think and say, but *you* don't think it's weird?"

Maddie rolled her eyes. "For the last time... no. I don't think it's weird. I like Ben. And who else is going to take care of your neurotic ass?" She smirked.

"Maddie!"

"Hey, you know I'm right."

"You girls ready?" Ben's voice echoed up the stairs, and I flinched.

"Crap! I'm not even dressed." I went back into the closet to grab the teal sundress from its hanger. After I pulled it over my head and studied myself in the mirror, I gave Maddie a wink. "You'd better be right, smart-ass."

She flipped her hair over her shoulder. "When am I wrong when it comes to fashion?"

I barked out a laugh. "I'll remind you of that next time I see you in the Cookie Monster getup."

"Knock, knock." Ben leaned into the room. "Time to go, ladies."

Natalie pulled me in for a hug.

"Thank you so much for coming." I gave her a tight squeeze then backed away to wipe at a stray tear. "I'll see you tomorrow."

"You got it. We're hitting the mall first thing in the morning." She grinned at Maddie. "And no backing out."

"I know, I know." I'd resigned myself to let them pamper me if it made them happy. "I'll be there with bells on. Just make sure you have my chai and vanilla bean hot and ready when I get there."

"Deal."

Natalie caught up with Father John and the rest of David and Sarah's friends, leaving our little group alone at the gravesite. A twinge of something resembling jealousy squeezed my chest as I stared down at the matching headstones. I didn't think I'd ever *really* be okay with having my husband buried beside his ex-wife, but for Maddie's sake, I'd never regret the decision. The look of pure gratitude on her face when she'd realized what I'd done made the gesture worth it.

Maddie and Grey had turned to walk away, hand in hand, so I hadn't expected Maddie to rush back, practically knocking the wind out of me with a crushing hug. "Thank you."

"Wow." I hugged her back, fighting against the urge to cry again.

She let me go and hugged Ben. There was a sparkle in her eyes as she whispered something in his ear. He nodded then kissed the top of her head before she joined Grey at the edge of the path, and the two of them wandered off together.

"What are you two up to?" I eyed Ben's secretive expression.

He ruffled his hair and dropped his eyes to his shoes. "I don't know what you're talking about."

"Uh huh." I took his hand and tugged. "You ready?"

"Actually…" He tilted his head and regarded me for a long moment. "If you wouldn't mind, I'd like to have a minute or two with David before we go."

My heart jumped. "With David? Why?"

"I just think he and I need a moment alone." Ben leaned in and pressed his lips to my hair. "I won't be long."

"Okay." I strolled toward an old bench under a nearby oak tree and sat to watch Ben out of the corner of my eye. I couldn't make out his words, but his body language and the set of his jaw told me he was having a serious conversation, the sort of thing one didn't take lightly. He faced Sarah's grave for a moment then he turned toward me, and his entire face lit up with a smile.

"Everything okay?" I asked as he approached the bench.

"It is now." He sat beside me and squeezed my hand. "I felt I needed to clear the air with David before moving on."

"Clear the air?"

"Yeah. I needed to let him know I would take care of his girls. Both of them. I know he'd do it himself if he were here, but since he can't be, I asked his permission to take over."

For the umpteenth time that day, I found myself fighting back tears. "And what did David have to say about that?"

"Well, I think he resisted at first. I had to convince him of how much I love you and how good we'd be together. Eventually, he caved."

I choked back a sob and a laugh at the same time. "He was always a bit of a softy."

"Oh, he was a tough sell." Ben fidgeted with something in his pocket. "But in the end, I'm pretty sure he gave us his blessing."

I nodded toward Ben's closed fist. "Whatcha got there?"

"What, this?" He held up his hand but didn't open it. "It's nothing." He smirked and moved to shove it back into his pocket.

"Oh, it's definitely *something*." I grabbed for his fist, but he was too fast. "Is it for me?"

"Yep."

"Well, can I have it?"

"Yes." He slipped his arm around my shoulder and tugged me toward him. "But not today."

"Someday?" I nestled into his warmth, staring out at the lilacs in full bloom around us.

"Definitely." Ben laid his hand on the slight swell of my stomach, reminding me that despite where we were, life carried on.

ACKNOWLEDGEMENTS

First and foremost, I'd like to thank Laura Kolar for being the best critique partner and sounding board a writer could ever have. Back before either of us had signed our first publishing contracts, I called Laura to tell her I had an idea for a book loosely based on my relationship with my stepdaughter, Mady. But I knew I could never tackle the project without her help. Thus began my journey writing this heart-wrenching story of love, loss, and discovering family. Thank you, Laura!

I would also like to thank everyone else along the way who helped make this book become a reality.

To my girls, Lauren, Alexa, and of course, Mady, for sharing their insights into the mind of a teenage girl. I would've never known what "molly" was without you. And you didn't even flinch when throwing yourselves under the bus when we needed help writing those scenes about sneaking in and out of the house undetected. Thank goodness, I found out about that after the fact, and not before.

To Lucy Carson for being kind enough to take the time to review the unpolished manuscript. Your invaluable advice helped make the story even better.

To Michelle Rever and Karen Allen—the best editors ever!—for taking the raw material that was Ashes of Life and polishing it until it shined.

To Erin Schirer, Lizzy Vance, Louise Flynn, Lauren Dean, Rachel Bongart, Marilyn Higgins, and Katie Moretti for being the best beta readers ever.

To Julie Wagner, who not only did a beta read, but also guided me in the right direction when I was writing those tough medical scenes. And to Nicole Moscou, for helping me stay on pointe with the ballet scenes.

To Red Adept Publishing—and the best publishing staff anywhere—for picking me out of the slush pile all those books ago and dusting me off. Without you, I wouldn't be where I am today.

To my families and friends, for supporting me in this crazy endeavor. Being a writer is often a thankless job. The outside world doesn't always understand what goes into that finished novel they pick up from their local bookstore, or online retailer, but to those who've watched my struggles (and triumphs) over the years… you get it. And I most definitely appreciate it.

And lastly, to all the non-traditional families out there struggling to make things work in a difficult world, here's to you. For fighting the good fight. Don't give up just because it's hard, because in the end, nothing worth having is easy.

ABOUT THE AUTHOR

ERICA LUCKE DEAN

After walking away from her career as a business banker to pursue writing full-time, Erica Lucke Dean moved from the hustle and bustle of the big city to a small tourist town in the North Georgia Mountains, where she lives in a 90-year-old haunted farmhouse with her workaholic husband, her 180 lb lap dog, and at least one ghost.

When she's not writing or tending to her collection of crazy chickens and diabolical ducks, she's either reading bad fan fiction or singing karaoke in the local pub. Much like the main character in her first book, To Katie With Love, Erica is a magnet for disaster and has been known to trip on air while walking across flat surfaces.

How she's managed to survive this long is one of life's great mysteries.

Printed in Dunstable, United Kingdom